USER I.D.

Books by Jenefer Shute

*LIFE-SIZE * SEX CRIMES * FREE FALL * USER I.D.*

U S E R I. D.

Jenefer Shute

Houghton Mifflin Company - Boston - New York - 2005

D- May, 06

ISBN 0-618-53906-9

Design by Melissa Lotfy

Printed in the United States of America

For Mark, Nel, Angela, and Geoffrey

U S E R   I. D.

1

VERA NEVER FELT like herself in LA. Whoever, she thought, that self might be, unrecognizable just then behind the wheel of a car. Certainly not the glamorous and self-possessed self she'd hoped for—a self that could plunge into traffic with aplomb—but, still, the only one she had. Or was likely to have, the way things were going.

The conference, for starters, had not been much of a success. Not much of a success at all, she thought, cringing as an enormous gleaming vehicle bore down on her, in that reckless, suicidal Angeleno maneuver known as the merge. Somehow, the limo missed her—they do this all day long, she reminded herself—and, trembling, Vera stepped on the gas, trying to get her speed up to something approximating that of the ambient traffic.

She must remember, she thought, settling for a sedate sixty-five miles per hour, never again to put the word "torture" in the title of a conference paper. It must send out the wrong subliminal signal—otherwise, how to account for the sparse attendance? And her performance, she suspected, had been less than stellar. She always felt befuddled in LA, dopey and dazed, as she did at that very moment, hurtling down the Santa Monica Freeway, dreading death by Humvee. It was something to do with the light, she'd decided years ago, the merciless light of LA. Entirely too intense for February. It made her feel weak and queasy, wrong in her own skin—overexposed, all of a sudden, like a snail without its shell.

Distracted by the billboards, with all those moving parts, she missed the first sign for her exit but, on spotting the second, swerved rashly across two lanes of traffic, managing to get down the ramp without actual bodily harm. It was always an enormous relief to exit the freeway alive.

Now, crawling down Sepulveda Boulevard in minimal traffic, squinting despite her sunglasses, all she had to do was find the Avis agency to return the car. But, though she knew where she was on the map, more or less, Vera felt lost. The day was just too bright—blindingly bright and blue, so bright that the glare hurt her brain. She didn't recognize anything around her—endless lube stations and taco joints—though she'd picked the car up from this very place just two days before. She experienced a sudden, vertiginous disorientation, the exact opposite of déjà vu. I should have sprung for the GPS, she thought, then at least I'd know where on the planet I was. Hell, with her sense of direction, she should have had GPS implanted at birth.

Even without the GPS, it was hard to miss the giant red and white Avis banner that soon came into view, snapping with a crisp, irritable sound in the breeze. With her turn signal on—it had been on for over a block now—Vera cruised along, peering molelike over the dash, trying to determine where the entrance was. She could see signs and flags everywhere, a superabundance of visual information, but it wasn't clear to her, in that dizzying array, where she should turn. All she was thinking of, really, was disburdening herself of this machine, this odd-smelling machine (as all rental cars are, as if they're sprayed inside with some fake aroma of cleanliness and newness), and catching the shuttle to the airport, making her flight.

She was sweating lightly now, her blouse beginning to adhere to the car seat—another way in which LA disagreed with her. She had the kind of skin—olive and slightly oily—that tended to sweat, and the kind of hair—thick and long and curly—that tended to cling damply and frizzily to the back of her neck. She should have pinned it up. She shouldn't have worn pants. She should have lost ten pounds before presuming to appear here, city of bionic bodies. She should, perhaps, just have stayed in New York, where it was a manageable forty degrees, and she wouldn't feel like day-old falafel, greasy and unappetizing and past its prime.

At last, a man in a short-sleeved white shirt, posted at one of the entrances, waved her in, this way, turn here, park here, in this small lot, ringed with thick shrubs. The sign said GUEST PARKING, but if she gave it a nanosecond's worth of thought she assumed that the other lots were full, busy time of day and so on. Leave the keys in the car, he told her. OK she said, but, experiencing a tiny prickle of doubt—just how far was the counter from there?—asked if she should take her luggage or come back for it. Take it, he said, with an abrupt jerk of his hand, so she retrieved her suitcase from the trunk and wheeled it, whining, over the pavement. Which way now? He gestured hastily at the narrow opening between two large shrubs. She noticed that he was sweating heavily, his bald head beaded, rivulets running down his face. But it was a hot morning. A hot bright Los Angeles morning.

Obediently, she dragged her suitcase along the narrow strip of pavement, which opened up, almost immediately, onto a scene of immense activity, four lanes' worth of cars pulling up at kiosks, people hopping in and hopping out, hyperactive attendants in, yes, white shirts, but red caps as well, nametags of course, busily handling keys and forms, an efficient conveyor belt of human beings and machines. With an inkling that, as usual, she'd ended up in the wrong place, she hauled herself and her bag to one of the kiosks and asked the attendant (busy, distracted, barely lending an ear) where she should go to complete the paperwork.

"Here," he said, "here—you bring the car here."

"But someone told me to park in that lot there," she said, pointing.

He shook his head impatiently. "No. Here. All the cars come here."

A twinge of unease came over her, an unnamed anxiety wormed its way to the front of her brain, past all the clutter in there, thoughts of shuttles, gates, flights, cabs, money, phone calls, messages, e-mails, classes, Colin. What if . . . ? But surely not. But then how . . . ? Mistake, that's all. Misunderstanding.

Faster now, stickier in the armpits, face tensed, right where the frown lines were forming—the idea of Botox no longer seemed quite as grotesque as it had a few years ago—she hurried back the way she had come, dodging across two lanes of traffic, dragging her bag down the path, through the narrow gap in the bushes to the small lot, quite clearly marked GUEST PARKING. And of course, but unbelievably, the car was gone.

She stared stupidly at the now vacant spot, and then at all the cars in all the other slots, as if the answer were simply that the car had moved itself from one to another, but of course it hadn't. It was gone.

She felt as if all her blood had drained, instantly, into her sandals' rubbery soles.

She'd been scammed. She'd been conned.

How was this possible?

Admittedly, Vera thought, she wasn't a connoisseur of car-rental agencies. She almost never rented a car, almost never traveled to places, like LA, where you needed one. So, granted, she'd been out of her element, distracted, befuddled, not exactly exuding street smarts or *savoir-faire*. But to be scammed so egregiously, to be taken for such a sucker . . .

And now what? Lawsuits and legal fees: some endless expensive nightmarish mess. She'd be liable, she assumed, for the loss. She'd have to make restitution, she'd have to pay up. What were her rights in this situation, anyway? Why hadn't she read any of the small print on the rental contract? Why did she never, in fact, read any of the print on any contract?

She could feel herself starting to panic now, big-time. Lawsuits, bankruptcy, public humiliation . . . Her face a rictus of anxiety, the linen of her blouse damp and wilting, she dragged the suitcase, yet again, through the narrow outlet—why hadn't it been immediately obvious to her that this wouldn't be an efficient way to channel large numbers of people returning cars? Why hadn't she paid attention to the sweat pouring down the man's face and the odd angle at which he stood, at an unnatural distance from her, obviously—now!—so he could watch for someone coming? why had she been so incredibly stupid?—and headed, this time, for a security guard in a booth, a young Latina, bottle blonde.

"I think something bad has happened," Vera told her, gesturing through the glass, speaking in a loud and agitated way. "Something bad!" The guard had difficulty hearing her at first, with all the cars swooshing past, so she came halfway out, listened to Vera's first few sentences until the words "Guest Parking," held up her hand, went back into the booth, and got on the phone. As she spoke, she regarded Vera through the grimy porthole with an air of jaded contempt. As in: Will the stupidity of these people never end?

Waiting out there on the traffic island, where it was gusty and fumy and loud, looking around hopelessly for the missing vehicle, which she wouldn't have recognized even if she'd seen it, Vera replayed the events in her mind, first enumerating all the ways in which it must have been her fault—she looked like a victim, didn't she, an easy mark, creeping down Sepulveda like an old lady, squinting into the sun, hapless and clueless —and then compiling a counterlist of all the ways in which it hadn't been—the entrance should be clearly marked, goddammit, what kind of security did they have here, it was their responsibility to guard against this kind of thing, how could a person be expected . . . and so on. She alternated rapidly between these two versions, the former with more conviction than the latter. Then the guard came out and pointed her towards the main office, across the four lanes of traffic.

"You have to see the manager," she said, "fill out a report."

"But I have a plane to catch," Vera protested, indicating her bag.

The blonde shrugged. "Second floor, ask for the manager."

The manager, having identified without much interest what brand of nuisance Vera was, called over another man, bureaucratic type in a blue shirt, who had something to do with security. He, too, seemed unperturbed. Vera wondered whether this was because they were Californians or because cars got stolen from their lot every day. He sat Vera down in a cubicle and told her to wait for the police.

"The police!" Vera said shrilly. But I haven't done anything, she wanted to protest. Instead, she asked, in an aggrieved tone, "How long is this going to take? I have a plane to catch . . ."

He shrugged.

"My plane is at one," she insisted. "I can't miss my plane." This was not strictly true. She had no classes until the following day, no compelling reason to be on this plane rather than the next. But it was suddenly crucial that she didn't miss this plane, her plane, the 13:10. She'd never missed a plane in her life.

He shrugged again, informed her that she couldn't leave the premises until she'd filed the police report. There was a slightly threatening tone in his voice, if one can be both bored and threatening at the same time. He didn't seem at all interested in hearing her tale of woe. He remained poised at the doorway, impatient to leave.

After he'd gone, a secretary, who'd been off to photocopy Vera's driver's license, returned and told her, in a confidential manner, that this—the scam—had happened before. She, too, seemed unmoved, unsurprised. Before Vera could ask any questions, the woman went back to her desk, in the opposing cubicle, and addressed herself to the unfinished business on her computer screen, Your Stars This Week. From what Vera could see, she was a Gemini with love troubles. Nobody seemed the least upset or agitated—nobody, Vera thought, except herself. Her blood was a bouillon of bad chemicals, agitation and anxiety, fight and flight.

As she waited for the police, in the bare gray office cubicle that itself resembled a cell, she began preparing her defense. I haven't done anything wrong, she reminded herself. I'm not the kind of person who has run-ins with the cops. I'm a responsible, meticulous kind of person, bordering on dull, the kind of person who flosses and recycles and returns library books on time. I'm Professor de Sica (sort of), from New York City, just minding my own business here, just trying to return a rental car. I'm guilty of nothing, she thought, except stupidity.

Well, she thought, staring dejectedly at the two pushpins that constituted the sole visual interest on the cubicle walls, that's bad enough. Stupidity, a.k.a. an increasingly inattentive relationship to reality. It was only a matter of time until something like this happened, until her stupidity, hitherto fairly well camouflaged, became a matter of public record. As she approached forty, she felt that she was becoming stupider every day, duller and more blurry, that she was losing her grasp on things. She wasn't sure if anyone else had noticed it yet—her students, perhaps, occasionally—but she noticed it every day. As she noted the effects of gravity on her face.

She pictured herself on a Wanted poster, not looking her best. Wanted for Impersonating an Intelligent Person for Thirty-eight Years.

After about twenty minutes, a young policewoman showed up, accompanied by a soundtrack of radio squawks and static. She was short and plump, and walked with an awkward, duck-like gait, encumbered by the arsenal of objects suspended from her belt. She also looked absurdly young: this must be the shit work they assign to the rookies, Vera thought, going down to the Avis agency on a Tuesday morning to take a car-theft report.

"Mornin', ma'am," chirped the recruit, as if on a social call. She plopped herself across from Vera, legs planted apart.

"Morning," Vera replied, warily. She had hoped for a little more gravitas from the LAPD. And she hated to be called ma'am: it made her feel middle-aged—which, she supposed, she was.

The secretary brought the cop a Diet Coke, which she popped gratefully, blotting the condensation from the can on her uniform sleeve. (Where's my Coke, Vera thought peevishly, I who have been sitting here for half an hour, after an enervating, not to say traumatic, experience?) Then, with both elbows on the desk and half an ear on the constant unintelligible crackling of her radio, the policewoman got down to business, filling out her form.

It soon became clear that Vera was not the injured party in this situation, not even a player. The issue was between the con artist and Avis, or, more precisely, Avis's insurance company. Vera, in legal terms, was not the victim. (Then why, she wondered, do I feel like one?) She was not even the character in the detective story who, combing her memory for significant details, has to describe the event. The cop took her name and address—Vera de Sica, 211 East Second Street, New York—but didn't ask for a narrative of what had happened. Vera felt cheated, as she had been rehearsing this very narrative in her mind and was now on the fourth or fifth draft, a model, in her opinion, of clarity and economy. Nor did the young woman even ask for a description of the suspect, which Vera had also been rehearsing, and which she provided anyway, using the lingo of TV cop shows—Caucasian male, mid- to late thirties, five eight to five ten, average weight, belly, baldish, well spoken, short-sleeved white shirt, no obvious scars or tattoos. She couldn't remember the color of his eyes. This bothered her. But the cop wasn't writing any of it down anyway: there was no place on the form for description of perp.

Although she felt robbed of her star-witness moment, Vera did establish, to her immense relief, that she wasn't liable for anything—that she'd have to pay the rental fee, two days' worth, nothing more. She didn't really understand this—she had, after all, personally handed the car over to a thief, thoughtfully leaving the keys in the ignition for him—but she wasn't going to complain. After the policewoman left, Vera gave her credit card to the secretary, who returned with a receipt and a paid-up copy of the rental agreement. Being cautious by nature, Vera asked for a written statement from Avis, signed by Mr. Manager or Mr. Security Guy, confirming that she owed them nothing. That she was guilty of nothing. Liable for nothing—no damage, no loss. She knew that, legally, the statement was probably on a par with a pawprint from her cat, but it made her feel better, like a doctor's note, a clean bill of health.

She got the statement—two lines—and that was that. No

one, she realized, wanted to hear her story. Nobody seemed surprised that she had been conned, or incensed by the con. No one even cared to know that she was in fact a sophisticated, street-smart New Yorker and that this was not the kind of thing that usually happened to her. Usually? Ever!

Leaving the cubicle at last, she felt angry. With the crook, with Avis, with herself. She felt humiliated. She still felt vaguely guilty.

She wouldn't tell anyone, she decided. She wouldn't tell Colin. She wouldn't tell Helena, even though Helena had got herself involved in some pyramid scheme a few years back and lost several hundred bucks. She wouldn't even tell Simone, her shrink. What for? This would remain a secret, strictly between the con man and herself.

For the moment, she channeled her energy, her sense of outrage, into getting Avis to take her to the airport on time. The next shuttle, in fifteen minutes, just wouldn't do, she told the secretary. She needed to leave *now*. This instant. There was some phoning back and forth (the secretary, a quiet middle-aged woman, proving, after all, wearily sympathetic), and then Vera was instructed to take her things downstairs and wait for the bus—a whole shuttle, just for her. They would ride in state to LAX, Vera and her bag.

As the shuttle pulled out of the Avis lot onto Sepulveda, she noticed that there were now uniformed security guards at every gate, waving hesitant motorists towards the correct entrance. Sure, she thought, *now* they're out there, in force. She tried to tell her story to the driver, a handsome young Latino, but his English wasn't up to the task, or so he made out. Otherwise, he was friendly and smiley and bursting with life; he handed her down to the curb with a chivalrous air.

She made her flight without difficulty, even with time to

spare. She was the type of person who, in order never to be late, was always early, always killing the odd twenty minutes or so before an appointment. So, even after an encounter with a con artist and a cop, even after the bizarre detour her day had taken, she'd still failed to be late, arriving at the gate with plenty of time to buy a *New York Times,* a *Vanity Fair* (a guilty pleasure, only on planes), and an overpriced bottle of water with a made-up Scandinavian name. As her flight was called, it was almost as if nothing had happened, just a slight diversion on the way to LAX.

But when, finally, she tilted back her seat in the loud, stale air of the cabin, gave the evil eye to her neighbor, a middle-management type who'd claimed the armrest as his God-given right, and tried to focus on the spring fashions (*Vanity Fair* thought it was April already), she found that her mind was still roiling, wouldn't let go.

The entire visit, she thought, had been a bit of a letdown. The conference had been even more third-rate than Vera had anticipated, sparsely attended even by the usual suspects, the ones who showed up, like her, at all the third-rate conferences and gave, like her, their third-rate papers. Her brief and highly speculative paper on second-language acquisition among torture victims, based on a sample of four at Brooklyn Multitech, where she taught, had been received with the indifference it probably deserved. She'd wanted to tell these people's stories — Haxhi and Nomsa and Carlos and Jean-Claude — but not through tabulations of syntax over time.

After the conference she'd drunk chardonnay from a plastic cup with people with whom she could have drunk chardonnay from a plastic cup in New York, then had dinner in Santa Monica with her old friend Lynn from graduate school, who'd wanted to talk of nothing but her dissolving marriage (her third), which had made Vera reflect, nervously, on the ever precarious situation between Colin and herself. Then, predictably, she'd got lost driving the glittering freeways back to the Biltmore, where her conference-rate room faced into an airshaft and the enormous bed made her feel lonely and small, as if she might roll right off it and into the void. And since the college was contributing only a pittance in travel funds towards this excursion, she was also worrying, subliminally, and, at times, liminally, about how much this was all costing her.

And then, on top of it all, to be conned, to be scammed, to be taken for such a sucker.

Guest Parking, no uniform, bizarre body language, sweating like a pig, unlikely system for returning rental cars — it was all so obvious, in retrospect. She'd been a fool, that was all, just plain naive. That was what hurt. This wasn't how she saw herself, never had. She lived in New York, after all: she was as skeptical and savvy as they came. No telephone salesman ever got further than three words into his spiel with her. No street-corner con artist ever tried to hustle her: he'd take one look at her, her stride, her frown, her distrustful air, and wait for the next mark to come along. She was wise to all this, all these scams and scammers, from the humble junkie in the East Village, peddling the stuff he'd ripped off on the very block where he'd stolen it, to the corporate data miners and niche marketers, with their mailing lists and discount cards and pop-up windows, their cookies and credit reports and extended warranties, purloining everyone's privacy, bit by bit.

And yet, she'd been had. While she'd been out of her element — in a car, in California, in the dazzling light — someone had taken advantage of her. Taken her for a ride, she thought — or rather, taken himself for a ride, at her expense. She felt enraged, and at the same time ashamed. Guilty. Foolish. Violated. As the plane groaned, tucking its various parts away, Vera stared out the window at the disappearing yellowish smudge of the San Fernando Valley and understood that, while technically she might not be the victim, something had, nevertheless, been stolen from her.

2

THIS ONE'S CALLED INVINCIBLE," Charlene said, demonstrating on the back of the customer's hand with a quick, deft stroke, "and honey, you better believe it is. You can eat dinner, drink three cups of coffee, smoke a pack of cigarettes, and it ain't going anywhere." Sometimes, depending on her gut-level assessment of the client, she would add, with a wink, "Even give a blowjob, if you feel like it," but the woman across the counter, a faded, sun-ruined sixty-something with an expression of chronic anxiety, was clearly not a candidate for that approach.

"It's very youthening," Charlene added, "because it doesn't bleed. Stays right where it is." The woman looked dubiously at the lilac streak on her yellowish skin.

"Here," said Charlene, briskly wiping the tester with a tissue, "let's try that on your lips. You'll see what I mean."

Five minutes later, the woman, looking dazed but gratified, was on her way, with one Invincible lipstick in Lilas, one in Peccadillo ("for evening wear," Charlene had insisted), and a $14 lip pencil, for the hell of it. She'd be back, Charlene knew—she looked like someone who had too much time on her hands, between tennis games and shrink appointments—and next time Charlene would push a big-ticket item, one of the "skin reconstructors" from the Age Annihilating line. You didn't want to emphasize the wrinkle situation the first time out.

The woman was a cheapskate, Charlene could tell, but a cheapskate with money. You'd be surprised how many rich women, even movie stars, would show up at the cosmetics counter at the Revco—the big Revco, near the Beverly Center, where they actually had testers for all the drugstore brands, with lab-coated reps for Max Factor, Revlon, and Oriole. Charlene was Oriole. Which, if people weren't so dumb, they would know also owned Lancôme and used many of the identical formulations. Maybe some of them did know. But most of them were just cheap. Charlene couldn't fathom that: if she had money, if she was loaded, like some of these women, who clearly hadn't worked a day in their lives—in the upright position, anyway—she would never set foot in a drugstore. She would shop only at Saks and Neiman's and Fred Segal, buy only Chanel and Shiseido and that Mer stuff that cost $150 an ounce.

Glancing at her watch—a fake Cartier that Howie had bought her after a drinking spree in Tijuana—she grimaced and eased her ass onto the high chrome-and-vinyl stool behind the Oriole display. Her feet hurt. Her doctor had told her that she needed to lose weight, but she didn't believe that was the reason her feet ached so bad. OK, maybe she could stand to drop a few pounds, but the pain was a kind of strangled, insistent throbbing, as if her feet were having a heart attack. How could that be from her weight? Poor circulation, more likely. Blood pressure. Next thing she knew she'd be having a stroke.

She heaved herself to her feet again, spotting a skinny blonde in exercise tights grazing her way down the long, curved counter from Revlon to Oriole. They didn't like to see you sitting down, wanted to believe you were at the ready all day long, on your toes, ready to hop to it. Without thinking, Charlene assumed "the expression," the alert, benign, vacantly expectant air that she could switch on and off like headlights, regardless of mood. The oncoming blonde looked vaguely familiar, with the ponytail, the overbite, and the tits, but Charlene wasn't sure if that was because she was a repeat or because Charlene had seen her on TV. LA could be confusing like that. The minor stars were OK: you could sell them truckloads of makeup because they were insecure. But the famous ones, sealed into their vacuum-pack of entitlement, were insufferable. Not so long ago, a big star—and Charlene didn't mind naming names—slumming with her girlfriend, Slurpee in hand, had casually pocketed a couple of Bisous testers while Charlene was bent under the counter, ransacking her supplies for a discontinued shade.

She looked at her watch again. One more hour and she'd be out of there. It was a Tuesday, slowest day of the week, and she was ready to leave. Shit, she'd been ready to leave since she'd arrived, at 9:00, with a low-grade Jack hangover, scratchy head, and that sick, queasy feeling, like morning sickness, that even her usual fried-egg-on-a-roll couldn't subdue.

The skinny chick wasn't buying. She was just looking to refresh her makeup at someone else's expense.

On the way home, bumper-to-bumper for an hour on the 405, Charlene always tuned in to Dr. Laura. She liked the way Dr. Laura bossed the callers around, giving it to them straight, no pussyfooting, just letting them know which end was up. "Oh please," Dr. Laura was saying to Whiny Steve, whose girlfriend wasn't getting around to leaving her husband for him, "you got yourself into this situation and now you have to get yourself out. Enough playing the victim, already!" This was the kind of talk that Charlene liked. None of this feel-good, higher-power, la-la-land stuff. She could imagine herself, in another life—a life where she hadn't dropped out of Dayton High at sixteen—as a Dr. Laura, a Dr. Charlene, telling people on the radio what was what. She had a knack with people, understood what made them tick, which was why she was so successful in sales. Winner of a thirty-two-inch TV from Oriole last year, Super SalesPerson, Greater Los Angeles area, third quarter. When you made SuperStar, you got a weekend in Vegas. Which she would, if only to beat that anorexic fashion victim at the Sherman Oaks Mall, the runner-up.

Clients tended to assume that, because she was fat and had a bad perm, she was stupid. (Which was, admittedly, part of her successful sales persona: the non-threatening presence at the makeup counter, to whom you could confess all your sins, from failure to exfoliate to fear of eyelash curlers.) But she wasn't stupid. She was fat because she drank too much and had a wicked Ho Ho habit (working at the Revco, with an endless supply on Aisle 6, didn't help), and she had a bad perm because, despite cosmetology school, it never came out right—kind of sheepdoggy. But stupid, no.

This car now, this car was stupid. This ginormous gas guzzler that Howie had acquired, Charlene didn't need to know how. She would have preferred an SUV, a get-out-of-my-friggin'-way Jeep or Explorer, but here she was instead in The Brontosaurus, as she privately called it, a 1985 Monte Carlo, Nile green. Howie had done the paint job himself, over at his friend Ray's shop in Van Nuys. Ray was an expert, could transform a vehicle in under an hour, but Howie was still learning, hadn't quite mastered the detail work. She hated this car, this distended monster with its sloping shoulders and its wide, crooked grin, but she had to admit that once she got a little speed up, got the Chevy sailing like a yacht down the 405, drawing curious or admiring looks from other motorists, she did feel kind of vast and invulnerable, almost regal. Howie liked big cars from the eighties, maybe because he'd been a teenager then, bagging groceries for doctors' wives at the A&P. Dr. Charlene could just picture him, too, a skinny, dyslexic kid, resentfully loading the weekly haul into those enormous trunks. Now he had his own 1985 Lincoln Continental, which he didn't allow her to drive—white with red interior, more limolike. They took the Lincoln when they went out at night, to TGIF's or to the multiplex. Made them feel like celebrities, though it could be a bitch to park.

Howie was home, she could see, pulling into the carport, where the Lincoln and the Chevy between them took up all four spaces, causing endless griping from the Filipinos upstairs. Hey, as far as Charlene was concerned, they could just park their Japanese junk-bucket on the street and be grateful they lived in a free country.

She glanced at herself in the flip-down vanity mirror on the passenger side: T-zone getting shiny, but that was what Mattinee Powder was for, wasn't it—for those on-the-go touch-ups. She felt she needed to prime herself, put her best face forward: she could never be sure, these days, what she was going to find at home. What kind of mood Howie might be in. Six-thirty was kind of early for him to be home, which might be a bad sign. Or, alternatively, a good one. Not that he'd had a fixed schedule for months now, but he did have his routines. His habits.

The apartment building was ugly, no way around it—a two-story shoebox daubed with that phony LA stucco, the color of Colman's mustard—and every time Charlene saw it her heart cramped, gave a ping of distress. This wasn't what she wanted, this wasn't what she'd planned at all, a seventies two-bedroom in Culver City. She'd clipped a picture of a big white Victorian from a magazine, a *Martha Stewart Living* that she'd "borrowed" from the checkout, a big white Victorian with a shingled roof and shutters and a herb garden out back—not that she would ever bother with all that faggy stuff, the basil and the rosemary and the rest of it. She just liked the look of the house, liked the idea of the garden, with its arbor and fishpond.

Charlene was an assiduous student of all the magazines the Revco stocked, from *Saveur* to *Soap Opera Digest,* from Italian *Vogue* to *The National Enquirer,* from *HG* to *GQ* by way of *More, Self,* and *Worth.* Though she scorned the self-help titles cunningly displayed by the diet aids (*Eat Right for Your Astrological Type*? Please!), she squirreled away useful information—how to pack a suitcase, what not to wear to a job interview, the five telltale signs of skin cancer and so on. Just recently, she'd read in *Psychology Today* that, in order to achieve your aspirations, you should begin to gather images of the things you wanted, in a collage or just in a special folder, to let the Universe know. Then the Universe would provide.

So far, Charlene had assembled photos of Pierce Brosnan, Donald Trump, Dolly Parton, a Parisian café, a Mercedes SUV, a slender blonde saluting the sun on a deserted beach, a Sub-Zero refrigerator, Monet's water lilies, a golden retriever, an array of Chanel logo earrings, a cozy dinner party for eight, and a businesswoman type in killer suit and heels (Charlene the Cosmetics Tycoon, CEO of the stunningly successful Get Real makeup line). Like they said in that ad for the New York lottery, Hey, you never know.

With Howie, on the other hand, she knew. Knew he'd always leave his stinky high-tops in the entryway, right where she would trip over them. She'd learned to send both shoes flying with a single smart kick.

"You're here," she said, dumping her purse and sunglasses on one of the cardboard boxes in the hall. "Here" meaning "right there," since there were only two places Howie would be if he was home: installed in front of the thirty-two-inch TV, or installed in front of the Gateway computer in the back bedroom. This evening he was in front of the TV, tipped back in the leather-look recliner they'd brought with them from Florida, watching QVC. He could watch the shopping channel for hours, said it was like meditation, a way to think about nothing. When they'd first got together, she'd thought it was weird—a guy hooked on the shopping channel, I mean, what does that tell Dr. Charlene?—but now she was fine with it. Liked to watch it herself, veg out to the mantra of ab-blasters and serveware and cubic zirconia, words you never heard anywhere else, like the lingo of a sect. And, let's face it, it was a lot less obnoxious than ESPN.

"Yup," he said, taking a swallow and replacing the can on his T-shirt, kind of braced against his gut. Charlene was relieved to see he was still on the Bud, which meant that the serious part of the evening, the Jack Daniel's part, had yet to begin.

"Well," she said, "my feet are killing me." With Howie, she always had to pretend that he'd asked her how she was, how her day had gone, because he never did. So she supplied his part of the dialogue in her mind and then responded to it. She shook off her sandals—the gold ones, to match her belt—and padded gratefully across the shag carpeting to the kitchen alcove, dropping the mail on the counter and rooting in the fridge for a Bud Light. "Fuckin' *killing* me," she repeated, popping the tab.

Howie nodded. Took a long swallow.

"Say goodbye to dangerous mold and other airborne toxins!" said the TV.

"Man," Charlene said, plopping down on the couch, to Howie's left. It made a rude noise, an air-escaping noise: the vinyl ones always did that when you sat down hard, as if surprised, huffy, at the arrival of your butt. She longed for real leather, creamy soft.

She put her feet on the coffee table and studied her toes. Puffy, corn-ridden, with chipped polish (Candyfloss Pink, from last spring's line)—not a pretty sight. Good thing the customers couldn't see them, except when she came out from behind the counter to do a makeover, and then they were too busy gazing at themselves in the mirror to notice her toes. Good thing Howie never really looked at her either.

"Act now!" said the TV. "Void where prohibited."

Charlene took a long swig of her beer. Then another. This was what she thought about all day at work and all the way home in the Chev. This was her reward for putting up with rich bitches and bimbos eight hours a day, for having to fawn over them, caress their skin with cotton pads, smell their starving breath. She sucked down about half a can's worth in one go—cold, bitter, gassy, no taste like it on earth—then glanced over at Howie.

"So?" she said.

"So?" he mimicked. " 'So' what?"

"So what you been up to? Today?" Sometimes—quite often, actually—he got mad when she asked him this, flushed from gold chain to bald spot and refused to answer. She watched him warily, but he just shrugged.

"Nuthin'."

"Nuthin'?" Now it was her turn to mimic him, skeptically.

"Hanging with Ray, at the shop, a little bit, that's all."

"Yeah right," said Charlene. Howie shrugged again, with a sheepish expression, a self-conscious smirk intended to convey false modesty. He'd copied it from some TV comic, Charlene couldn't remember which one.

"Well," he said, "I did bring Ray a little present." She waited. "A present from Mr. Avis." A silent alarm, an all-points bulletin, went out through her nervous system.

"I thought that was over, Howie," she said quietly. That was the one she hated most. The riskiest, the dumbest, if you asked her. With so many variables, so many things that could go wrong. Why not just go out there with a big sign on your chest, she'd asked him once, saying ARREST ME?

"Hey," he said, maintaining the same, fake smirk. "Once in a while. Can't hurt. Easy money. Which I don't hear *you* complaining about." He'd got the idea when he'd worked, very briefly, for Budget in Daytona Beach, saw how people always wanted to turn in the wrong gate. Howie was sharp like that, always figuring an angle, spotting a weak point. She had to give him credit for that. It was a gift. She'd read in a magazine once that there were seven kinds of intelligence, but Howie had the eighth.

"You'll be the one complaining," she said. "You and Ray. When they catch up with you."

"Nobody's going to catch up with me," he said, with a sly grin, genuine this time. "Because I'm the best."

She sucked gloomily on her beer. There was nothing left, but she didn't have the energy to get up and fetch another.

"Hey, don't get all pissy on me now," he said, tipping himself out of the chair and to his feet. "I brought *you* a present too." He did the smile that was supposed to be charming, and sometimes was.

She made a moue, lips downturned as if to say, This better be good. Howie disappeared into the back room, which he used as his "office," and came back bearing a small Blockbuster bag, which looked almost empty.

Charlene, regarding the bag without interest, held out her Bud can. "Willya get me another, while you're up?"

He handed her the bag and a fresh beer, popping one for himself while he was about it. As he leaned over her, she caught a strong whiff of him, the rank, adrenal stink that he always gave off after doing a job. Even when he didn't tell her, she knew. She could smell it on him, his fear, his excitement, the whole huge rush.

Without much interest, Charlene dumped the contents of the bag onto the coffee table: a brochure of some kind and two quarters. Then, with a final shake, a crumpled receipt.

"This it?" she asked. "This is nothing." Often people left the car-rental agreement in the glove compartment, and then they were in business. "This is nothing," she repeated, smoothing out the credit card receipt, fifteen bucks for gas at a Mobil on Sepulveda. "No address, nothing."

"Check out the brochure," Howie said, indicating it with his chin. He'd remained standing over her, jiggling one leg slightly, in that hyperactive way he had.

On the back of the booklet was a map, downloaded from the Internet, a blurry bowl of spaghetti with the UCLA campus highlighted in yellow. On the front, in hot-pink type, *Language, Identity, and the "Self": Articulations and Disarticulations. The Larry King Center for Communications, University of California, Los Angeles, February 9–11.*

"Language and the 'Self,'" Charlene read, in a highfalutin manner. "Articulations and—what the fuck is disarticulation, anyway?"

"Look inside," Howie said, impatiently.

She looked. Schedule, registration fees, keynote address, blah-blah-blah. List of participants. She ran her finger quickly down the alphabet, then stopped.

"Aha," she said, looking up at Howie, who was smirking again. "A college professor. Now you're talking."

3

O F COURSE THE FIRST THING Vera did was tell Colin. On the phone, that evening, after she'd had a hot bath and a glass of wine. Not, of course, in that order.

"I wasn't going to tell you," she said, propping her legs up on the arm of the sofa and twirling her feet around to guard, retroactively, against that deep vein embolism thing that people got from sitting cramped on airplanes for hours. Usually on trips to Australia, she knew, though one couldn't be too careful. "But something happened to me today."

"Why weren't you going to tell me?" he asked, not particularly curious or put-out. Colin, for all his intelligence, wasn't psychologically minded. He assumed transparency and just waited for people to get to the point.

"Because it's embarrassing," Vera said. "Promise you won't laugh."

"I won't laugh," he said. "What happened?" He sounded mildly curious now. She could imagine him scrolling through the options in his head. She wondered what Colin would consider embarrassing, indifferent as he was to most social norms in the realms of dress, sex, and ideas.

"I got conned," she said, reluctantly. "Scammed."

"You?"

She told him the story, but she lied, a little. She said that the man had been wearing a shirt with an Avis logo. She'd decided, on the plane, that this single detail would make her behavior seem more plausible, less idiotic. Henceforth, this was to be her version.

Colin didn't laugh. Nor did he, as she'd anticipated, point out the flaws in her thinking that had led to this particular outcome. He didn't, as far as she could tell, immediately get on the Web to see if other scams like this had been reported elsewhere. He was thoughtful, sympathetic, feeling out the implications. He suggested, which hadn't occurred to her, that the con artist probably had an inside connection on the Avis lot, somebody paid to look the other way or take a coffee break.

"Good thing you got your luggage out," he said. "You didn't leave anything in the car, did you?"

"No, nothing."

His tone was unusually gentle and solicitous—so much so that Vera found herself wishing he'd offer to come over, though it was already past 10:00 and by the time he got the train from New Jersey it would be 11:30, and then she wouldn't feel so much like seeing him. The distance between Basking Ridge, New Jersey, and Alphabet City, which had initially appealed to her as a moat of privacy, meant that sometimes, by the time they met, the impulse to see each other had already flickered out.

She knew that, if she asked him to, he'd probably get on the train and come over, but, given the perversity of the human species, the point was not to have to ask.

He didn't offer. She didn't ask.

After they hung up, Vera, feeling mildly grumpy and out of sorts, poured herself another glass of wine, threw the dirty clothes from her suitcase into the laundry bag, tossed her mail— all junk and solicitations from credit card companies—into the recycling bin, and checked her e-mail again: a virus alert, forwarded by Helena, which Vera had already received three times and knew to be a hoax. She had decided that virus alerts were themselves a kind of pox, eating up time and space and memory on the Web. Then, while she was on-line, she paid some bills—Visa, AT&T, dentist—with the sick, anxious feeling that activity always generated, partly because her bank balance was so dismal and partly because she still didn't feel right conducting her financial affairs in the open air of cyberspace. Nor could she ever remember the random alphanumeric sequences she was supposed to use as passwords, so she'd humbly changed them all to the name of her ex. Ex-pet, that is.

Feeling ragged and frayed, in a state of minor disrepair, she decided to go to bed. The cross-country flight had worn her out, the Darwinian struggle for a cab at LaGuardia had worn her out, the mildly depressing and anticlimactic experience of coming home to her stuffy little apartment had worn her out—dead flowers in the hall, Chinese menus under the door, faint odors of cleaning powder and day-old garbage. Not even, since Lulu's death, a cat to welcome her. Coming home from a trip, even a short one, had become something of a chronic disappointment, she realized, as if she expected something to have changed—herself or her life—by virtue of her absence. But her absence from her life failed to change it, as did her presence. My life, she thought, has a life of its own.

Increasingly, these days, she'd find herself looking around her—at her apartment, at Colin, at her *Das Boot*–like office at the Multitech—and thinking, So this is it, then? This is my life? When, exactly, did I sign up for this? At what exact moment, she wondered, had the improvisations of her twenties and early thirties—move to New York from Boston; take the ESL certification rather than the arts degree so she'd have steady work for a while (and travel the world, she'd told herself, though she hadn't got much further than San Juan); avoid any man who looked as if he might "tie her down," though she wasn't going anywhere anyway; stay in Alphabet City even though she no longer had the slightest interest in nightlife and tattoo parlors and salsa music all summer long—when had these improvisations hardened into a choice? And when had that choice, if it was a choice, ceased to be one?

Enough already with the Existentialism 101, Vera thought: the unexamined life might not be worth living, but neither is the unlived life worth examining. She'd recently almost begun to envy people—her brother, Ernesto, for instance—who, apparently unplagued by doubt about how best to spend one's allotted time on this planet, infallibly had a Five-Year Plan in place, a Ten-Year Plan, a Fifty-Year Plan. Well, she'd had plans, too: the Be an Artist Plan, the See the World Plan, both of which had gradually morphed into the Teach for a While Plan. Now, after twelve years, the plan—if it could be called that—was to make it from paycheck to paycheck without going broke. Like many New Yorkers, she'd come to realize that maintaining her life in the city (which never sleeps, and never allows anyone else to sleep, either) required so much energy that, in the end, none remained for transforming it.

To quash that line of thought—which led predictably to further thoughts of destitution, adult diapers, and a lonely death—she turned off the lamp. But, on closing her eyes, she immediately saw that face again, in eidetic detail, down to the last trickle of sweat. The bastard, she thought. The scumbag. What kind of person would do such a thing? And what a risky, distasteful, scummy way to make a living. It couldn't be easy, judging by the way he was sweating. And he wasn't that young—mid-thirties, she'd guessed—though still young enough to find another line of work. Did he get any pleasure from it, she wondered, from the con, some sense of power and potency? Was that what kept him going? His contempt for his victims and their misplaced trust? Or had this just, somehow, become his job, the way that teaching English as a Second Language had become hers?

Snapping the light back on, she sat up and checked, unnecessarily, that the alarm was set for 6:00, then, subsiding, killed the light, flipped her pillow, plumped it up, and instructed herself to sleep. But her mind wouldn't slow down and began instead to run a tedious checklist of everything she had to do the next day:

1. Correct exercises from Intro class first thing in morning
2. Iron gray pants
3. Get train by 9:30
4. Teach Intro and Intermediate classes back to back (don't forget to photocopy assignment for Intermediates)
5. Office hours from 2:30 (expect a steady stream of students because of test next week)
6. Take sandwich because there won't be time for lunch (Correction: 2b. Make sandwich. Shit, no bread)
7. Fill out reimbursement form for conference in LA

Oh, and

8. Go to gym if not too tired

Well, you will be too tired if you don't go to sleep soon, she reprimanded herself, wondering, once again, when her life had turned into an endless to-do list. Perhaps everyone's is, she told herself, perhaps that's what's meant by "adult life." Once again, she shut down this line of thought, the unlived, et cetera. She tried to turn her mind to something more stirring — tried, half-heartedly, to have an erotic fantasy about Colin (she was on top of him, stretched out over his long lean warm body, holding his hands over his head, they were gazing into each other's eyes, he was whimpering)—but couldn't sustain it. She tried to have an erotic fantasy about someone else but couldn't think whom. Her thoughts kept returning, in a guilty, uneasy, rageful way, to the man in the Avis lot.

The pig, she thought, the predator. She pictured him again, gesturing to her from the entryway. It hadn't taken him long— a split second—to peg her as a loser, to corral her in Guest Parking like the weakling of the herd. But what, she wondered, had marked her as prey? Images of "downer" cattle from the recent BSE outbreak began flickering through her brain. Was she, in some way, a downer human? And, if so, what—in that split second—had the stranger seen in her?

The next time she saw Simone, in Simone's pleasantly cluttered office on the Upper West Side—Guatemalan wall hangings, Zulu baskets, unsteady heaps of well-thumbed books— Vera brought the subject up, though she had already resolved not to. She'd learned, by now, that for her to decide not to say something was pretty much a guarantee that she would blurt it out on some later occasion. Perhaps, she thought, as she heard herself launch into the story, this marks a new phase in my relationship with Simone (and, through the miracle of the transference, with others as well), a new phase of openness and honesty and such. She doubted it, but you never knew.

Simone listened, with the grave, skeptical empathy that was her trademark, the direct, humorous intelligence that had endeared her to Vera from the start, after decades of failed relationships with therapists, along with just about everyone else. Nor did Simone, as Vera had half anticipated, and, she realized, half desired, embark on an analysis of all the various ways in which Vera must have had "Victim" inscribed all over her; she took the incident at face value, as a con, to which anyone, under the circumstances (preoccupied, unsuspecting, in a hurry), would have been vulnerable. Having made her confession and received her absolution, Vera felt better, unburdened, but at the same time obscurely disappointed, as if she'd wanted, somehow, to be blamed.

That evening, over sushi with Colin in the East Village—it was a Friday, an evening they often dedicated to sushi and sex—she listened with half an ear as he described in great detail some major security flaw some hacker in his research group had discovered in some major Microsoft product. Colin worked for Lucid Technology, out in New Jersey, ostensibly as a specialist in Internet telephony, but in practice, it seemed to her, as a kind of freelance hack-artist, who went in to work when he felt like it, worked on whatever problem seized his imagination that day, wore whatever he liked (accessorized, always, by army boots), and was paid, at the age of thirty-one, more than triple Vera's pittance from the public university. He didn't seem particularly interested in money, which was one of the things Vera liked about him, and, apart from the spacious suburban house he rented, so as to have plenty of garage room in which to restore his precious old Rileys, he lived very much like the grad student he had so recently been.

"Which shows, once again," he concluded, "that anyone who's stupid enough to rely on Windows is asking for it."

She agreed, lazily, topping up his sake cup and then her own. She preferred Macs, anyway. Colin had tried to introduce her to Linux, but she'd told him she couldn't be bothered learning a new system at her age. He was always trying to upgrade her technological know-how, and she was a fairly willing student, interested in computers and the on-line world, wanting to understand more, but only if it didn't involve major investments of time. Or too much exposure to boy culture.

"Shall we get another?" she asked, lifting the empty sake jar and looking around, in the hyperactive throng, for something resembling a waiter. As she did every week, she wondered why they came there, to be crammed elbow to elbow with strangers shouting their business, mainly flirting and boasting, over the din. The man next to her, pierced and buzz-cut, was describing to his date, also pierced and buzz-cut, a noteworthy erotic dream.

"So what's he going to do about it?" she asked, reverting to Colin's colleague and the security flaw.

He shrugged, picked up his chopsticks. "Probably post something on Slashdot," he said, "get the word out." He seemed to have lost interest in the topic.

At this point in the conversation, according to Vera's stubborn inner sense of things, it was time for Colin to turn to her and express some reciprocal interest, whether real or feigned, in her—her day, her work, her life. She had, after all, just spent twenty minutes listening to a highly detailed and mildly tedious account of something that had happened not even to him but to a colleague. But she knew he wouldn't and he didn't; he addressed himself instead to his sushi.

Even after six months with Colin, she still experienced this predictable (and apparently inextinguishable) pang at his disregard for the ritualized niceties of a relationship—the various formulaic versions of so-how-was-your-day and so-what's-new-with-you? They had discussed this, in various ways—sometimes under snuggly and intimate conditions, other times not. Colin, though receptive, seemed baffled. He'd professed himself unable to understand why she needed him to perform this, to him, meaningless routine. She knew he cared about her, didn't she? Yes. She was an intelligent woman, wasn't she? Yes. So he could safely assume that if she had something to tell him, she would? Well, yes . . .

He made her feel silly sometimes, silly and needy. She yearned to be neither.

Leaning back in her chair, and then forward again, as she banged heads with the diner behind her, she watched Colin attack his tuna. He ate delicately and at the same time voraciously, the way he made love, and it gave her pleasure to watch his hands at work, his long brown monkeyish fingers scarred and nicked, as always, from various misadventures with various tools. Colin was never happier than when elbow-deep in a dismembered engine, filthy, sweating, and bleeding—all of this, however, in a peculiarly non-macho way. There was something regressive about it, Vera thought. Something to do with Colin's absent father, a technician and tinkerer, who'd abandoned the family when Colin was ten. She'd offered this theory to Colin, who'd accepted it matter-of-factly and had continued, untransformed, to tinker.

Watching his hands made her want to have sex. She tacitly vetoed the option, which they'd discussed earlier, of catching a movie at the Angelika after dinner. She hated the Angelika on weekends, anyway. No, she decided, they would go back to her place, open a bottle of wine, take a languid hot bath together. She would rub oil into his smooth young skin, he would rub oil into her smooth but not so young skin. Then, as part of their pre-lovemaking ritual, he would allow her to shave him, which she did slowly and tentatively and not too well. About a third of the way through, he would lose patience and finish the job himself, but she didn't mind: he was the first lover she'd ever had (and she'd had quite a few) who was willing to shave each time they made love, so her skin wouldn't be sandpapered by his stubble. His trust touched her, his vulnerability, as he raised his soapy chin to her, as he bared his neck to her, a woman with a razor in her hand.

She liked that about him, his openness, as she liked his looks: his curly dark hair, seldom washed and kept in a vanity-free hacker's ponytail, his greenish-blue eyes, which in certain lights caused her an odd spasm in the solar plexus, and his long, lean young body. There was a lot to like—his intelligence, too— so perhaps the other stuff, the age difference, the occasional sense of utter disconnect, of emotional malnourishment, didn't matter so much after all. Even the long disquisitions on technology. Even what she privately thought of as his Hitler Youth wardrobe, consisting mostly of army surplus. He didn't own a single pair of jeans that hadn't been eaten through by battery acid. He didn't care, so why should she?

"If you aren't going to eat that . . . ," Colin was saying, eyeing her leftovers. He'd demolished everything he'd ordered, down to the last fatty scrap of eel. She pushed the wooden platter towards him. A squeamish eater, she actually wasn't that keen on sushi. She would have preferred a steaming bowl of pasta.

On the way back to her place, she snuggled under Colin's arm, feeling amorous but also a bit chilly in the crisp winter air. They could never walk that way for long, arms about each other, because of the difference in height: either she would be taking giant, seven-league strides to keep up with him or Colin would try to match her pace with tiny, mincing steps. Either way, they looked ridiculous. She tried not to see this as symbolic, their failure to walk in step, to find a rhythm.

As she bolted the door behind them, Colin was already on the sofa, unlacing his boots, having dumped his Arctic-quality parka on the floor. She took off her coat (made in Italy, where they didn't understand winter) and hung it neatly in the hall closet. She took off her shoes, aligned them next to the door, pulled off her sweater, creating weather in her hair. Colin dropped his boots with consecutive thuds on the hardwood floor, a sound that made her cringe for the people downstairs, and then headed, as usual, straight for her desk.

"Look," he said, waiting impatiently for her Mac to wake up, "there's something I want to show you."

"Look here," she said in a sultry voice, unbuttoning her body-warm blouse, "there's something I want to show *you*."

He glanced in her direction, grinned appreciatively. Then he turned back to the screen. "Jeez, this thing is slow," he said, scrubbing the mouse across the mousepad like a dried-up pen. Colin waged a constant guerrilla campaign for Vera to go broadband—mainly, she suspected, for his own convenience—but, late adopter and crypto-Luddite that she was, she had no problem with dial-up. She even liked the high-pitched mating song of the modem as it went on-line. "Ah, there we go . . ." He began hitting the keyboard at hacker speed. "Come take a look at this."

"Come take a look at *this*," she said, shimmying stripper-style. It was partly a game they played, partly deadly serious, her trying to lure him away from the computer.

Again he smiled. "Come here, you."

She sidled over and sat on his lap. He put one hand down her bra, playfully, and, peering over her shoulder at the screen, used the other to point and click, until the page he wanted appeared.

"OK," he said, "give me a name."

"Do I *have* to?" she asked, pretending to whine. "Can't we just have sex instead?"

"No, really, Vera, give me a name."

"Oh, I don't know—Helena. Kowaleski." Her best friend. They'd met in Intro to Visual Arts at UMass, and, since both were solitary and unsociable by nature—and seemed to think this was normal—their friendship had stuck.

"What's that—K-O-W-A-L . . ." He entered the name fast and inaccurately, backed up, corrected it. Clicked a few times. "OK," he said, "watch this."

Hel-*lo!* Vera wanted to say, this is not the time for a demo. Not the time to illustrate, once again, how nobody has any privacy on the Web — Colin's current hobbyhorse. His screen saver was a notorious quotation from some software CEO, which Colin had programmed to replicate itself rapidly, then self-destruct: "You have zero privacy anyway. Get over it." He'd recently hacked thousands of credit card numbers "lying around" a Champ Hardware site, just to show it could be done. He'd also spent hours intercepting images from security cams in shopping malls, an enterprise Vera had found mildly amusing.

The screen filled up with names and addresses, a big block of text.

"OK," he said triumphantly, "120 Kent Street, Brooklyn, correct?"

"Well, duh," Vera said. "I could have got that from the phone book. Or from my very own address book." I need a grown-up, she thought, as she'd thought so many times in Colin's presence. A grown-up, not a gifted kid. But a grown-up would be dull, she reflected, her thoughts following their familiar groove: dull and paunchy, middle-aged. But *I'm* middle-aged, she thought, and then, with a stab of anxiety, killed that thought. She killed it at least five times a day, but it wouldn't stay dead.

"Yes, but you see these other names and addresses?" Colin asked, absorbed in the screen. She nodded dutifully.

"Her neighbors. Her nearest twenty neighbors."

"But that's creepy," Vera said, her interest now piqued. "You just enter someone's name, you get a list of all their neighbors?"

"Yup. Addresses, phone numbers. You could call them all up, if you wanted to. Ask questions about Helena. What kind of hours does she keep, does she have a boyfriend, a dog —"

"Yikes," Vera continued, imagining an army of anonymous human beings somewhere assembling such a database, such a mass of information. "But who would want to do that?"

"Skip-tracing services," Colin said. "When people run out on their bills. Normally you'd have to pay a fee . . ." But not me — Vera finished his sentence in her mind — because I'm a hacker and hackers don't pay.

"That's creepy," she repeated, though she couldn't have specified exactly why. Too much visibility, as if a stranger were peering through the walls of your house. The houses of everyone around you. And you had no idea.

"So what else d'you want to know about her?" Colin asked, reading from a menu. "Search for Social Security Number? Cellular Number Lookup? Bankruptcies, Liens, and Judgments?"

"No, that's enough now," Vera said. "This is sick."

"Death Locator Database?"

"Honey," she said firmly, turning to face him, so that she was straddling him, "are you going to play with the computer or play with my tits?"

"Your tits, of course," he said, hitting Disconnect. Whatever else could be said about him, Vera thought, when Colin gave something his attention — a microprocessor, an engine, or the female body — he applied himself to it with wholehearted, fearless, and highly ingenious concentration. This was not altogether a bad quality in a lover.

4

ONCE HOWIE HAD LEFT that Sunday afternoon, sailing off in the Lincoln to do the rounds of the mailboxes, Charlene could get down to business. The house fell suddenly, blissfully silent; she could feel the muscles of her face relax, her neck unknot, could switch off the channel in her brain that preempted all the others, the one dedicated to unscrambling Howie's static, his moods and silences, his surges of rage.

Sundays, when she didn't work at the Revco, she liked to sleep late, until noon or one, and then eat a big pancake 'n sausage breakfast over at the IHOP on Culver. Sometimes Howie would join her, but if he had a really bad hangover he would sleep all day. Then she would put on her pink sweatsuit and do a few desultory rounds of "power walking" on the track of the local high school, because Howie was always after her to get off her fat ass and get some exercise. Not that she noticed him doing anything about that beer gut of his, but never mind. She actually sort of liked the walking routine, because she and Judith from down the road would just end up sitting on a bench in the shade, shooting the shit. They never got into anything personal, but Judith liked to hear about makeup, new products, the inside scoop: how all the lipsticks for all the brands came from the same two factories, and so on. It was the only time Charlene ever saw her—a trim housewife with two overscheduled children—but it was nice all the same, like having a real friend.

Now, still in her workout clothes—God forbid she should ever actually work up a sweat—Charlene had fetched herself a beer, turned on the AC in the back bedroom, and settled herself in front of the computer. She thought of this as her second job. Howie was always hustling her to quit the Oriole gig and work full-time on this other "venture," as he called it, but she wasn't stupid. When you'd grown up—solo—with an alcoholic mother who racked up frequent flyer miles in the psych ward, you didn't underestimate the value of a steady job. Charlene had already done way too much time as the Avon lady and as a data-entry clerk at the DMV, enterprises that, for various reasons, hadn't ended well. Plus, she was pretty sure that Howie was going to land in jail, and she was equally sure that she wasn't going to join him there.

She needed, what was it called, an "exit strategy." The words just came into her mind, like that. Exit strategy.

The computer was ready, alive, purring softly, its lucent blue screen like a window into another world. A world where she could be anyone she wanted to be, where she could slip free of Howie, and slip free of Charlene, too. She imagined herself as a sleek, quicksilver fish, darting through the aquamarine waters of cyberspace. That was where she felt truly agile, truly alive.

Taking the Blockbuster bag out of the desk drawer, she carefully extracted its contents, minus the two quarters, which had gone towards the weekly load at the E-Z Wash. Not much to work with: the credit card slip and the conference brochure. She smoothed out the crumpled yellow chit on the surface of Howie's desk, an ugly fake-woodgrain thing from Ikea that she would never have chosen in a million years.

This scrap of canary-colored paper was a starting point: it gave you the credit card number, expiration date, name, and signature. By itself, it was good for a short, intensive burn-through on the Internet. But the brochure gave you one additional piece of information: institutional affiliation. With that, Dr. Charlene was in business.

So, let's see, who was she going to be this time? This moment always filled Charlene with a strange, electric charge: the moment of finding out who she was, the other one—the stranger who didn't even know that Charlene Cummins existed, let alone that she was about to do her some serious harm. It filled Charlene with a nervous, expectant rush, like the instant before you set eyes on your Match.com date.

Vera de Sica. She copied the name on the back of Howie's liquor store tab, then looked at it. What kind of name was that, anyway? Not American, that was for sure. An immigrant, most likely, enjoying her free ride in the US of A. Flying to California whenever she felt like it, renting a car, staying at the Biltmore, obviously not hurting for money. Charlene had gleaned the Biltmore information from the brochure, from which she also copied the entry under "Conference Participants": "*De Sica, Vera:* Adjunct Asst. Prof., Brooklyn Multitech, Department of ESL and ESL Education." Whatever that might be—something to do with English, she knew, English as a Foreign Language, something like that. But then it would be EFL, wouldn't it? English for Stupid Losers, she thought. English for Slimy Latinos.

English had been Charlene's favorite subject at school, despite their teacher, Mrs. Milford, a narcoleptic depressive counting down to retirement, who'd tacitly given up on the whole notion of education, permitting a roomful of throwaway kids to run wild while she read despairingly from Longfellow. Even so, Charlene had won a prize in the third grade, for a poem about snow. "Snow, oh snow," it began. She couldn't remember the rest. She still remembered all the states in the Union, though, the U.S. presidents, the capital of Ecuador, and the names of all the planets, in order (much good they did her now): Mercury, Venus, Earth, Mars, Jupiter, Saturn, Uranus, Neptune, and Pluto.

So here was *de Sica:* Professor of English. What exactly, she wondered, did the Professor profess? Pity there wasn't more of a bio. Even a nugget of information, such as where our esteemed Professor had earned her fancy degrees. These alumni associations could be a gold mine. But the Multitech catalogue would tell her that, or the departmental Web site. They always listed the faculty's credentials: degree, university, year. It was a form of institutional bragging. Howie had used this before, when *Who's Who* hadn't known what was what.

The first thing was to get an address. Which would be a piece of cake, now that Charlene had a city. With the fast typing of the former data-entry serf, she logged on to her AOL account and entered her password, which even Howie didn't know: the name of her favorite lipstick, a frosted blue-pink from Clinique (*not* from Oriole, even though she had to pay retail). Double Trouble, it was called, for the durability plus the frost, hence her password: doubletrouble. Much higher quality than Oriole, which tended, despite what she told the clients, to cake or bleed.

Straight to the on-line directories, New York, Brooklyn—two seconds flat. De Sica, Vera: no entry found. That was odd. Either she had an unlisted phone number, or she didn't live in Brooklyn. You could find an unlisted number, but it was more work, plus you had to wait. Dan over at Docusearch.com did an Unlisted Telephone Number Lookup for thirty-five bucks, twenty-four hours, guaranteed. But Charlene wasn't in the mood for waiting: she was all revved up and ready to go. So do me a favor, Prof, she thought, live in one of the other boroughs, why don't ya?

The Manhattan directory, within seconds, yielded a de Sica,

V, at 211 East Second. Bingo, thought Charlene, with a proleptic adrenaline surge, the first, she anticipated, of many. Of course the V was Vera: women always listed themselves under their initials, so as not to announce their gender to serial killers idly scanning the phone book—thereby definitively flagging themselves as female.

Well, Professor de Sica, now I have you. Gotcha. You're screwed, except you don't even know it yet.

Charlene had never been to New York, but she knew enough to know that Second Street was downtown, SoHo or the Village or one of those high-end, ever-so-artsy kind of places. She pictured an enormous loft, with skylights and columns and discreetly burnished stainless-steel fixtures, like she'd seen in a movie once. She pictured people draped around drinking red wine, she pictured them admiring some god-awful painting on the "distressed" brick wall. She hoped that, at the very least, our Prof had received a lungful when the towers burned.

With a name and address in hand—hell, even with just a name, but Charlene liked to get the address herself, to prevent mix-ups—there was nothing she couldn't find out about our Miss V. Or Mrs. V, as the case might be, though Charlene had a strong gut feeling that our Prof was single—she couldn't have said why. The loft, maybe. The lack of a first name and an ampersand in the directory listing. Something.

Anyway, she would soon know for sure. Down to business: the credit report, God's little gift to people like Charlene and Howie. Ray's little gift, really—because (among other things) Ray sold cars, he was legit. An authorized subscriber, an auto dealer who needed access, 24/7, to credit reports—customers, potential customers, anyone who walked onto the lot and was naive enough to give Ray his name. Ray would be in the office checking on the guy while he was still eyeballing the vehicles, to see whether he was good for the asking price—and therefore worth Ray's sales pitch—or just a Looky Lou. And Ray bought the credit reports from a reseller, who never visited the site like he was supposed to, and never asked any questions about Ray's "employees," Ms. Cummins and Mr. Cash. Howie's little joke.

Charlene liked to plug the name du jour into all three bureaus, TransUnion, Equifax, and Experian, because one would often contain some tidbit that the others didn't. Whether the info was accurate or not was another story, not Charlene's problem. What appeared on your credit report became the truth about you, whether you knew it or not, whether or not it was true. Once there, it could never be removed. All you could do was put a statement in your file disputing it, but, really, who read those? Forget the book of Judgment: your credit history was forever.

And here it was.

LEGAL NAME: Vera Migone de Sica

PLACE OF BIRTH: Somerville, Massachusetts

SOCIAL SECURITY NUMBER: There it was, all nine digits. The keys to the kingdom. The Open Sesame. The Decoder Ring.

Well, wasn't that nice. If Migone wasn't the mother's maiden name, then Charlene was a rabid yak. Another big adrenaline surge: our Prof, through her touching attachment to Mama, had just saved Charlene hours of searching on genealogical Web sites, the hassle of applying for a duplicate birth certificate, or the dubious thrill of "social engineering." That was when you got on the phone and wangled information out of those minimum-wage, minimum-IQ "customer service representatives." And how hard was that? They assumed, poor babies, that if you knew someone's name, address, telephone number, Social Security number or mother's maiden name, then you must *be* that person.

"Oh, hi, I'm Vera de Sica, but I've forgotten my password again . . ."

"Oh, hi, this is Mr. de Sica calling, Bob de Sica. Listen, my wife is away on a business trip, but I just have a couple of questions about our most recent bill . . ."

"Oh, hi, this is Vera de Sica. Listen, I'm on the cell phone, in the car, so I don't have my account number handy, but . . ."

CURRENT AND PREVIOUS ADDRESSES: Despite an unsightly slew of previous addresses, our Prof was now a nester, nine years at the Second Street address. That was all Charlene needed to know. She could search the property tax records later, get a sense of the market value.

CURRENT EMPLOYER: Brooklyn Multitech, Metropolitan University, New York, New York. Well, Charlene already knew *that*. Twelve years on the job: nice and stable, just what Charlene liked to see, upstanding citizen, gainfully employed, not a job-hopper or a rent-skipper. PREVIOUS EMPLOYERS: Kinko's Copies, Ristorante Da Nico, Hostos Community College, La-Guardia Community College. So our Prof had done some time as a waitress. Yet another line of work at which Charlene had failed: she didn't like being told what to do, especially by cranky people—which was, pretty much, the job description. At least as a cosmetics "consultant," she got to call the shots: you could tell some woman with a law degree to put cow cartilage or putrid toxin on her face, and she would.

There were recent inquiries in the file from Bloomingdale's, Sunshine State Leisure Timeshares Inc., and American Airlines. That didn't tell you much, just who was interested in pitching something to Upstanding Citizen de Sica.

The real nitty-gritty, the heart of the matter, the ham in the sandwich, was the banking and credit card record, which Charlene printed out to explore at her leisure. But she did notice that something seemed off: just a checking account at Citibank, opened in 1994. Charlene would have expected, at a minimum, a cash management account at Merrill Lynch or Morgan Stanley. Her experienced nose smelled a big fat rat. She'd have to look into that.

On the face of it, Charlene thought, our Prof just did not like to spend money: only two credit cards, each carrying a modest balance, a few thou apiece. Plenty of room for growth there— five, ten cards at least. Our Prof had never missed a payment, never paid late, not even once. No delinquencies, bankruptcies, tax liens, monetary judgments, overdue child support.

Charlene had a hard time imagining a life like that. How it was done. How you kept it up. How the whole thing didn't come crashing down on you.

She'd tried, God knows, but the system just wouldn't give her a break. She'd been passed over twice for promotion at the DMV, and she knew it wasn't because she lacked the skills or the smarts (hey, a trained gerbil could do the job). No, the higher-ups hadn't liked her big mouth, that was all, her "bad attitude." She just hadn't fit in with the other data-entry clerks, timid, skinny, single-mother types, who would take any kind of crap to keep a job—never mind that their acrylic tips basically impeded them from typing.

Well, screw them anyway. It was around that time that she'd met Howie, who'd presented her with other opportunities. A chance, at last, to make something of herself.

Not everyone in this world had everything handed to them on a platter like little Miss "Never-Missed-a-Payment" de Sica. Let's face it, you didn't buy even a "starter" apartment in Manhattan without family money, and you didn't get into fancy colleges without connections. Charlene understood only too well how the class system worked. But what if, she wondered, someone just happened to take a wrecking ball to the Prof's house of cards?

Her credit rating was excellent. She was a professional, owned property, had a steady job. She would do very nicely.

And then, running her eyes over the report again, Charlene noticed something that she hadn't registered at first. DATE OF BIRTH: June 10, 1964. That was creepy: Charlene's own birthday was June 11 of the same year. Very creepy, she thought—as if, somehow, this was meant to be.

5

A FEW EVENINGS LATER, with the Brooklyn jazz station playing softly and a glass of red wine to hand, Vera was tackling a small heap of receipts, nasty accordioned slips that wouldn't lie flat. Even though the college would refund only a laughable amount, she still had to chronicle every penny she'd parted with in LA. Airfare, conference registration, hotel, meals (her pitiful sandwich, her pizza slice), car rental (quick squirmy flashback), gasoline. Gasoline? Where had she put that receipt, then—that $15 worth, or whatever it was, to fill the tank? She searched again in her wallet, but she'd already emptied it out. She looked in the pockets of the pants she'd been wearing, in the various compartments of her briefcase. Damn. She was usually so meticulous about these things—partly by nature, and partly out of a kind of free-floating paranoia, as if she might at any moment be required to produce evidence. Of what, she couldn't have said. That she'd been where she said she'd been, done what she claimed to have done. That she'd kept accurate records. That she'd left a trace. That, after all, she existed.

If this was a new symptom of aging—losing things—then she did not care for it at all. Losing it, on the installment plan: first bits of information, names and dates and phone numbers, then objects in the physical world, and then, she supposed, one's mind. Along with one's continence and the use of one's limbs.

Perhaps this was another symptom of aging, she thought: to be always thinking about aging. She tried to turn her attention back to the task at hand.

Otherwise, she had everything she needed for the reimbursement form. If she weren't so broke, she wouldn't even waste her time filling it out. But she was so broke—broker even than she needed to be, since, out of pride (and also, admittedly, to avoid the inevitable It's-Not-Too-Late-to-Apply-to-Law-School lecture), she habitually misrepresented her financial situation to her parents. She had, after all, a lifetime's worth of practice in telling them what they wanted to hear. And what they wanted to hear was that she was self-sufficient, doing well; Carlo and Francesca hadn't toiled all their lives to raise a whiner.

They'd sweated it out at De Sica Cleaners & Expert Alterations without complaint—until, after decades of exposure to dry-cleaning chemicals, even Carlo had to admit that his lungs were shot. Only then had they sold the business and moved to a summer-camp-like "retirement community" in Arizona for people like them, people who'd worked fourteen hours a day for forty years and had a horror of unstructured time. Under this regime of administered leisure, where Carlo occupied his days with Scrabble and golf, and Francesca occupied hers with Oprah, petit point, and visiting even older ladies for the church, they seemed—almost—to be enjoying life. So what was Vera going to do, call them up and confess that she couldn't pay her bills? On the contrary, during their weekly phone calls and biannual visits, her brief was to convince her parents that she was doing splendidly (despite the lack of a husband and a law degree), that she *loved* teaching, that she still had great plans to write that screenplay, or complete that photo project, and that all their sacrifices, therefore, had not been in vain.

So at that moment she had little choice but to tot up her

petty expenditures, photocopy the form, submit it to her department chair, wait a few months (administrative time being different from ordinary human time), and then receive her pittance. Which might, if she were lucky, cover cab fare to La-Guardia plus a pack of gum.

This had all taken much longer than it should have. She still had a set of exercises to correct. She dreaded it, as she dreaded pretty much everything she had to do these days, with the possible exception of her time with Colin. And with him, too, she dreaded the inevitable moments of disconnect, when her spirits would drop the way the elevator in her building at Brooklyn Multi sometimes did, with a sudden, heart-emptying lurch.

The next day, arriving at her office with an unexpected fifteen minutes to spare, and noticing, as she passed it, that Roberto's door was open, Vera decided to hand-deliver the reimbursement form. Things tended to get lost in the main ESL office, especially requests for money, but Roberto could usually be counted on to work his way, within the lifespan of a single human being, to the bottom of the pile of papers on his desk. Roberto, the departmental chair, was a genial, gregarious Dominican who liked to spend his days chatting with colleagues and students and then complain that he could get nothing done. He was on the phone, listening intently, when she appeared at his door, proffering the manila envelope and requesting, with a tentative gesture of her eyebrows, permission to enter. He smiled broadly, waved her in, and then pointed, with an exasperated grimace, towards the receiver, making a yak-yak motion, hand opening and closing like a duck's bill. But his voice, as he concluded the conversation with a few reassuring Yeses and No Of Course Nots and Talk to You Soons, was patient and kind.

"So Vera," he said, swiveling his chair to face her, "sit down, sit down. How's it going? I feel as if I haven't seen you for ages."

"No, well, you know. Well, actually, I was at that conference in LA last week, which is why I stopped by—"

"Oh yeah, that Language and Identity thing at UCLA. Did you run into my old friend Guillermo Mendoza there, from San Francisco State? I think he was supposed to be on one of the panels, something about truth commissions, I think. The language of truth commissions. And Lacan. Just think of a topic and add 'and Lacan,' and there you have Guillermo's career in a nutshell."

"No, actually, there were so many—"

"And your talk? Go well?"

"Oh, fine. The three people who were there got a lot out of it, I'm sure . . . Anyway, Rob, I just wanted to drop off this form for the travel money. If you could just sign it and send it on its way up the food chain, that would be great."

"Sure, no problem," he said, taking the envelope from her and slotting it blindly into the bottom of the tall, messy, but, she'd discovered, relatively systematic stack that overflowed his in tray. "Anyway, it's good that you stopped by. There's something I need to talk to you about. Do you have a minute?"

She looked at her watch. "Um, about ten minutes," she said, "then I have class."

"No, it won't take long," he replied, getting up and squeezing past her—for all his good qualities, slenderness was not among them—to close the door. This action alarmed her. Roberto conducted most business, except that of the most dire and confidential nature, with his office door open. Most of the faculty did, in fact, at the cost of their own and their students' privacy, because the new anti-sexual-harassment codes had put the fear of God into them and they wanted, at all times, to be seen to be doing no wrong.

She waited, tensely, for him to resume his seat, to squeeze back in behind his desk. She recrossed her legs. She chewed the inside of her lip. She adjusted her spine against the hard plastic back of the chair.

"I wanted to talk to you," he began, rubbing his hands together, as if they were cold, "before the department meeting next week."

Oh God, she thought, what had she done? Had some student complained? Had she been harsh? Had she been unfair? Had she, worse still, said something racially or ethnically or genderly insensitive?

"You've probably heard the rumors," he said, with the ghost of a shrug.

Of course she hadn't. Rumors? About her?

"About this new board . . ."

It took her a moment to understand what he meant. For a second she misunderstood him to have said "broad." And then it made sense: the board of trustees of the Metropolitan University, a gang of political appointees and geriatric industrialists, handpicked by the mayor. A new mayor this year, flamboyantly right-wing, hence a new board.

She nodded, just to keep the conversation going, while she waited to understand—the way she bided her time while a student struggled with a sentence, awaiting the word or phrase that would unlock his intentions.

"Well, it looks like they're really going to do it."

"Do what?" she asked. "I'm sorry, I'm so out of it . . ."

"Get rid of all the so-called 'remedial' courses, Vera. Which includes, of course, ESL. Basic composition, basic math, ESL. The students will have to take them somewhere else, at the community colleges or who knows where."

"Oh yes, I have heard something about that. But surely—"

"But surely what? This is what this new mayor is all about, classism and racism. God forbid we should actually teach at a public institution. God forbid the sons and daughters of immigrants should actually get an education here. It was fine in the thirties and forties, when they were all white—nice Jewish boys who could win the Nobel Prize. But now . . ." He didn't have to finish his sentence. But now they were black and brown and everything in between, now they spoke every language under the sun, or, depending on latitude, under the ice.

"But surely—"

"No, I think they're really going to push it through, at their next meeting, in April."

"But surely the union—"

"Oh, we're going to fight it of course. All the faculty, at all of the colleges. But I think we're going to lose. I think it's a done deal."

Vera tried to gather her thoughts. She stared, without seeing it, at the Frida Kahlo poster to Roberto's left, at a patch of parrot green. First, a generalized sense of outrage: as the daughter of immigrants herself (Carlo and Francesca de Sica from the outskirts of Naples), as the first woman in her family to go to college, let alone get a graduate degree, she identified fiercely with her students. She wanted them to succeed, to get a leg up into the middle class; some of their stories, cobbled together in laborious and imperfect English (Tell the story of your life, 250 words, use the PAST tense, please!) routinely broke her heart. And then, with a sudden icy sensation, she realized what this might mean. What Roberto was trying to tell her.

"You mean . . . ?"

He nodded, sorrowfully. "The department would be eliminated. Just like that. The people who have tenure, the Ph.D.s, they'll probably be absorbed into the language departments, Spanish and Russian and so on. But the rest . . ."

The rest, like Vera, who, with their modest M.Ed.s, weren't

even eligible for tenure, and who had chugged along on yearly contracts at the lowly rank of Lecturer, would be out on their ear. (*Lecturer*, at Metropolitan U, meaning a member of the vast academic underclass that taught far more than full-time professors and was paid far less.) Never mind that she'd worked there for twelve years and that her student evaluations were positive ("Prof de Sica is a very dedicatted teacher. She is funny, but she gives too many homeworks"). Never mind that she still went to conferences, gave talks, applied for grants, even published something every now and then. Never mind that she had a mortgage and credit card bills and . . . thank goodness Lulu is dead, she thought, irrationally.

"You've been here the longest, Vera, so I wanted to make sure you were in the loop. Before it comes up at the meeting next week. And of course we're going to organize, we're going to fight this tooth and nail. It's an outrage—it goes against everything Metropolitan U stands for. But I have to say, I'm not optimistic." He shook his head. "Not optimistic at all."

She trusted his political judgment. Roberto was an old Sixties organizer, with a background in the unions and the antiwar movement. He was usually patient, sanguine, resourceful, and savvy. If he said a battle couldn't be won, then it probably couldn't.

"Whew," she said, with what little air remained to her. "Jeez."

"I know," he said, with an empathetic gesture somewhere between a nod and a wince.

"Wow. Well, this certainly concentrates the mind . . . Thanks for the warning, Roberto. Thanks for making my day."

"I know," he repeated. "The thing to remember, Veracita, is that even if they do push this through, it can't possibly go into effect until September. Maybe even the September after, if there are legal challenges and so on. So, best-case scenario, you'd still have eighteen months."

"Gee, thanks. Eighteen months to find a nice, strong cardboard box to live in. And a new profession—definitely too late to become a call girl. But maybe a dominatrix? I could abuse people in different languages and correct their grammar when they beg for mercy."

He laughed, with an appreciative plosive sound. "I can just picture that, too. But Vera, come on now, you know you'll find another job. At one of the other campuses. Or, uh, one of the community colleges."

"Sure, as a tutor, at twelve bucks an hour." They both knew this was true. They both looked, simultaneously, at their watches. "Well," Vera said, standing up. "The condemned woman has to return to her cell now."

He nodded. "Hang in there, OK? It isn't over till it's over."

"Sure," she said, with a skeptical, downturned pout, one she'd acquired, she realized, from her Francophone students. Even the prettiest ones could make themselves ugly in an instant by pulling this face, as if they'd just smelled something foul and that something was you, their interlocutor.

At the door, realizing she'd been abrupt, even rude, she turned and added, "Oh and thanks for clueing me in, Rob. I really don't mean to . . . It's just . . . you know."

He showed both palms, as if to say "don't mention it," then blew her a kiss. When she looked back, through the open door, he was already hunched over his computer, logging on.

She sleepwalked back to her office—a windowless incubator for sick building syndrome that she shared with two other people and their crumbs. Luckily, neither Joon Seok nor Flora was there, as she absently gathered the folder, videotape, and piece of chalk (a rare and precious commodity at Metropolitan U) that she would need for her class. Someone had abandoned a half-empty take-out coffee cup on the black plastic casing of her videotape, which lacked a box. The tape appeared undamaged, but even through the fog of distraction Vera felt her daily stab of irritation at the presence of a Starbucks concession in the lobby downstairs.

She was going to be a few minutes late for class. She hated that. The students, on the other hand, loved it, as it robbed her of the right to chastise them for arriving late, as some of them habitually did, with a Starbucket of latte in one hand and a cell phone in the other. She wondered how they afforded it. Any of it.

And she wondered how they were going to react to the news, when they heard it. Obviously, she wasn't going to say anything yet. With any luck, by the time the cuts were implemented—by the time the bloodletting was over—most of them would already have passed the ESL test for which Vera was supposed to prepare them. She would just have to work extra-hard, that was all. To make sure they passed.

As for her, her future, she'd worry about that, Scarlett-like, tomorrow. She could already hear Simone's voice telling her that it was all a question of how she looked at the situation, that this might in fact be a gift, an opportunity to take stock of her life, to make some changes, and so on. To reinvent herself. To decide, at last, what she really wanted to do, take charge of her fate. To become a photojournalist (one of her persistent fantasies) or drive a Jeep for Médecins sans Frontières (another, though she could barely work the gears) or take a course in Web design and become hip and young again (a notion she'd vaguely assimilated from Colin). To start work on that script about the Triangle Factory fire that she'd been planning since college. Or even perhaps to tackle—for real—the photo project she'd begun in a burst of enthusiasm a few years earlier and now pursued halfheartedly and intermittently, if at all. Deciding that anyone could call herself a street photographer, she'd begun systematically documenting the myriad hand-printed, misspelled signs that she noticed all over Manhattan, signs posted by immigrant shopkeepers and greengrocers, and that, for some reason, wrenched her heart: TOMOTOS, RIE & BEANS, MESCAL IN, IAM. She'd devoted all her weekends to this project for several months, then something had come up, she forgot what. When it was done, the collection would be installed in a gallery (yet to be found) and entitled "Signs of (Dis)Location." She'd even bought a digital camera on her credit card.

Well, there was the rub. It's all very well, she heard herself tell Simone, but before I can reinvent myself, I'd first have to re-invent my mortgage and my bills and my student loans. Not to mention, of course, my monthly tab for such sage advice from you.

"OK," she said, dumping her chalk-streaked briefcase on the table at the front of the classroom and noting, with relief, that the VCR and monitor were still bracketed to the wall—two had somehow liberated themselves and walked out of the building in the past three months. "We have a lot to do today. Let's get this show on the road."

6

CHARLENE was taking Vera shopping. That's how she liked to think of it, anyway, as she sat down at the Gateway, armed with a printout of the credit report. There were so many things, Charlene thought, that our Prof must need—about five more credit cards, for starters. A good selection of high-end electronics. Accounts at Saks, Neiman Marcus, Barney's perhaps, though Charlene had to admit she'd never dared walk into the Barney's on Wilshire, where they carried Swedish and Japanese makeup lines she'd never heard of and not one item above a size six. Well, she thought, let them look down their pointy noses at her: Vera de Sica would just stroll right in with her new charge account and buy some Louis Vuitton luggage. That always sold well on eBay.

Vera de Sica probably was a size six, Charlene realized, or even a size four. These New York types were always skinny and neurotic, drank coffee all day, never ate. Spent half their lives on the psychiatrist's couch. Charlene made a mental note, once she was into the bank account, to look for something that looked like the name of a shrink. One always liked to know which meds one was taking.

From the living room came the sound of the shopping channel, extra-loud. Charlene had learned to block it out most of the time, but occasionally she'd find that a phrase or two had infiltrated her brain and was repeating itself in an endless loop: Antibacterial Body Lotion, she found herself thinking, Three-Stone Princess-Cut Diamond Ring. Get-Up-and-Go Spray-On Toupee. It was annoying to find yourself thinking thoughts you didn't want to think, that weren't even yours, when you were trying to think about something else. This was a problem that preoccupied Charlene, living with Howie: how to hear her own thoughts, find out what they were—if, indeed, she still had any of her own. Perhaps she could just sneak in and mute the TV. Howie had probably passed out by now—it was after 11:00—and Charlene wanted to get this job done tonight, at least the applications. Everything could be done real quick, round the clock, on-line or on the phone, and she knew that, given the Prof's most excellent and virtuous credit rating, each card would be good for at least $7,500—hell, $10,000, $15,000 apiece. And once you had the cards, you could keep getting more, keep paying one credit card with another. Charlene had always loved that idea. So why waste time?

There was, however, an art to the applications—it wasn't as if any loser could get on-line and start applying for credit in someone else's name. Even the credit bureaus, total fuck-ups that they were, purveyors of garbage, might get suspicious if there were a sudden flurry of inquiries on one name, if they suddenly received twenty requests for the credit report of, say, oh, Vera de Sica. So Charlene and Howie had painstakingly determined which of the three bureaus each of the major credit card issuers subscribed to. Then they would rotate the applications, so that the requests were spread out among the three bureaus, causing not even a blip. That was smart. They were smart. They weren't amateurs.

And they preferred to do things the old-fashioned way—the mom-and-pop way. Ray was always after Howie to update his techniques, always trying to hook him up with the Russian Mafia, or Web site spoofers in China, but Howie preferred to do his business by hand, as it were. It had always worked just fine, he said—kept the operation on a reasonable scale, something just the two of them could handle. And he didn't trust those Communists, no offense.

Howie had figured out the logistics of his "enterprise" long before Charlene even met him. In person, that is, f2f: they'd met on-line, through the Yahoo personals. She'd been taking step classes three nights a week then, and she'd had her friend Desiree at Avon do her makeup for the photo, but, still, she wondered what exactly had drawn Howie to her: her looks, her smarts, or her previous association with the DMV.

Their first encounter, in the flesh, had been awkward, as it always is after a man and a woman meet on-line. When they finally get together, their apprehensions are mismatched: she's afraid he'll be a serial killer, he's afraid that she'll be fat. And Charlene hadn't been exactly skinny, nor had Howie exactly lacked a criminal record. She'd seen him glance at his cell phone several times during the first half hour, checking the time or, perhaps, praying it would ring. That was when, trying to show that there was more to her than met the eye, she'd brought up, once again, her data-entry days at the DMV. Howie's gaze had immediately stopped darting around the busy bar; he'd fixed her in the intense, flattering beam of his attention and asked her to elucidate certain technicalities, which she was glad to do. This led to a couple more dates, over which Charlene gradually heard Howie's tale of woe.

The way Howie told it, he'd had no choice: he'd lost his license on a drunk-driving charge, and he'd needed to keep driving to keep his job. Those were the days when he actually had a job, selling advertising for the *Daytona Beach Savvy Shopper,* a weekly throwaway that soon went under. Before that he'd sold advertising for a small local TV station and before *that* he'd worked as a "customer care associate" at Budget, both jobs that he'd lost, according to him, because his bosses had been assholes who objected to a guy having the occasional beer. Now, with the DWI conviction, the system had done its best to screw him. As it had, he claimed, his whole fucking life.

But Howie, with his eighth type of intelligence, wasn't about to give up so easily. He needed a driver's license. His had been suspended. Therefore, he needed someone else's. Therefore, in the eyes of the law, he needed to *become* someone else. And why not, anyway? Being Howard J. Hoffner was no great shakes. It had become something of a drag, frankly, dragging Howie around for these thirty-some years. He'd be quite happy to lay that tired old self aside, give it a rest. A new self, a new start: it was the American way. He could reinvent himself, remodel himself, do it right this time. Perhaps, he confided to Dr. Charlene, he'd even quit drinking, or, at least, drink less—get up early in the morning, work out with weights, take evening classes in real estate, become an entrepreneur. He loved that word: entrepreneur.

The only question was, who to become? The answer, again, was obvious: if you wanted to know who was who, where would you look but *Who's Who in America*? Unfortunately for the fat cats profiled there, the bios listed enough information—birth date, place of birth, mother's maiden name—for the diligent reader to request a copy of a birth certificate. With birth certificate in hand, the diligent reader could then show up at the local DMV, take a driving test, and be on his way: photo ID with his own face and someone's else's name, an identity makeover in half an hour. You needed a driver's license not merely to drive, Howie had found, but to navigate contemporary life. In the face-to-face world, or RL, photo ID equaled identity. You were who a laminated two-by-three-inch piece of plastic said you were.

And really, Charlene thought, why not? Everything about identity was arbitrary, accidental, anyway: you didn't get to choose your genes, any more than Howie had gone shopping for his bald spot, his dyslexia, or his deadbeat dad. Any more, come to think of it, than Charlene herself had elected to grow up in Armpit, Ohio, with a mom who couldn't get out of her bathrobe most days, "schools" where no one noticed if you went AWOL for weeks, and no friends worth mentioning (who could you bring home? who could you trust?). And then, on top of all that, a major deficit in the looks department. Self-pity wasn't Charlene's style, but hey, just think about it: another twist of the DNA, and she could've been Princess Di.

It was all random, fundamentally unfair. So why not cash in on it, as Howie had, on the arbitrary and free-floating nature of identity: Why not become an entrepreneur? An entrepreneur of identity?

From that modest start-up, the enterprise had, in one of Howie's favorite words, "proliferated." He was managing multiple identities now, multiple P.O. boxes, multiple accounts. It was like a real job, with real stress, which, he complained, Charlene didn't seem to appreciate, always nagging him to get off the couch and get a life. He had a life—several, in fact. He handed over the extras to her, the accidental females. Plus, he kept a small sideline in simple cons, just to keep his hand in. And because it was so easy, so addictive, people practically begging you to take their money, take the car. Only thing was, you had to keep moving: you could never stay in any one state for too long. They had pretty much used up California.

Howie was smart, Charlene thought, waiting for the chronically sluggish Chase site to download its screenful of bloatware, but not smart enough. He was lazy, got greedy—didn't always do things right, took stupid risks. He was going to get caught, no doubt about it. She just had to make sure that she didn't get caught alongside him. That she was somewhere else by then. Or someone else.

Half an hour later, by the time Charlene shut down the computer for the night, our Prof was the proud, though unknowing, possessor of five new credit cards, total available credit $75,000. She also had a brand new P.O. box, though she didn't know that either. In fact, Charlene thought, our Prof needs a new address for all her other mail as well—the credit cards she already uses, her bank accounts, and so on. Surely, with all that lofty thinking she was doing, the Prof wouldn't want to be bothered with those statements every month, with mundane matters like where the money went. Charlene would take care of that for her, Charlene would keep track. From across the continental divide, she would become a devoted student of the Prof's, researching every detail of her life: where she shopped, where she traveled, which restaurants and bars she patronized, which gym she belonged to, which magazines she subscribed to, which Internet service provider. Whether or not she had a pet, and, if so, dog, cat, or iguana. What her liquor store bills looked like, where she got her prescriptions filled, whether she used a dating service, whether she ordered sex toys or Bendover Boyfriend videos by mail. And so on. Not to mention Charlene's natural curiosity about Vera's paycheck, her weekly cash withdrawals, her mortgage payments, and—interesting question—where her savings might be.

You could know so much more about someone you'd never met, Charlene thought, than about the hundreds of people you saw every day—gliding past you in their urban tanks, brushing shoulders with you at the hypermarket, offering their faces for you to make up, sharing your bed. She felt that she knew Vera more intimately already than most of the people in her physical world—the Filipinos upstairs, Cindy from work, Judith from the Sunday power-walking, even Ray from the chop shop, Mr. Shoot-Off-at-the-Mouth Meth Addict. When you changed IDs every couple of months, close friends weren't part of the package. And as for Howie—who knew Howie?

This one could be a keeper, Charlene thought. Vera Migone de Sica, professor of English. Why not? She'd seen professors on talk shows, whose job description—as far as she could tell —seemed to involve traveling the world, taking the summers off, writing a book or two, and then delivering the same sound bite for the rest of their lives. How hard could that be? It could have been her, in a different world, a parallel universe, one that was fair.

Just for the hell of it, before calling it a night, she went back on-line and bought herself a present. Something nice and shiny, a touch of class. For herself. For Vera.

7

A s VERA WATCHED her colleagues trickle into the union meeting, she wondered, as she always did, how it was that academic life reduced everyone sooner or later to the same basic silhouette: the same stooped posture, the same harried expression, the same unwieldy burden of briefcase, raincoat, textbooks, lecture notes, and, these days, Starbucks cups whose sippy lids coughed stale coffee onto your hand. The profession—or was it just the light?—made everyone look old and gray and tired. She assumed she must be starting to look like that too, like a superannuated candidate for the Fresh Air Fund.

She would sit at the back of the room—understanding, anew, why her students fidgeted in these chairs—reading her mail or correcting homework, attending with half an ear, like a dog that doesn't understand human speech but has one ear cocked for a change in tone or the jingle of the leash. Her livelihood was, after all, on the line. But though the proposed cuts were discussed in a general climate of outrage, and though the mayor was freely called a fascist and a racist and a corporate lackey, little else was achieved. A decision was taken to picket the board meeting in April, but, otherwise, she thought, she might just as well have stayed home.

Vera spent a lot of time at meetings giving her colleagues

makeovers in her mind. She had no doubt that the students did too, that that's what they were really thinking about when they gazed searchingly at their teachers. Academia was not a profession that tended to attract attractive people, she had noted.

"But you're an academic," Colin pointed out when she repeated this observation to him in her kitchen that evening, as they put some kind of dinner together. She was the hunter-gatherer, he was the cook.

"I am not!" she replied, pretending to slap him with the dish-towel. This distinction was crucial to her, always had been. "I happen to teach—for the moment, anyway—at an academic institution. But it's not my vocation, it's not who I am."

"What is your vocation, then?" His tone was neutral, genuinely curious. As always, he took what she said at face value, didn't challenge or dismiss. At times she was grateful for this, after too many years with too many men who'd had too much therapy (and yet not enough).

"Um," she said. "I don't know. I don't have one. Much to my parents' distress." She thought about it while she rinsed the lettuce, then patted it dry, solicitously. "They just never understood why I wouldn't go to law school. 'But you *love* to argue,' my mother would always say," and here Vera mimed Francesca making the sign of the cross. "'Did we work all those hours in the dry cleaners for you to live in a tenement?' was my dad's line."

"Well," asked Colin, not unreasonably, "they might have a point. Why wouldn't you?"

"And become a *lawyer*? Grubbing for money all day? Like Ernesto, except without the rubber gloves? No thanks."

Colin looked at her skeptically. "But then, by default, this *is* your vocation—this teaching gig. It's what you do."

Her skin didn't like this idea; she felt it flush. "You know I only took the ESL degree so I could earn a living for a few years, travel . . . ," she said, avoiding his gaze. She ushered the lettuce into a wooden salad bowl, where it huddled at the bottom, looking strangely cowed. She hoped Colin would refrain from mentioning that, so far, she'd accomplished neither goal. That the "few years" had somehow stretched into twelve, that she wasn't exactly going anywhere.

"You know how it is," she temporized: "first generation. I could hardly come home one day and announce to poor old Carlo, bagging the shirts, that I wanted to be an *artiste.*" She said the word in a deliberately fey and pretentious manner, striking a pose. Then she wiped her damp hands on the back of her pants. "He would have had one of those Italian asthma attacks" —and here she mimed an operatic bout of breathlessness. Over the years, she'd developed a successful routine of "doing" her parents, performing them as caricatures, mainly (as now) to deflect unwelcome interrogation. "So it didn't seem like such a bad idea to stay on at UMass, get the accreditation, move to New York, and then figure out what I wanted to do." This wasn't strictly true, either. The truth, she suspected, was that she'd lacked, not the courage of her convictions, but any convictions at all.

Why else, she thought, would she have been so easily derailed from her artistic aspirations? True, everyone at twenty wants to lead a "creative" and "meaningful" life, as Vera had. And true, her drawing teacher had called her work "wispy," her painting instructor had damned with faint praise her "solid technique" —but that same instructor, a notorious drunk, had derided Helena's collages as "dogshit," and Helena had persevered. Vera, on the other hand, had quietly switched her major to French Lit. She'd also quietly downsized her ambitions—OK, then, if not Art, why not documentary filmmaking or literary translation? Why not digital photography or graphic design? Why not, indeed? She knew she had the skills, the eye; her photo project, as far as it went, was pretty damn good. So what she lacked, it seemed, was the guts. Sometimes, had it not been a physical impossibility, she would have given herself a swift sharp kick in the pants. When she'd discussed this impulse with Simone, Simone, sagely refraining from delivering it herself, had referred Vera to a scholarly work on the "Impostor Syndrome." Which, Vera had said after a cursory glance, couldn't possibly apply to her, because she really *was* an impostor.

Now, slapping the lettuce around in the bowl, she glanced over at Colin to gauge his response — but, Colin-like, he'd ceased to pay attention. Instead he was attacking an eggplant with great vigor, slicing it in a surprisingly skillful manner, so that it fell open like a flower. "Who taught you to do that?" she asked, surveying the result.

He shrugged — meaning, Vera knew, she-whose-name-could-not-be-spoken, Colin's ex, Chloe, who had dumped him for her history professor. She had trained Colin well, in bed and in the kitchen. Vera would have been grateful to her, if she hadn't been so very young and so very pretty. And if Colin hadn't still kept a stash of photos of her amidst the chaos on his desk.

"Anyway," she said, officially terminating the discussion, which was producing a queasy, panicky feeling throughout her body, a vertigo that afflicted her whenever she thought about the future (not to mention the past), "that gig is up. I'll be on the dole soon, plenty of time to finish my photo project. Plenty of time to collect Coke cans out of the gutter for the nickel. Plenty of time to greet you at the door dressed in Saran wrap."

"Ve-ra," he said, lifting her hair and kissing the back of her neck, which infallibly gave her gooseflesh, "you know you can always get another job if you want to. Though I actually wouldn't mind seeing you in —"

At that moment, the phone rang, shrilly, and Colin stopped. He raised his eyebrows in the general direction of the living room, and Vera shook her head, meaning, no, the machine would pick up. As she reached, on tiptoe, for the olive oil on the high shelf where Colin always put it, she heard a man's voice and then, she thought, the words "Fraud Protection Unit." She thought instantly of the police, of Avis, of the missing car. A current of alarm zapped through her. Now what, she wondered, dashing through the doorway and diving for the phone on the desk, damn, no, on the sofa.

"Yes?" she barked.

"Ms. Vera de Sica please," the man said, mispronouncing her name, Sick-er.

"Speaking."

He repeated his spiel, da capo. He was blah-blah-blah from the Fraud Protection Unit for her Visa account. Damn, she thought, fooled: he's going to try to sell me something.

"Look," she said, "whatever it is, I'm not interested. I'm in the middle of making dinner."

"Ma'am," he said, "this is for your own protection. I just need to verify a change in your account information."

She'd paid her bill, or, more precisely, the minimum monthly payment, she was sure of that. She was never late. She lived in fear of Bad Credit, an evil American ghost whose very name had haunted her immigrant parents. Bad Credit, and Bad Neighborhoods.

He verified her phone number, date of birth, mother's maiden name (Migone). Vera looked impatiently through the door into the kitchen, where Colin was throwing handfuls of eggplant into what looked like too much oil. He took up a lot of space in the tiny kitchen, she noticed, his long arms and legs in perpetual motion, performing all his actions as if in an enormous rush. Sometimes, especially first thing in the morning, his incapacity for stillness exhausted her, frayed her nerves so that she just wanted to weep.

"We just want to verify a change in billing address for your account," the man recited, and then read off a P.O. box in Van Nuys, California.

"No, no," said Vera, irritated. "There's been a mix-up. That's not my address." Just last week her phone had been cut off because the telephone company had confused her line with her upstairs neighbor's. And for the past six months the post office had been conscientiously delivering mail for a Mr. James Wood, who, as she'd repeatedly informed them, had never lived there. She was sick of this shit, this rampant incompetence. Her body chemistry was all stirred up, thanks to Colin's tactless choice of topic, and she was hungry and cranky to boot. She was sick of people calling at the dinner hour.

"So you did not request a change of billing address from 211 East Second Street to P.O. box blah-blah-blah?" the man repeated, though Vera was barely listening.

"No," she repeated, grimacing and rolling her eyes for Colin's benefit. "There's been some mistake. I use an on-line service, PayThoseBills.com, so maybe, I don't know, they wanted the bills to be sent to them. But I want everything to come here. And anyway they should have told me. I've already had this conversation with them, I don't know what their problem is."

"Very well, ma'am," he said, "we'll reinstate the original address." *Very well*, she thought, *reinstate*: who taught these people to talk like that? They were, she knew, these customer service representatives, a small army of the underclass, installed like prisoners in their cells, row upon row under constant surveillance, a panopticon of productivity, each worker tethered to headset and screen, each call timed to the fraction of a second, each sentence scripted, each keystroke recorded. She'd had students who had worked these jobs and had come to class numb and languageless, their humanity on hold.

"OK, thanks," she said, already hanging up. "Bye."

The kitchen smelled pungently of garlic, which meant that the whole apartment soon would, and then the hallway outside. Colin didn't believe in moderation, with, among other things, garlic and sex. She didn't mind. She hoped the neighbors didn't, either. She stole a black olive from the pile that Colin was hacking away at, then asked him to reach her down the vinegar. Salad dressing was about the only thing she knew how to make. Otherwise, her role was to choose the wine, to pick up a loaf from the Italian bakery on Tenth, to think about things like candles and music and table napkins, which would never cross Colin's mind. He didn't really understand why you shouldn't eat standing up in the kitchen, since it was more efficient (less distance from stove and sink, hence less energy expended).

Even with the candles lit, a fresh bunch of daffodils on the windowsill, and Ibrahim Ferrer on the boom box, the apartment looked dismal to Vera in the waning light. She looked around the small room that served as her living/dining/work space, making the familiar inventory. She needed a new couch: Lulu, bless her heart, had done an Enron-sized shredding job on the current one. She needed a human-sized (as opposed to leprechaun-sized) dining table. She needed more rugs, new curtains (the old ones were gray with city soot), something to replace the faded Cindy Sherman poster on the wall. She needed . . . What she really needed, she knew, was not to be sitting here in her apartment, staring at the walls—which themselves needed a paint job.

And the worst part was that this apartment—this dispiriting container—was the only thing she owned, her only actual asset. She'd bought it almost a decade earlier, with the proceeds from a buyout from her former landlord on Canal Street (he'd been doing something illegal, she wasn't sure what). With that lump sum and a couple of extra courses over the summer, she'd scratched together a laughably low down payment for the Second Street apartment, in retrospect the only smart financial move she'd ever made, though at the time her parents—and most of her friends—had been aghast: nobody wanted to live in the East Village then, in the early nineties, when it was still Heroin Central, when you had to step over dirty syringes to get to your door. When Tompkins Square Park was an ex-squatter encampment, when Avenue B represented the boundary of the known world, when the only bars around were scary places for hardcore drinkers. Now the apartment was worth close to triple what she'd paid for it—but so was everything else, so she couldn't afford to move.

She'd hoped to get away, go somewhere for Spring break, even if just for a weekend, but given the dismal state of her finances, and her even more dismal prospects, she'd decided it would be more prudent to stay home and update her CV. Make some phone calls. Network, or whatever it was that you were supposed to do when you were looking for a job. Anyway, even if she'd wanted to go somewhere, Colin could never be pinned down: he hated to make plans. Sometimes he would go on seventy-two-hour work jags and barely sleep and barely eat. Sometimes he'd stay home all day and eviscerate his Riley, showing up at his office, if at all, around 9:00 P.M. Sometimes he'd arrive in Manhattan at 3:00 in the afternoon and drag her off to the movies. "Let's see how we feel," he'd always say, if she tried to make plans. But she knew how she'd feel. She always felt pretty much the same way (fair to middling, shades of gray). She liked to have plans, deadlines, and then work backwards from them.

Well, now she had a deadline, she thought. Imminent unemployment was undeniably a deadline. She didn't like the "dead" in deadline.

"Shall I put the pasta on?" Colin asked, from the kitchen. "Are we ready to roll?"

"Sure," she said, reaching for the corkscrew. "I'll open the wine, let it breathe."

"You know, that's such a fallacy," Colin said, over some loud crashing sound, which was his way of interacting with cookware. "Most wines don't need to breathe these days. Just as nobody needs to sniff a cork."

"I know," she said. "It's just a . . . figure of speech." The wine might not need to breathe, she thought, but I do—just sit quietly somewhere and breathe. "You sure you don't want to go somewhere this weekend, just drive out somewhere in the country?" She tried to think of something Colin might want to do in the country. "You could take your laptop, test out that wireless antenna, or whatever it was, that you made from that Pringles can . . ."

"Let's see how we feel," he said, clanging the lid of the pot. She felt, right then, like a big glass of wine, which she duly poured herself. Then, as an afterthought, poured him one.

As an experiment, in the spirit, almost, of anthropological inquiry, she had actually gone on an interview, at a private language school for "businesspeople," off Fifth Avenue, in the expensive Fifties. The very receptionist had intimidated her, with her casque of coppery hair, her perfect stockings, her perfect smile. Even in her best black Italian jacket, bought at a discount at Daffy's and still reasonably chic, Vera had felt shabby, down-at-heel, as if she must have lint on her, dandruff, as if her ensemble were held together with safety pins. The school itself was hushed and elegant, with thick carpets and recessed lighting, a warren of small, glassed-in classrooms and state-of-the-art media labs, each one discreetly veiled with Italian blinds, like a celebrity dentist's office, or a place where women came for Botox injections on their lunch hour. Vera felt a surge of class resentment on behalf of her students: she would have killed for some of this equipment, for a single soundproof room.

The Director of the school was an extremely brisk, and extremely blonde, Englishwoman, wearing a suit in some bright news-anchor color that didn't do much for her reddish skin. Vera had the feeling that she had consulted an image consultant, and had, as a result, emerged looking like a cross between a corporate CEO and a politician's wife. She sat Vera down in one of the private classrooms, across a small, gleaming table on an ergonometrically correct chair, and gave her CV a quick once-over. Having established that Vera did in fact have the necessary qualifications, not to mention twelve years' worth of experience, she proceeded immediately to the "Four Do's."

"These are the four things I absolutely insist on," she said, holding up a surprisingly large hand to enumerate the Do's on her knobbly digits. She was a big-boned woman; without the image consultant, she might have looked like a cross-dressed character from Monty Python. Come to think of it, Vera thought, even *with* the image consultant she looked like John Cleese in a dress.

"Punctuality," she said, with her index finger. "Our clients are very busy people, their time is worth a lot of money. They cannot, ever, be kept waiting. Classes must start and end on the dot."

Vera indicated, with a modest shrug, that this would be no problem, that she was punctuality itself.

"Professional dress," she continued, adding her middle finger. Oh shit, Vera thought, a whole new wardrobe. Pantyhose. The full-body equivalent of foot binding. "By which I mean business dress. That's just our rule."

Vera nodded and again shrugged modestly, indicating her outfit, as if to suggest that she never wore anything else, that she washed the very dishes in suit, stockings, and heels.

"Number three, client's interests come first." Number three was the ring finger, which posed a bit of a coordination problem for the baby finger, which had to be held down by the thumb.

Vera nodded sagely—but of course.

"We don't use textbooks here. Everything is individualized, tailored to the client's needs. If the client is interested in scuba diving, then you'll have to find materials to do with scuba diving. Or hedge funds, or IT, or whatever it may be."

Hedge funds, no problem. She'd make a point of finding out what they were. At Brooklyn Multi they talked about green cards and deportation hearings and what to say when you took your mother to the hospital.

"And number four," liberating the baby finger, "no fraternizing with the clients. Absolutely no social contact, I mean, outside class time. A lot of our teaching takes place one-on-one, or on the telephone, as you know. Boundaries must be clear. There have been legal problems in the past, questions of liability . . ."

She left the sentence hanging, while Vera tried to imagine who might have sued whom for what.

"Of course not," Vera said. "I wouldn't dream of it." Which was true. The idea of fraternizing with busy, important businessmen who wanted to talk hedge funds held zero appeal for her. She'd never got over the idea that spending one's life— one's one and only life on this planet—chasing a buck, simply chasing a buck for its own sake, was about the lowest form of human activity. Her immigrant parents, predictably, did not understand this attitude at all. They still lived in hope—Vera suspected that her mother actually prayed for this daily—that she might still outgrow it, just as they hoped, against ever diminishing odds, that she might yet change her mind about marriage and children. A sad paradox, Vera thought, since it was their own arduous lives that had led her to equate "family" with "ball and chain."

Vera wondered whether her lack of a wedding ring, at her advanced age, was somehow a danger signal to the Director, whether she should make some discreet allusion to a boyfriend or a fiancé. Fuck it, she thought, this is the twenty-first century. Sometimes it was hard to remember that.

The Director stood up, signaling that the interview was over, and made some ritualized remarks to the effect that no actual positions were open at that actual moment but that the school's needs were ever-changing—"Just today," she said, "I received a call from a Brazilian lumber company, which wants intensive language training for thirty PR officers in New York, so we have to hop to it"—and that they would be in touch. Vera was pretty sure that they wouldn't be, though she couldn't have said exactly why. And that was before, with her chronically impaired sense of direction, she had blundered into a closet on her way out, mistaking it, in that high-gloss maze, for the front door.

Just thinking about the hypothetical businessmen made her feel unusually tender towards Colin, who had, after all, just cooked her dinner, even though he was now in the process of inhaling his, without even waiting for her to sit down at the table with him. There was a time when she would have brought this to his attention, attempted to re-educate him. Now she simply wandered over from the window and sat down too, her knees touching his under the rickety little table. He was jiggling his right leg, an unconscious spillover of energy, which grated on her, just a little, as it always did.

"Thanks for cooking," she said, unfolding her napkin. "Looks great." He nodded, mouth full, stabbing noisily at some stray rigatoni. His plate was almost empty and soon, she knew, he'd be leaping up from the table, dumping his plate in the sink, firing up her Mac. She tried to think of some way to distract him, detain him at the dinner table. Or should she just let him go (it was only across the room, after all) and eat her pasta in peace?

It was always like this with Colin, she thought, a constant series of minor irritations and adjustments, a constant free-floating sense of unfulfillment. But perhaps, she thought, that was what intimacy was. She wouldn't know: she'd always had more success with students and cats than with actual human beings. Simone, of course, attributed this to Vera's solitary childhood, the long hours alone in the triple-locked apartment while Carlo and Francesca ran the business, and Ernesto—being six years older and a boy—had the run of the neighborhood. Vera was secretly more inclined to blame temperament, an unfashionable notion in New York. Whatever the reason, she just didn't seem wired for pair-bonding; short bursts of serial monogamy were more her style. But how long could that continue? And what, she wondered, watching Colin drain his wineglass, was compatibility, anyway? How would you know it when you had found it, since it could never be flawless, never complete? And which were the truly important things, the things to hold out for?

Sometimes, watching Colin when he didn't know he was being observed, incandescent with concentration over his rivet gun, or blissfully applying the principle of capillarity to his strawberry smoothie, her heart cramped, seemed to spasm in her chest. Why not, she would think then, why not? Why not make this for real? Colin was unconventional enough that it just might work, that they might be able to invent an oddball life together. He wouldn't crowd her, she was sure of that, would never turn into the cartoon hubby slumped on the couch. He made her laugh. He made her come. He was capable, on occasion, of tenderness, of puppyish joy. And, above all, he rarely bored her — she saw Colin as a new species, evolving before her eyes, a pre-post-human being, happily jacked into a vast circuit of information and machines, carbon-based and silicon-based alike. His brain was wired differently from hers — hence the occasional system failure when they tried to connect. Yet he seemed, in spite of everything, content with her, had never hinted that he was in it for the nonce or for the sex, that he'd prefer a flashier flesh-machine. It was she who was always doing the hinting and the complaining, the behavioral management. It was she who always had one foot out the door.

How did you know, she wondered, how did you know when something might be workable, might be real? When it might be, despite its imperfections, worth holding on to? Or whether you were, once again, simply settling for less?

8

"IS THAT NEW?" asked Cindy, tidily packing Q-Tips into the Lucite container next to her makeover mirror, which was framed by subtly pink, subtly flattering movie-star lights. "I never noticed it before." Cindy was Revlon, a college student who worked afternoons and wore hardly any makeup, which Charlene thought was totally unprofessional. She was a physical therapy major, with big, rough hands and dog hair on her skirt, and Charlene could not for the life of her fathom how Cindy had ever got this job. When there were so many pros out there, people who'd been to cosmetology school, like Charlene herself.

"Yup," said Charlene, with an air of false modesty, extending her right hand like a client inspecting her manicure. "It's new. Howie bought it for me." Howie, in fact, had never set eyes on it: she could only wear it at work, where it was always in the way, sometimes even scratching the customers' faces when she applied their blush. But Howie would hit the roof if he ever saw her wearing it. The point was to burn through the credit, sell everything on eBay or return it for cash, not swan around wearing a Three-Stone Princess-Cut Diamond Ring. And Charlene should have been patient, should have waited for the new cards rather than running up the old. But fuck it, Charlene thought. She'd felt that it was something Vera would like, Vera would wear. And why shouldn't Vera have something nice, once in a while, if she wanted it?

"Cool," Cindy said, appearing to lose interest. Charlene was pretty sure that Cindy was a dyke, though they never really talked about anything like that. They mainly talked shop—shiny eye shadows in little tubes, like finger paints, were going to be big this spring—and borrowed cotton balls from each other when they ran out. "Was it your birthday?"

"No," Charlene said, polishing a cluster of greasy smears off her hand mirror, "my birthday's in June. June tenth."

Cindy, Charlene thought, had something of an attitude problem, asking personal questions like that, giving Charlene —or so it seemed—the occasional odd look. Maybe it was just Charlene's imagination, but Cindy seemed standoffish some-times, like something was up. Even on rainy afternoons, when there wasn't a client in sight, and they'd sharpened every last eyebrow pencil in the store, she *still* wouldn't accept Charlene's friendly offer of a makeover—a major breach of cosmetics-counter etiquette. Instead, if she wasn't busy highlighting some textbook, Cindy wanted to chitchat about current events (like Charlene gave a shit), or her dog, Deltoid, or things that were none of her business, like why had she never met Howie, and had Charlene ever thought of taking evening classes some-where, and what was that bruise on Charlene's wrist.

Charlene liked to keep her private life private, always had; compartmentalization, she believed, was the key to sanity. When she was at work, even when things were slow and she was bored out of her mind, she tried not to think about her other "venture." It was too confusing, made her feel too schizoid, to be recommending a good silicone-based foundation to a client ("Silicone's what they use to clean up oil spills, honey, so imag-ine what it does for your T-zone") while at the same time scheming to devastate someone else's financial life. Which required concentration, resourcefulness, smarts.

For instance, just yesterday, a slight glitch had arisen in the de Sica situation. The simple but elegant change-of-address technique had been thwarted by an over-zealous Visa employee —it worked about 70 percent of the time, Howie had found, depending on how conscientious the credit card companies were about checking—and Charlene most definitely did not want our Prof scrutinizing her Visa bills so early in the game. In fact Charlene, for various reasons, wished to scrutinize them herself. Therefore, a little social engineering had seemed in order:

"Oh, hi, this is Vera de Sica, account number so-and-so. Listen, I'm in LA for a couple of weeks on business, but I just got an audit notice from the IRS and I urgently need copies of my last six statements. Official copies, they say, from you. Could you do me a favor and FedEx them to the Biltmore Hotel for me?"

"Oh hi, this is Professor de Sica. I was at the hotel a few weeks ago, for a conference? Listen, there's been a bit of a mix-up, and somebody's going to FedEx some important documents to the hotel instead of to my university, like I asked them to. They should get there in a day or two. Would it be OK if I sent my research associate, Ms. Cummins, over to pick them up? Thanks so much. That's D-E, S-I-C-A."

Damn, she was good, Charlene thought: She had the lingo down pat. She was too smart to be spackling concealer onto menopausal bitches at the Revco, too smart to be living in a shoddy apartment with shag carpeting, too smart to settle for a lowlife like Howie.

Why, then, was she doing so? Dr. Charlene asked herself this question almost every day, usually in the stern tones of Dr. Laura, but the answer, she knew, would get her booted right off the show. Dr. Laura was all about self-esteem, about not "playing the victim." Charlene aspired to high self-esteem, but seriously, Dr. Laura: who else would have her? Before Howie, she'd barely had a date—dating wasn't one of the skills you acquired when you'd spent your adolescence doing laundry, working the night shift at Burger King, and checking that Mom hadn't set the couch on fire again by "falling asleep" with lighted Marlboro in hand—and here, in LA, forget it. If you weren't skinny, implanted, and blonde, or at least majorly highlighted, you were invisible. A non-person, a non-woman, a non-being. Men didn't look at you, not even through the tinted glass of their SUVs; store clerks—from the teenager at the Gap to the transvestite at the MAC counter—failed to see you; even the drive-through teller at Wells Fargo stared right through you as she handed you your change. You had become, as you had always feared, not quite human and not quite real.

Glancing over at Cindy, who was now engaged in a listless comparison of two beige streaks on the back of a client's hand—which, hello! is not the same color as your face—Charlene wondered if Cindy ever felt the same way. It beat the shit out of her that Cindy didn't do herself up more, take better care of herself—an SPF-15 moisturizer, for starters, a few dabs of concealer, a dollop of blush. Plus, really, how long would it take to slap on some mascara and lip-gloss? And this was supposed to be an intelligent woman, someone who was trying to make something of herself. Charlene now, given half the chance, would have ordered up the full menu, from Botox and liposuction to Dolly Parton–style implants. Hell, if she could've afforded it, LASIK, eyelid lifts, dermabrasion, collagen injections, rib removals, cheekbone engineering, a nose job, a tummy tuck, a hair weave, and porcelain veneers on every goddamn tooth.

Her favorite show, not surprisingly, was *Extreme Makeover;* she'd even gone so far as to download the fourteen-page application form for would-be participants. Why not? God knows she could use *a truly Cinderella-like experience,* just like Jackie and Lori and the rest of them, *a real life fairy tale in which people's wishes come true, not just to change their looks, but their lives and destinies.* And what a luxury it would be, she thought, to hand her body over to the experts, to await, stoically, the moment of transfiguration, the new self reborn from its chrysalis of bandages.

But the Participant Questionnaire, she'd discovered, asked entirely too many questions, the kind of questions a two-bit shrink would ask:

Tell us about your relationship with your parents?

Tell us about your relationship with your siblings?

Tell us about your relationship with your mate/significant other?

Tell us about your relationship with your friends?

Who could answer questions like that? Not to mention the killer, number 46: *Besides altering your appearance, what is your biggest dream?* Charlene the CEO of Get Real cosmetics, Dr. Charlene with her wildly popular call-in show, Professor Charlene living the literary life in New York, Charlene the single woman fending off suitors with a stick—those were fantasies. A dream, on the other hand, was something you thought might conceivably come true.

Like leaving Howie. Leaving Howie, getting your own place, living your own life. The thought was unthinkable, taboo, and yet—look—she had thought it.

But for that, Charlene knew she would need money—start-up capital, it was called. And smarts. She had to keep reminding herself that she was the smart one. Smarter than Howie, smarter, even, than Vera (because, after all, whose identity had gone missing?). All she really needed was the paperwork to prove it: the bachelor's degree, the master's degree, the Ph.D. All the little pieces of paper and plastic that procure you some options in life.

Yes, Charlene thought, the Prof definitely needed to get her self together, her degrees, her birth certificate, a California driver's license, maybe even a passport. And then—eventually—a nice new apartment in Santa Monica, all to herself, in her own good name. All to herself? Charlene began to feel light-headed and tingly, the way you felt right at the apex of the Superman ride at Six Flags. Something was fizzing in her veins, a new sense of possibility. There was so much to do, starting right *now*. Our Prof was going to be a busy girl, with all this paperwork to attend to. She was hardly going to have a moment to read those weighty tomes or attend those literary cocktail parties or sit in cafés with her PowerBook, all those important things a Prof had to do.

"Hey Miss," a voice said impatiently, "you work here?"

Charlene nodded reluctantly, moved towards the rack the client was ransacking, and assumed, without thinking, "the expression."

"I'm looking for that lip stain," the woman said, a secretary type on her lunch hour (suit, hose, and sneakers, harried expression). "That one that's supposed to stay on for eight hours?"

"Ah," said Charlene, beaming beatifically, "you mean Overtime?"

The woman shrugged. "I guess. I saw it in a magazine . . ."

"Step right over here, honey," Charlene said, patting a tall chrome stool, "and let me show you how good it looks on you. Trust me, it's not called Overtime for nothing. It works even harder than you do!"

In short order, Charlene had sold the woman two units of Overtime ("one for your purse and one for your desk drawer"), a "turbo" lip liner, which was identical, except in price, to the non-turbo lip liner, and a tube of Done Deal "sealant" (which had essentially the same ingredients as Saran wrap). You had to sell more than one item to get a commission, on the theory that if the customer had come in looking for a specific product, and you just rang it up, you hadn't done any actual selling. Charlene had upped the ante, had set a personal goal of three items per sale—which she usually met. But what difference did it make? She could be the best cosmetics saleswoman in the solar system, and she'd still never get promoted, to Lancôme, say, in one of the high-end department stores, because she just didn't have the right style—the right wispy, peaches-and-creamy, Daddy's-girly style. And she never would. That's why she had to move on, create new opportunities for herself.

Howie, of course, didn't need to know any of this. Howie needed to know what Howie needed to know: that Vera's new cards were arriving, credit cards and department-store charge cards, and that they could go shopping. That they could drive up to Tahoe, to the casinos, and get a cool few thou in cash advances there, instead of the measly $500 per day you could get from an ATM. Same story at the racetracks, Santa Anita and Hollywood Park. That they could do the usual Electro City routine: finding the "gift" in "gift certificate," Howie called it. You used your shiny new plastic to buy high-denomination gift certificates (Howie always signed them "Mom and Dad," Charlene preferred "Your Loving Wife"). Then you bought something—a VCR, say, or a satellite dish—that cost just a little more than the gift certificate, so the receipt would reflect a cash payment. The next day you returned the merchandise for a refund—*et voilà*, cash in hand. They never went back to the same branch twice, of course. But there were over fifty Electro Citys in the Greater Los Angeles area alone.

Howie had figured that one out, too. With his smarts, he should have been rich by now, he'd complain, reliably, after the third or fourth beer. Maybe, Charlene would reply (sometimes out loud, sometimes not, depending on whether Howie was on the upswing or on the mean downswing), if you didn't piss away every dollar that came into this house. Howie liked to brag that he was a gambler at heart—"Hey, I'm a gambler at heart," he'd say, when he did something rash—but omitted to mention that he usually lost. Or that he gambled, incontinently, on anything that moved—the dogs, the horses, and, in East LA, the fighting cocks.

So, Charlene thought, applying a dab of sealant to her own lips, let Howie know what Howie needed to know—which, let's face it, wasn't much. Let him think that it was business as usual. Let him think that they'd be burning through de Sica in a couple of months, then moving on. Vera had other plans.

9

MARKING EXAMS always made Vera feel like a failure, because, surely, if she'd done a decent job of transmitting knowledge to her students, they wouldn't be making such abysmal mistakes. She felt sometimes as if she should be receiving the F, not them—an idea that always made Roberto laugh, shaking his head at the over-subtlety of women. "Veracita," he'd say, "it's really not that complicated—the reason the students do badly on the exams is because they don't study." Male teachers, Vera had noticed—even generous, conscientious, and empathetic male teachers like Roberto and Joon Seok—tended to feel little guilt, and less responsibility, where their students were concerned. Whereas female teachers, even the tough or crazy ones, tended to over-invest. Teaching, for women, turned into a grand theater of transference—she knew this not least from her own experience—while men, though susceptible of course to the ego blandishments and the sexual possibilities, managed, in general, to keep things compartmentalized. Which was more unhealthy, she couldn't say.

Well, she wouldn't have to worry about any of this when she was driving a jeep for Médecins sans Frontières, she thought, writing a reluctant C at the bottom of one exam and drawing a thick circle around it, as if to keep it from floating away.

But even Médecins sans Frontières wouldn't accept such a

bad driver, she thought gloomily—one, moreover, with zero sense of direction.

Only two more exams to mark, then she could break for lunch, coffee, newspaper, a patch of late-March sunlight on her favorite—and, if truth be told, only—armchair. Until then, the creeping sense of failure, of waste, of having been part of some horrible charade, of having impersonated a teacher while they impersonated students. Had nobody, but nobody, been listening when she'd explained, for the millionth time, about "say" versus "tell"? And as for nominalization . . . what a debacle. What a shambles. She should just throw it all in, quit her job . . . wait, that was going to happen anyway. She couldn't even fantasize about quitting, because she was already on the way out. Another reason to be depressed . . . and ha! This student, one of the better ones, had fallen right for the *faux ami* in the comprehension exercise. She looked despairingly at the remaining two exam books, one with an elaborate manga-style doodle on the front cover, never a good sign. She shuffled the manga exam book to the bottom of the pile, reaching for the other one instead—but this student dotted her i's with tiny circles, even worse.

Having given Manga Man a C and the annoying i-dotter a reluctant B–, Vera neatly recorded that day's marks, stacked the papers in alphabetical order, capped her pen, and pushed back from the desk like Lulu shooting out of her cat carrier after a particularly harrowing session with the vet. She tuned the radio to the jazz station and went into the kitchen to make herself a cheese and tomato sandwich on sunflower rye, her lunchtime staple. It was the only thing in her life, she thought dourly, that she could count on to provide a predictable, if modest, dose of satisfaction. Especially in combination with a good cup of coffee, something interesting, even gossipy, in the Arts section, and a friendly parallelogram of sun.

After lunch, she strapped on her sandals, tied her hair up in a messy ponytail, put on a dash of her favorite lipstick (Oriole's Insouciance), and sauntered forth to buy Helena a birthday present. Helena, an artist who worked in mosaics—minute pieces of glass and tile glued into gargantuan scenes of violence —was Vera's closest friend, but, in the manner of New York friendships, they didn't actually see each other that often. Helena lived in Williamsburg, slept until noon, and worked in her studio until 4:00 A.M., so their potential area of overlap on an average day was pretty scant. They communicated mainly by phone and e-mail, but, on important occasions—birthdays, career crises, and breakups—would meet for a meal in the East Village. Over Helena's protestations that she was fat and depressed and should just stay home, Vera had made reservations at Holy Basil for a birthday dinner on Saturday night.

Which raised the problem of the gift. Left to her own devices, Vera would have bought everyone a book, but experience had taught her that this predilection was not always shared, that for some people receiving a book was like getting extra homework. Helena, she knew, was one of those people: she read only on planes, and then only paperbacks with raised, glitzy type and some obvious connection to TV or the movies. So, against the dictates of her own utilitarian nature, Vera was going to buy something froufrou for Helena, something in the toiletries or lingerie line, something girly and frivolous and entirely unnecessary. There was no shortage of little boutiques in the newly yuppified East Village that specialized in precisely this kind of thing—when, Vera wondered, had "gift" become a separate category of commodity, signifying something highly scented and essentially devoid of function?

The spring sunshine was tender on her bare arms, the sky a freshly laundered blue, the trees, even in Alphabet City, a luminous, transient green—the kind of day, in other words, when a person lingers over her errands and invents new ones, just to stay out in the world. So she took her time wandering from boutique to boutique, testing various unguents on the back of her hand and holding various lacy items up to the light. Eventually she decided on a particularly sheer and silky camisole, which—she couldn't quash her practical side entirely—would be useful under a sweater if its services were not required in the boudoir. Helena, she knew, hadn't had a lover in a while, another of those New York mystery stories.

As the clerk was folding the camisole, origami-style, into yards of tissue paper and then placing this package into a box and the box into a bag—Vera tried not to calculate the number of trees involved—Vera handed over her credit card and wandered to the back of the shop to look at the rack of birthday cards. They were all too hip and cynical, even for her, in that deeply jaded, postfeminist "girlfriend" mode she'd never come to appreciate.

"Excuse me," the salesclerk was saying, trying to catch Vera's eye, "excuse me, over there."

"Yes?" Vera said, making her way back between a display of Barbie dolls in dominatrix gear and a line of votive candles designed to ward off bad haircuts or worse dates.

"Card's been declined."

"What do you mean—?"

"Card's been declined," the girl shrugged. She had spiky blonde hair, bad skin, a cute navel, and an indifferent expression. "Card's no good," she explained, pointing to some message on the scanner, which Vera couldn't read from where she stood.

"But how can that be?" Vera asked, a sensation of mild panic rising from her gut. "Has it been demagnetized?"

"No," the girl said. "It works OK. It's just been refused, that's all. Do you have another one?"

"Well, yes, but that's not the point. Why would this one be refused? There shouldn't be any problem." She ran through the possibilities in her mind: yes, she'd paid the minimum due, though not the whole balance, a couple of weeks ago; at that time there'd still been a fair amount of usable credit, several thou in fact. She kept track of it, in a vague kind of way. It was for emergencies. Or birthday presents. Or dentist bills—whatever didn't fit into the normal cycle of life, or, more precisely, whatever didn't fit into the constraints of her monthly budget. "I know I just paid it," she said, "just last week."

The girl looked down at the cash register, bored, as if she'd heard this all before. Come to think of it, Vera thought, in this neighborhood, she probably had. She'd probably heard everything.

"I just paid it," Vera repeated, stubbornly. "I just paid the bill." The girl shrugged again, an eloquent nonverbal rendition of "Whatever."

"Can you try it again?" Vera asked.

"I already tried it twice."

"Well, would you mind trying one more time, because I know that card should be good. Maybe there was a glitch with the computer or the phone line or something."

The girl looked pointedly around the shop, as if to indicate that she had other pressing business to attend to, but, as both she and Vera could see, there was no one else there and nothing else to do. She shrugged again, swiped the card with an exaggerated flourish, waited for what seemed an excessively long time, and then shook her head again. "Nope. See, same message."

"So now what do I do?" Vera asked. "This has never happened to me before." She felt mortified, alarmed, but, at the same time, vaguely guilty, as if she had at last been found out, caught out —for what, she couldn't have said. For crimes against fiscal responsibility. For her bad relationship to money and credit, her bad faith on the whole question of consumerism (here she was, practically broke, charging a camisole to her credit card). Her low income, her low aspirations, her nonexistent 401K. Her lack of prudence and sound investment strategies.

"Well," said the girl, and from her tone and the way she shifted her weight around, she might as well have said "duh," "you pay with another card or with cash, and you call the credit card company when you get home. Unless you want to call them now on your cell, but it usually takes forever to get through and hit all those buttons and wait for a human being and blah-blah-blah."

"I don't have a cell," Vera said, shortly. "I'll pay cash." It was more than she could actually afford to part with, with payday two weeks away, but she'd manage. She'd get by. She wasn't going to risk humiliation with another piece of plastic. She just wanted to pay and leave and find out what had happened.

When she finally got off the phone with her Visa "account executive" that afternoon—having begun the conversation in attack mode—she was chastened and deflated, close to tears. She'd had plenty of time to build up a head of steam while waiting on hold, listening to endless menus, none of which contained the option she wanted, entering endless numbers and typographical symbols, hearing the same message repeat incessantly how important her call was, while her heart pounded, her mind raged, and evil chemicals coursed through her blood. At last a human voice came on and asked her, in a tone of deep ennui, to re-enter all the numbers she'd already punched in. She'd lost it then, begun yelling like what the police call an Emotionally Disturbed Person. The human being had had to talk her down. He'd clearly had training in this. He'd assured her that he understood her feelings. He'd asked for her mother's maiden name. And then, tapping quietly, he'd given her some very bad news.

She sat staring at the grain of her oak desk, noting how the finish had been marred by her habit of sliding her laptop out of the way when she wasn't using it, leaving permanent skid marks. She felt, at that moment, as if something like a Bradley armored vehicle had driven over her, leaving skid marks of its own.

Then, reflexively, she dialed Colin, who — she could hear as soon as he picked up — was in his impatient and distracted, i.e., non-chatty, work mode.

"What's up?" he asked. She could hear his keyboard clacking away as he spoke, something that she always tried — but failed — not to take personally. Like the cartoon character flattened by a steamroller, she tried to reconstitute herself, spring back, as required, into three dimensions.

"Guess what, honey?" she warbled, in her best ditzy-house-wife voice. "I bought a diamond ring and a satellite dish!"

"You what?" he said, still clacking. "A satellite dish? In Manhattan?"

"Well," she said, coyly, "maybe I don't live in Manhattan."

Even that failed to stop the clacking. "What do you mean? Are you moving?" She noticed that he didn't sound exactly heartbroken.

"No, no," she said, dropping the silly voice. "Someone's been using my credit card. Maxed it out." Saying the words out loud made it real, somehow, the bizarre, insidious violation.

"Who?"

"Well, obviously, I don't know. Someone's been ordering things from catalogues and the Internet, having them delivered to an address in Van Nuys. A P.O. box at Mailboxes Inc."

"Van Nuys, California?"

"Yeah. But the mailbox has been closed already. It was opened in my name, just for a few weeks. Can you believe the nerve! *My* name."

"A satellite dish—?"

"A satellite dish, a diamond ring, kind of a big, tacky one, apparently, from Zales, a camcorder, all kinds of stuff from the Gap . . . and that pretty much maxed me out. Over limit, actually."

"Hmmn. Well, you have to close that account right away."

"Done that. And I'm only liable for the first fifty dollars, if I can prove I didn't order these things."

"But how," asked Colin, ever the logician, "do you prove a negative?"

"The address, apparently. Though I don't really see why, in principle, I couldn't have ordered those things for myself and had them sent to a mailbox in Van Nuys . . ."

"And of course there wouldn't be any signatures, if it was on-line or on the phone—"

"All within the last week, apparently."

"Your account should have been flagged, then. For unusual activity. Someone should have called you."

"Apparently it had been flagged. Apparently the Fraud Unit or whatever it's called was supposed to call. Don't know what the hell took them so long."

"Maybe," Colin said, not unreasonably, "it has something to do with the fact that you never pick up the phone."

That evening, over dinner in the garden at Miracle Grill, they rehashed the subject at length, trying to determine how the credit card information could have been purloined. Vera, with her crypto-Luddite instincts, immediately blamed the Internet: it must have been when she ordered those books from Amazon.com, or those pants from Lands' End, or that printer from MacMall.

"I just *knew* it couldn't be a good idea to have my credit card info floating around in cyberspace," she said, pointing at Colin, as if he were somehow to blame. "Anyone could steal that information."

"Rubbish," said Colin, who had grown up in the UK and still said things like "rubbish" and "bollocks" and occasionally "tripe." "The information on those sites is probably more secure than if you just hand your card over at a restaurant or give the number to some random person on the phone. That's probably the least likely explanation."

"Then what's the most likely explanation?" she asked, broaching her quesadilla.

"You have some guacamole on your face . . . there, over a bit, OK. The most likely explanation—I don't know. When did you last use it?"

"Well, I've hardly been using it at all, because I've been trying really hard not to run up any more debt. A couple of restaurants. Tickets for Pina Bausch at BAM. I ordered that printer in February, when my other one died, but that was only a couple of hundred bucks. And the pants a couple of weeks ago, for the spring, because those are the only kind that fit me properly and also I don't have to pay to have them shortened."

"Well, the shipping fee is probably more than it would cost you to have them shortened but never mind."

"Whatever," said Vera, annoyed at his pedantry, when empathy was so clearly the way to go. "So, the pants in March, the printer in Feb, late Feb. Before that, it was the hotel in LA . . . oh my God."

He looked up, quizzically, from the construction project that his fajita had become.

"The car! That damn car!"

"Which car? The one that got stolen?"

She nodded, emphatically. "That rental car. In LA. It must have something to do with that."

"But how could it?" He pondered the question briefly. "They stole a car that wasn't yours. There was nothing of yours inside it. How could they even know who you are?"

"Well, that's true," she admitted, sagging back in her chair. "The car was registered to Avis, not me. They'd have no way of knowing my name. Unless, I don't know, he had an inside connection at Avis and . . ." She let that line of thought trail off: it all seemed too elaborate, too unlikely.

Colin thought for a moment, his fajita forgotten and beginning, in slow motion, to disassemble itself. "It must have been at a restaurant or something," he said, "somebody who works there, rips off the carbons, has a little sideline going. Or someone with a skimmer."

"A skimmer?"

"That's when they have a little device, where you can't see it and their boss can't see it, and they scan your card twice. Once for the real transaction, the other to steal the info for themselves."

"Christ," she said. "It could be something like that. I mean, who's keeping tabs, every time you pay with a credit card?"

They both considered this question with a meditative sip of beer, then Colin began, patiently, to reconstruct the deconstructed fajita. He corrected a flaw in the design, so that it maintained its structural integrity even when he took his fork away. Satisfied, he sawed off a piece.

"Technically," he said, "they're not ripping you off, anyway, they're ripping off the credit card company."

"Doesn't matter," Vera said. "It's such a horrible feeling. You feel, I don't know, violated. Like somebody has done something really unclean to you. It's like the time I felt this guy opening my bag on the crosstown bus, really crowded bus, and yanked it away, just in time—he'd begun to work the wallet out of its compartment. Another couple of minutes and he would have

had it." Her body still remembered the shock, the dispropor-
tionate sense of defilement.

"I hope you got the cops on him."

"No. By the time I'd gathered my wits, he'd disappeared, of
course."

"Well, no harm done. To you, anyway."

"I guess ... ," she said, feeling, obscurely, that this wasn't
true. She picked a seedpod out of her sour cream, then, running
her hand through her hair, discovered another couple of pods
that had alighted there, clinging with sticky little feet. The garden at the Miracle Grill, though a soothing oasis in the asphalt
wastes of the East Village, posed a definite seedpod hazard in
the spring. "I hope this stuff isn't poisonous," she said, shaking
her head. "It's all over my hands now, and all over my food.
What kind of trees are these, anyway?"

Colin shrugged, without even looking up at the green haze
over their heads. He professed not to know any North American
trees and not to care.

"Well, anyway," he said, "even if somebody did get your account number, the account is closed now, so that should be the
end of that."

"Should be," Vera said. "Bloody crook. Rotten bastard."
When she was with Colin, she liked to speak in Britishisms, the
more antiquated the better. They reminded her, privately, of the
books her Anglophile father used to read to her, on Sundays
after church — Dickens and Stevenson and Sherlock Holmes. It
was part of the project for Vera to become middle-class, part of
the grand scheme that had included ballet classes on Saturday
mornings in the community hall at Sacred Heart and six years'
worth of piano lessons from Mrs. Ferrone downstairs. All to no
avail, as Vera turned out to be tone-deaf, with feet that had been
designed, over generations, for crushing grapes.

"But you know what really gets me?" she asked, after a pause.

Colin looked up, interrogatively.

"That the stuff they bought was so damn tacky. You should see that ring—I went on-line, to Zales, to see a picture of it—to see what 'I' had bought. It's a fucking monstrosity!"

"How so?"

"Oh, I don't know, just huge and flashy and clunky. Really horrible. It's kind of embarrassing to have that on my card, you know, as if I had chosen it!"

"Vera," Colin said, shaking his head, "I think you probably have better things to worry about than whether this crook has good taste. Just be glad it's over, with no harm done."

"You're right," she said, "but it just, I don't know, rankles. Like, why couldn't they have bought something decent, at least?"

"Well," he repeated, "it's over now. Unless you think they might have some other information about you . . . ?"

"Nah," she said. "How could they? And honey," she added, reverting to the ditzy-blonde voice and reaching for his hand across the table, "I do hope you're paying for dinner. That diamond ring has quite wiped me out."

10

THE TROUBLE WITH YOU, CHARLENE," Howie said, "is that you're a moron." He replenished the puddle of ketchup on his plate, steeped a couple of fries in it, and then pointed his fork at Charlene, spattering the tabletop between them.

"The trouble with you, Howie," Charlene replied evenly, "is that you eat like a hog. It makes me sick to watch you, honest it does." She took a deep, bracing sip of her Hawaiian Volcano. Another one of these and she'd be OK, wouldn't feel so much like wasting good liquor by spitting it in Howie's face.

"I'm the hog? *I'm* the hog?" Howie asked, gesturing towards her plate. "Who's having the Triple Jack Combo with extra onion rings? It ain't me, babe." And it was true: his bacon cheeseburger looked frugal, almost dietetic, next to her platter of shrimp, chicken, and ribs, but fuck it, she was hungry. And angry.

"Give it a rest," she said, after gnawing on a rib for a while, "just give it a rest, OK?"

"You'll *get* a rest," he said, "a nice long rest at Club Fed. Maybe you'll finally lose some weight, eating that prison chow every day." It was amazing, Charlene thought, how men always managed to believe they looked OK, as if their mirror images were digitally altered en route to their brains. Whereas women never saw anything but the flaw.

"Yeah," she said, shrugging, "well at least I'd get some peace and quiet that way. Without you always on at me."

They ate in silence, Charlene excavating her mound of mash, Howie conveying his fries robotically to his mouth. Charlene could still feel the occasional current of anger zigzag through her veins, but, thanks to the Volcano, less frequently now. OK, so maybe she had messed up a little by going to the Biltmore, in person, to pick up the statements Visa had so obligingly FedExed there for Vera. She'd been proud of the maneuver, proud of the poise and self-possession with which she'd strolled over to the concierge, identified herself as the Prof's "research associate"—which, let's face it, she was—and signed for the packet. So proud, in fact, that she hadn't been able to resist bragging, just a little, to Howie, who'd promptly gone ballistic. Right there in the TGIF's.

"What did I always tell you," he'd yelled, then, conscious of the Friday-evening crowd around them—the bickering family so close that one of the feral brats kept making a grab for Howie's fries—had lowered his voice and continued to berate her, sotto voce. "What did I always tell you: watch the fuckin' cameras. Stay away from the fuckin' cameras! But no, Charlene wants to be a movie star. Charlene has to go 'n pose for her mug shot in the fuckin' lobby of the fuckin' Biltmore."

Howie had an obsession with security cameras and was convinced that, one day, one of them was going to do him in. He'd heard a statistic that the average city dweller was recorded seventy-five times a day on hidden cameras, a statistic he constantly quoted to Charlene as he pointed out the electronic eyes wherever he saw them, in lobbies and parking lots and at the 7-Eleven, on lampposts and lintels, in the very emergency room where she'd taken him last year with his bleeding ulcer. Whenever he knew he was on camera, at a bank or casino or, crucially, at Electro City, he kept his baseball cap pulled low over his face and ducked his head in a manner that he'd cultivated to look gauche and ungainly rather than suspicious. Charlene looked terrible in a baseball cap—not to mention what it did to her hair—so she went with the big Jackie O sunglasses instead. Never mind that she could barely see indoors like that.

"And what for?" Howie had wanted to know. "What the fuck for?" It was a good question. Other than temporarily diverting the bills, so de Sica would take longer to catch on, the ploy served no real purpose—none that Charlene could admit to, anyway. She just wanted to know, that was all. Know everything she could about the Prof.

"I'm fishing," she'd told him, weakly, "fishing for information."

"What information? We got all the info we need. And the rate you're going, the cops are going to have all the info *they* need, too."

"I'm fishing," she'd repeated. "Trying to figure out where the money is. I don't see no savings account, no CD, no money management account, nothing. This woman is a professor, right? She owns an apartment in Manhattan. And she lives from paycheck to paycheck? I don't think so."

At that Howie had shrugged, unconvinced yet covetous, his greed piqued the way another person's curiosity might be.

"Well don't take too long," he'd said. "A few more weeks, then we blow through everything, cash her out. If we can't clean this one out by the end of May, we're amateurs. Amateurs," he repeated, pointing what little chin he had at her.

Charlene had shrugged, a gesture Howie took for acquiescence.

She had to be careful, she knew. Despite everything—despite the mood swings and the Jack Daniel's and the occasional whack—Charlene was afraid that Howie might leave her before she got around to leaving him. She'd long ago given up hope of remodeling him, fixer-upper that he was, but that didn't mean she was ready to leave just yet, ready to gather up her car keys, her credit cards, her Oriole tote, and walk out the door. She had often pictured herself doing just this (she'd be wearing a smart red suit, like Connie Chung), but the image, though exhilarating, filled her with a strange, vertiginous dread.

Where, after all, would she go? And what would she do? Frankly, she had no idea how "normal" people lived, what they did from one moment to the next behind closed doors. She'd tried to glean what she could from sitcoms and the soaps, but, by definition, they didn't show what people did when they had nothing to do. And much as Charlene dreaded coming home to Planet Howie every night, she couldn't quite imagine living alone either—literally couldn't imagine how it was done, how you would proceed, what you would do after you'd walked in the door. Put down your purse and keys, OK, look through the mail (a pile of mail just for you, in your own new name), walk into the silent, empty living room, hit the remote—then what? This was the point at which her imagination faltered, failed to provide. TV, beer, Internet, yes—but then? How did other people do it? How did other people live with themselves?

Vera would know, Charlene thought. Vera had been doing it for years, and successfully, too, by the look of things. You didn't end up with an advanced degree, a job, and an apartment in Manhattan without also being in possession of a viable self. So, Charlene thought, the Prof would teach her; by studying Vera's life, she would learn what she needed to know, the nitty-gritty, the basics, the stuff you couldn't get from *Cosmo* or *Sex and the City*. How, in other words, to construct a life. "Get a life," Howie was always telling her, especially when she complained. Well, now she would.

Vera's Visa bills, Charlene had discovered, made edifying reading, though not nearly as glam as she'd hoped, no competition for her nightly Danielle Steel. Our Prof, to Charlene's regret, turned out to be something of a cheapskate, not one to spend big bucks on high-end goods, not a designer name in sight, no Prada, no nada. Charlene sincerely hoped that the $49.95 purchase from Lands' End—*way* down-market—had been an aberration. Or a pair of pajamas.

Our Prof, Charlene noted, had a penchant for Thai food, which Charlene couldn't stand—too spicy, too salty, made her eyelids puff up—with sushi at Sandobe running a close second, usually on Friday nights. (Raw fish? In Manhattan? What could this woman be thinking?) And that modest, recurrent tab from Tien Fu Gong?—Charlene was guessing *The Sopranos* or *West Wing* plus kung pao shrimp. Vera was definitely more of a shrimp girl than a red-meat girl, Charlene suspected, whereas she, Charlene, could barely get through the day without a Big Mac. In an interesting symmetry, Vera's monthly restaurant bills and her monthly gym fees (New York Sports Club at Union Square, Basic Membership Plus Pilates) came out about even— as did, in all likelihood, the Prof's caloric account. Perhaps Charlene should really consider getting back on the treadmill, back to the step classes—not for Howie this time, but for Vera. So as to be able to slip more elegantly into her life.

Vera had a Mac—judging by a $200 charge from MacMall in February—which Charlene could have predicted: someone who considers herself artsy and independent-minded, what else would she have? Probably one of those crappy little iBooks that looked like a tangerine-colored toilet seat. A monthly charge from AOL cleared up the question of the Internet service provider, a crucial question for anyone with mischief on her mind. And just wait and see if the e-mail address wasn't something unsurprising like veradesica, or vdesica, or vdesic: this wasn't going to be one of those naughtykitty or leathergrrl situations, Charlene felt sure. She had a sudden, vivid image of herself scrolling invisibly through Vera's in box, opening anything that looked interesting, invitations and confessions, declarations of love, acquainting herself with the cast of characters in Vera's address book. Perhaps even sending a few mails herself, just to mix things up.

For that she was going to need a password, though. She'd read somewhere that "password" and "god" and "sex" were the most common passwords, but she gave the Prof more credit than that. Knowing our Prof, she probably was one of those people who did what she was supposed to do, used some random alphanumeric string that looked like the name of a Polish fungus. But you never knew.

Every month, Charlene saw, Vera charged the same amount at the same drugstore, which suggested a prescription. The CVS on Second Ave.: worth a call to see if we were talking allergy pills or Thorazine, Ritalin or Retin-A. Probably just Prozac, but it was possible, Charlene supposed, that our Prof was falling apart. Some of her spending certainly made no sense: a monthly Metrocard, when she could simply take a cab? $120 for tickets at BAM—whatever that was—when you could rent a movie for three bucks plus a coupon for popcorn? Charlene couldn't fathom this. And why you needed to get your hair cut at "Gabrielle's Organics" beat the shit out of her—a haircut was a haircut, right? So how could it be "organic"? Vera had also recently spent $50 at L'Occitane, nasty overpriced French stuff, in Charlene's opinion—these so-called natural product lines, she could tell you a thing or two. Vera needed to wise up, unless she actually liked smelling like expensive cat pee. Speaking of which: going back now to December and November, Vera had dropped a bundle at St. Marks Veterinary. Assuming she wasn't abusing animal tranquilizers on the rave scene—the image tickled Charlene momentarily, our Prof in a rainbow-colored beanie, fucked-up on Special K—one could only infer that Vera was excessively attached to her sickly pet. Sick puppy, sick kitty. It wasn't the kind of money you blew on a hamster.

Amazing what you could find out about a person from a few dollar amounts printed out from a computer somewhere in Delaware or Des Moines. You are what you spend, Charlene thought—and identity? Identity equals access.

11

VERA WAS LATE, and her shoes hurt, two of her least favorite conditions. She could blame the lateness on a faculty union meeting that had dragged on even longer than usual, with all the details to be organized for the board meeting the following week—the sign-painting teams, assembly points, and Abraham Lincoln Brigade–like marching formations—but the shoes . . . well, the shoes were just a mistake. They had seemed broad and soft and geekily chic when she'd tried them on in the shop, but a week of cohabitation had revealed them to be cunningly designed torture chambers that revived an ancient bunion from decades of dormancy and turned each step into searing, Hans Christian Andersen–style agony. And she couldn't afford to buy another pair right now, either.

It was strange, she thought, mincing gingerly along Second Avenue, how, when your feet hurt, you couldn't think about anything else. She could hardly wait to reach the restaurant, where she could relieve her feet of their thirty pounds of pressure per square inch, order a perfectly chilled martini, and discreetly unstrap her shoes under the table. Helena wouldn't mind. Helena, having been fat and depressed the week before, was now happy and thin, apparently—flying high. The birthday dinner had been postponed because she'd been invited, unexpectedly, to fly out to Seattle, where, even more unexpectedly, she'd received a large commission—a mural in the private Pilates studio of a twenty-six-year-old Internet billionaire. Helena had had all kinds of design concepts involving dismemberment, which the billionaire had deemed "way cool." So Helena was celebrating that as well: money, work, dismemberment. Whereas I, Vera thought, gratefully spotting her destination, have nothing to celebrate besides the imminent prospect of sitting down.

At that moment she passed someone on the street, a large woman with unmistakable magenta hair, whose eyes met hers fleetingly in one of those urban encounters where each recognizes the other but cannot, in that moment, recall the context. Vera was idly scrolling through the possibilities—former student? someone from the gym?—when the woman turned back and said, smiling, "I *thought* that was you."

"It is indeed," Vera said, playing for time. Someone who lived in her building? Waitress somewhere?

"How've you been?" There was an overtone of empathy, of gravitas, in her manner that flagged the question as more than routine.

"Oh, great," Vera said, nervously. "Great, thanks. And how about you?"

"Oh, you know how it is . . ." The woman made the defeated moue of the overworked, and in that instant Vera recognized her: the receptionist at St. Marks Veterinary, the one who kept the appointments and the books. She was probably just leaving work, a block away on Ninth Street, at this tender twilight hour of 7:00 P.M. Vera had got to know her quite well, by sight, in the course of repeated visits to the vet during Lulu's last illness and had in fact spent long periods in the waiting room watching this woman with grudging respect—her unharried demeanor, despite phones that never stopped ringing and stressed-out animals that sat shivering or snarling at one another across the narrow divide, her kindly attention to each pet's name and predicament, but most of all, Vera thought, the simple fact that she hadn't long since been driven insane by the clinic's door, which buzzed loudly every time someone came in—hundreds of times a day—and slammed even more loudly each time someone left.

"Busy, huh?" Vera asked. "As always."

"Crazy," the woman said, shaking her head.

"Anyway," Vera replied, glancing at her watch, though she knew the time, "it's good to see you. Got to run . . ." and she pointed in the general direction of the restaurant.

"Good to see you too," the woman said, turning as if to continue on her way. "You take care, now." Then she swung around, struck by a thought. "Didn't you move, though . . . ?" she asked, uncertainly. "I thought you'd moved."

"Moved?"

"Out West somewhere?"

"Oh no," Vera said airily, "still here, a prisoner of the East Village. Can't afford to stay, but can't afford to move either. I'll probably die in that little shoebox of mine."

The woman nodded ruefully, real estate being the universal language and the shared human condition of all New Yorkers.

"Anyway . . ." Vera said, shifting her weight meaningfully in the direction she'd been headed.

"Anyway . . ." the woman said, shifting hers, dubiously, in the opposite direction. They repeated their valedictions and Vera hobbled hastily down the block and up the stairs to Holy Basil, twenty minutes late. She knew that Helena would be agitated, not because Helena was a model of punctuality herself, but because Helena, a formerly fat person who had lost fifty pounds at Weight Watchers, was unable to focus on anything else when there was food in the room. Until she had decided what to eat and had eaten it, she would be awash in anxiety, abuzz with desire, deaf to all other concerns.

Sure enough, when Vera arrived, Helena had already installed herself at their table with a glass of water and an open menu, and was craning her neck around to inspect the plates of other diners.

"Sorry," Vera said, collapsing in an exaggerated manner into her chair. "First this stupid faculty meeting, which ran late, and then running into this woman on the street—"

"No problem," Helena said. "I didn't order, but I'm thinking the pad thai, if they'll leave out the egg, and then the yellow curry, but do you think that's got coconut milk?"

"Probably," Vera said, absently. She, on the other hand, had difficulty focusing on anything else when there was a large martini in the offing.

When the martini arrived, accompanied by a wan spritzer, which was all Helena—a former red wine and bourbon fiend— drank these days, they toasted her commission, and then, belatedly, her birthday.

"Oh, don't talk to me about birthdays," Helena said, running a hand disgustedly through her hair. "You know, if a face-lift didn't actually involve *cutting*—"

"You don't need a face-lift," Vera said, loyally. "You look great. The only thing you might possibly need is some sex." This was partly true: Helena had the kind of looks—strong features, high cheekbones, deep-set eyes—that, according to her mood and her general well-being, could appear either striking or severe. When she was happy and well fucked, she turned heads on the street. But today was a severe day, bordering on grim. Also, her short blonde hair, depending on how recently she'd washed it, could look either boyish and tousled, or what the French call *triste*. Today was *triste*. Vera decided to present the camisole at the end of the meal, when her friend's mood might be lighter, more playful.

The pad thai seemed to help Helena's spirits. The second drink helped. Listening to Vera's problems with Colin definitely helped, as, when one is loverless in Manhattan, one can always console oneself with the imperfect situation of everyone else, the relationships born of desperation and high rent, the massive concessions, the losers, the liars, the sex offenders, the cohabitation in tiny apartments with the cat's dish on top of the refrigerator and the fold-out bed.

"The thing is," Vera said, leaning back in her chair and picturing Colin naked at her Mac, as he liked to disport himself, "that he drives me crazy a lot of the time, just gets on my nerves. Like having a hyperactive child around, or, I don't know, a puppy."

"What percentage?"

"What do you mean, what percentage?"

"What percentage of the time?" Helena asked, indicating a block of time with her hands, like a fisherman showing the size of a fish.

"Gee, I don't know. I never thought about it that way. Um, twenty percent, thirty percent, maybe more."

"Well," said Helena, in a grave, mock-scientific manner, "I'd say that's well within the normal range for your demographic."

"Maybe." Vera shrugged. "I wouldn't know."

"And the rest of the time?" Helena had met Colin only once, briefly, at a crowded opening for one of her murals in a SoHo lamp store, not exactly the best context in which to appreciate his good qualities, air kissing and small talk not featuring among them.

"Well, the rest of the time he's great. Very smart, knows a lot of interesting things. Funny. Nonconformist. Great in bed." She left it at that, not wanting to appear to brag, but the fact was that Colin was a highly skilled lover, although—she sometimes felt—he approached the female body, and his own sexuality, as if it were a science project. In that same spirit, he'd also matter-of-factly revealed a few areas of kinkiness, which didn't particularly interest her, though she didn't object to them either.

"So then what's the problem, honey?" asked Helena, with a leer. "Sounds pretty damn good to me."

"The problem," Vera said, "is that there's no future in this. I'm almost ten years older than him. And he's at that stage of life where nothing is fixed yet, you know, everything is open, up for grabs. Where, in a sense, you feel as if your real life hasn't started yet."

"And you? I suppose you're ready for the old folks home? Picked out your burial plot yet?"

"*Moi*?" Vera thought of the daily collateral damage of living—the wear and tear of gravity, the gradual encroachment of forgetfulness, the slow, inevitable hardening of personality. She thought about entropy, about radiation, about how things fall apart. She thought about the way her hands, in certain lights, looked like those of an old woman. "Any day now."

"Oh please," said Helena, impatiently.

"No, it's more—you know. At this stage of one's life, what's the point in going on with something that you know will have to end sooner or later?"

"Everything ends sooner or later. Sooner, if you make up your mind that it's going to."

"You know what I mean," Vera said wearily. "I'm certainly not sitting around waiting for Mr. Perfect to come along. But why sign up, voluntarily, for another go-around through the wringer? And it always ends up being the wringer. After a certain point, there's no such thing as a fling anymore."

"Maybe," said Helena, "but why can't you just enjoy it while it lasts?"

"Because I know it won't."

"Oh please," Helena repeated. "There's a defeatist attitude if ever I heard one. And an ungrateful one, I might add. At least you're getting some, on a regular basis. And fairly high-quality stuff, from what I hear."

One couldn't argue with dearth, Vera thought. And perhaps Helena was right, she just needed to lighten up, have fun, carpe diem, and all those other things she'd never succeeded in doing. The children of Carlo and Francesca de Sica weren't raised to seize the day: they were raised to work hard and to worry. Her brother, Ernesto, had become a dentist because, he reasoned, people would always have teeth.

"Speaking of high-quality stuff," Vera said, producing the bag that held the box that held the tissue paper that held the camisole, "here's your birthday present, Miss Thing. May it see plenty of active service."

Helena, who had body-image issues, had to be convinced—by the simple expedient of holding it up to her torso and stretching it over her breasts—that the silky scrap would actually fit her. During this maneuver, Vera noticed two men at a nearby table giving them the eye and wondered, briefly, whether she owed it to Helena to give them the eye back, in an ironic, noncommittal way. But they were tie-loosened young Wall Street types, drinking green apple martinis, with cell phones at the ready like guns in a saloon. Helena wasn't that hard up, Vera decided, and ignored them.

In another era, she thought, she would have had to take her pickings from bar flotsam like this, or, worse still, from her downtrodden, distracted colleagues at work. In another era—even five years earlier—she and Colin would never have met. But maybe they shouldn't have, she thought: they'd met in cyberspace and while their virtual selves had hit it off, their embodied selves were now bumping, with the stubborn irrationality of meat machines, into real-life obstacles, contradictions, incompatibilities.

As Helena refolded the camisole into its wrapping (where, Vera suspected, it would remain forever), Vera signaled to the waiter, a lovely Thai lady-boy, for the bill. Producing her brand-new credit card, she realized she'd forgotten to sign the back, which she did quickly as the lady-boy moved away.

"Oh and you know what," she said to Helena, eyeballing the total and trying to calculate the tip, "somebody ripped off my credit card. Well, my credit card info, anyway."

She explained, briefly, about the satellite dish and the diamond ring, the phony address. She had rapidly turned the story —as, she realized, she turned just about everything that happened to her—into an amusing anecdote, just another of life's little jokes against herself.

"Bummer," said Helena, taking out compact and lipstick for the ritual postprandial application. "Same thing happened to my dealer, except apparently these guys were rifling through her trash. Fishing out her mail—all those credit card applications she'd tossed, bills, business correspondence, God knows what. She's got a paper shredder now."

"I've always wanted one of those," Vera said. She pictured herself feeding sheet after sheet into the machine—her bills, her junk mail, her students' papers, her mortgage, her diplomas, the memos from the curriculum committee—pictured the satisfying spaghetti coming out. "Except I wouldn't know where to stop. I'd shred everything. My whole life." When, a few years earlier, her colleague Maureen had lost everything in a fire, Vera had, perversely, envied her—a sentiment she knew better than to express.

"Identity theft," Helena said sagely, through stretched-out

lips. She could talk and apply lipstick at the same time, no problem. She blotted top and bottom lip together, then snapped the compact shut. "It's really common these days. You have to be careful."

"Yeah, but who would want to steal *my* identity? They'd be welcome to it. I'd *give* it away."

"No but seriously," Helena said, "you should check your credit report, make sure there's no other weird shit going on."

"Check my credit report? What a horrendous idea."

Helena shrugged. "You're entitled," she replied, as they both stood up to leave. "You can just request a copy."

"Request a copy of my credit report? And actually look at it, see what a low score I have? See what a loser I am?" Vera asked incredulously, brushing a couple of stray bean sprouts off her lap. "I don't think so." Her bunion, she noticed, had begun to throb the moment she stood up again. She'd been hoping it would have been miraculously cured by resting, au naturel, under the table for two hours.

It was still throbbing a week later when she assembled with the members of her department in Central Park to march, in what they hoped would be a dignified formation, towards the administration building. Her colleagues were all dressed, as agreed, in their academic gowns, but Vera refused point-blank to wear such a thing: pretentious and unflattering, she thought, and, worse still, polyester. She wore black pants and a black T-shirt instead, to blend in.

Standing next to Roberto and Flora, almost unrecognizable in their somber robes, she felt oddly underdressed, as in one of those dreams, increasingly frequent of late, where she'd show up for class unprepared, befuddled, and pajama-clad. As if she were already unemployed, she realized, with no compelling reason to get dressed.

The banners behind which they were to march read WE ARE ALL IMMIGRANTS! and ENGLISH AS A SECOND LANGUAGE: NOT REMEDIATION BUT A RIGHT! This latter sentiment had defeated the sign painter, so that the word RIGHT was inelegantly squished, curving upwards to fit the sheet.

"Catchy, huh?" Vera murmured to Flora, who, being tall, was positioning herself to hold up the top left-hand corner of the REMEDIATION banner.

Flora, an earnest, tender Colombian, seemed stricken by this remark. "But Vera," she said, pushing her silky hair back behind her ears, where it would not stay, "the point is to convey our political message, not to think in sound bites, not to become part of the culture of sound bites."

"No, no, you're right," Vera said hastily. "Only kidding." In penance, and to demonstrate her solidarity with the Colombian people, she took hold of the lower-left corner of the offending banner.

As they progressed towards the elegant Upper East Side townhouse where the administration was housed, they dutifully chanted "What do we want? EDUCATION! When do we want it? NOW!," but it was clear, even as they chanted, that the battle was lost. That, in fact, it had been lost from the start. The student contingent, with whom they were supposed to merge in a single, unstoppable wave of the proletariat, had been corralled by the police into a block near the precinct house, and the faculty group was permitted no further than the DMZ of Park Avenue. A few stick-thin old ladies in Chanel suits watched the demonstrators with blank attention while their Yorkies idly poisoned the early tulips, but then moved on, equally blankly, to nowhere in particular, and by the time the group had disbanded, with hollow, hearty handshakes and slaps on the back, the board had already issued a press release stating that all "remedial" courses—composition, mathematics, and ESL—were to be abolished at Metropolitan U by September next.

"September next?" Vera asked Roberto, who was relaying the news in real time. "Does that mean this coming September?"

He nodded dolefully, head cocked to decipher incoming intelligence from his cell phone.

Vera found herself on the 6 train heading downtown, out of blind habit, before she realized that that wasn't at all where she wanted to be. She wanted to be with other people, with Flora and Roberto, in a loud bar somewhere, although it was only two in the afternoon. She wanted to be knocking back beers, bearing up bravely, defying fate in the lusty, gravelly manner of a French chanteuse. But Flora had had to get home to relieve the babysitter, and Roberto was "caucusing" with other union officials, and everyone else had dispersed in a furtive, sheepish way, so here she was, on a crowded downtown train, clinging to an unclean pole. Like a stripper at the start of her act, she thought, except this is curtains for me.

What to do next? She'd call Colin when she got home, of course—he'd be sympathetic but brisk, she predicted: to him, losing a job would represent no more than a temporary inconvenience, a small blip in the immense grid of other possibilities. She'd probably have felt that way when she was thirty, too. Maybe she'd call Simone—no, she had her usual appointment the following day, so she'd save it for then. Calling the shrink was for dire emergencies, in Vera's opinion, moments of barking existential panic, not the mundane fact of hearing one would soon be unemployed.

She had the impulse to call her parents, as she still did whenever something major happened, but, as usual, she quashed it. Why invoke the predictable avalanche of parental concern? Why trouble them out there in their precarious, hard-won paradise?

Surely, after a lifetime of work and worry, they deserved a little peace of mind. It was already bad enough that she wasn't (a) married and (b) a lawyer. That she had no kids. That all she owned on Planet Earth was a couple of rooms in a former crack house.

Once home, she yanked off her sneakers and threw them, for no particular reason, across the room. Then she tried Colin's work and home numbers, with no response from either—Colin didn't believe in voice mail—which meant that he was either in the middle of a code-writing binge or up to his elbows in his Riley. Or he might simply be breaking for a chicken-and-mango-salsa wrap at the staff cafeteria at Lucid, which, she recalled resentfully, was fitted out with a juice bar, jazz pianist, and gumball machine, all for the little princes of the computing world.

Having Colin in her life, she reflected, felt, too much of the time, like having no one at all. She'd believed, at the outset, that she'd liked it that way. Now she wasn't so sure.

She dialed Helena but got the usual grumpy-sounding message. ("This is the disembodied voice of Helena Kowaleski. You know what to do, so do it.") She tried Flora, for a thorough debriefing, but Flora hadn't yet arrived back in Queens. Her officemate Joon Seok was at one of his other teaching jobs (he had three). The people she knew in New York were not, by and large, the type of people who had time to listen to your worries during the workday. And no way was she going to give Ernesto the opportunity of being right, with his eternal fixation on job security. As she wondered whom to call next, Vera recognized, reluctantly, the true measure of her isolation: nobody to tell her story to.

That was what e-mail was for, she thought, that's what it was really about: that momentary gratification when you hit "Connect." Which, waking her Mac from its cyberslumber, she proceeded to do. Or tried to do. After a few seconds of electronic dithering, the machine appeared to throw a hissy fit, spawning, at last, a sullen little box: *"User authentication failed. Check your user name and password and try again."*

Fuckin' hell, Vera thought, fuckin' AOL. Always some problem, some glitch, some annoyance when you were least in the mood for it. In the past, admittedly, she'd received the same error message after Lulu had sauntered over the keyboard and turned the log-in window into alphabet soup, but this could hardly be the case now. She checked her user name—*vdesica*—re-entered her AOL password—*lulu*—and hit Connect again, emphatically, as if prodding the machine to respond. Same dithering—during which Vera occupied herself by blowing crumbs and cat hairs off the keyboard—then the same box: *"User authentication failed. Check your user name and password and try again."*

She perseverated. So did the machine.

"User authentication failed. Check your user name and password and try again."

"User authentication failed. Check your user name and password and try again."

12

T HIS WASN'T HALF as much fun as she'd thought it was
going to be, Charlene saw—more than half the messages
in Vera's in box were work-related, uninspiring memos
about the time and place of the next Curriculum Committee
meeting, reminders about textbook orders for the fall, the new
University policy on plagiarism, questions or excuses from students: "Proffesor, I'm sorry I missed the final but my brother
was picked up by the cops in Queens and I had to get over to the
precinct because my stepmom doesn't know English. PS: Driving While Black." Charlene didn't know what the PS meant—
some New York thing, presumably—but she figured Vera must
be doing a decent job if her students could spell "precinct."
Howie—well, one day she would ask Howie to spell *precinct,*
just for a laugh.

But, really, Charlene fretted, scrolling through Vera's in box,
if the contents of your in box reflected the contents of your life,
this vdesica character must be dull as day-old mascara. No se-
crets, no spice, not even the usual solicitations to enlarge your
penis or collect millions from a Nigerian bank. Knowing our
Prof, she'd probably installed every spam filter and firewall that
money could buy, probably updated her virus protector every
day. She probably flossed daily, too, used sunscreen, took cal-
cium, had regular mammograms. Whereas Charlene, excuse

her, was fucked if she was going to let some stranger perform the yearly equivalent of slamming her boobs in a refrigerator door.

But where, Charlene wondered, was the passion in this woman's life? Where was the sex? Where were the invitations to art openings and book parties and fashion shows, to weekends at the Hamptons and cocktails at the . . . Charlene tried to remember the name of a hotspot she'd read about in *People* magazine, the Moola or the Roomba or something like that. Could Vera be—surely not—some kind of nerd, some kind of geek? Some loser with no sex life? Charlene wasn't going to stand for that. Especially now that she, Charlene, *was* vdesica@aol.com, having changed the password that very day to doubletrouble2.

As for Charlene, she thought about sex much of the time, except of course when she was with Howie. When Howie had passed out at night, or during long boring stretches at work, she'd imagine herself on a beach in Cozumel with Brad Pitt, or sometimes in a threesome with Brad Pitt and Hugh Grant. Sometimes even—though she knew this was sick—with Brad Pitt and Madonna, during her pointy-bra phase. They'd all be in a huge bed at the Beverly Hills Hotel, Charlene herself, miraculously thin, in some kind of Frederick's of Hollywood lace-up bustier, with cleavage like the Grand Canyon. Then she'd get so turned on she'd have to go and take care of herself in the middle of the day, in the skanky employees' restroom at the Revco, under the indifferent gaze of a wet mop.

So where were the men in Vera's life, in her in box? Honey, Charlene imagined addressing Vera in a girlfriendly way, your "in box" needs some action, know what I mean? There was a "C. D. Evans" at Lucid.com who sent several messages a day, but they were terse and unpunctuated, usually no more than a line or two, technological bulletins or links to other sites (the BBC,

Slashdot.com, Nerve.com, Whatis.com). So C.D. was probably some kind of technogeek that Vera consulted on computer issues, no one important. More promising was a "Roberto" who had sent numerous messages in the past few days, establishing a meeting place in Central Park. In the middle of the day. He'd also specified that Vera should wear her "gown," which seemed promising, even kinky. Charlene decided that he deserved a reply.

"Dear Roberto," she wrote, "have I ever told you how I dream about that big thing of yours? Wet kisses where you want them most, V." That should cover most eventualities, Charlene thought, clicking "Send."

She also responded to the Curriculum Committee memo, hitting "Reply to All." After a few seconds' thought, she typed "Frankly, my dears, I don't give a damn—Vera de Sica." She'd always wanted to say that to someone—her clients at the Revco, her former boss at the DMV, Howie in mid-rant. "Do you really think I care about your gangsta brother?" she wrote to the student. "I hope you realize that this means you've flunked the course." She was on a roll now, but running out of material. She felt a twinge of irritation with Vera, Vera and her undernourished in box. It was only a matter of time, a couple of hours max, before the Prof figured out what had happened and closed her account. Charlene had hoped to wreak a whole lot more havoc by then, cluster-bombing the smug edifices of Vera's annoyingly manageable, annoyingly middle-class life.

But now that she had, through astute guesswork, gained access to Vera's account, she couldn't really think what to do with it. That was sad, Charlene thought. That was fuckin' pathetic. She knew how to screw up someone's finances, but not really, when it came down to it, their lives. She had hoped, by occupying Vera's cyberspace, to inhabit her identity: to find out who she was by the way she was networked to others. To try on this vdesica persona for size, hang out in that cyberskin for a while, maybe make a few changes, a few nips and tucks. Hey, didn't it say right there, under User Options, "Edit Your Identity"? But there was only so far you could go with the Curriculum Committee, the textbook orders. She placed an order with the campus bookstore for thirty copies of *The Joy of Gay Sex.* Under Instructor, she wrote "de Sica," under Sections, she wrote "All."

Then another inspiration seized her: our Prof's address book. First of all, to print it out for future reference. Then to scroll through it, composing messages at whim. There was an edesica@dentassocs.com, who she assumed must be a family member. "What's up with you, you big fat loser?" she fired off. A Simone Foucault, M.D., simfou@mindspring.com, might be concerned, Charlene thought, to receive the following: "Doc, I feel as if my personality has been invaded by another, please help us, Vera ©." To Hugo at carlsontravel.com, she requested immediate reservations for a three-week trip to Bali, first-class flight and five-star accommodations. Charge, please, to the credit card on file.

Charlene paused in her typing and scrolling, scratched her nose, inspected her nail polish. She was running out of steam, running out of ideas. She couldn't tell, just from their names, who most of the people in the address book were or what role they played in Vera's life. So many names, so many addresses, so many of them ending with .edu or .fr or .uk, whatever that meant. Then she thought about her own address book, which contained no names at all, because Howie was paranoid about leaving any kind of trail. She thought about how she didn't even have a phone number for Judith from the Sunday power-walking or Cindy from the Revco. How even her mother was dead— cirrhosis, big surprise—and Howie wouldn't let her get a dog.

How, as far as she knew, neither she nor Howie had a single piece of paper in the house with their real names on it, though they had drawers full of bogus IDs.

They'd been married twice, in two different states, under names not their own—the quickest, cheapest way for Charlene to get an identity makeover. Just like the Sunday-paper wedding announcements, where the bride is always referred to as "the former so-and-so," as if that person no longer existed. You paid your $25, Charlene thought, and in ten minutes you were somebody else.

At the beginning, she'd wanted Howie to marry her for real. She'd thought it might make some kind of difference—but then she realized that he wasn't going anywhere anyway. Though he daily threatened to dump her, Charlene knew he wouldn't be able to keep his "venture" going without her. She was the one with the sales skills and the legitimate job—who'd rent an apartment to Howie otherwise? With his furtive manner and no visible means of support? Who would even give him a cell phone contract, when he neglected all bills and routinely forgot his *nom du jour*? Howie believed he was the brains of the operation, but Charlene knew the truth: she was front-of-house, he was strictly back-office. Otherwise why would he make her do all the talking—at Electro City, at Bloomingdale's, at the frigging Gap? While he stood by, head ducked under his baseball cap, lips slack, eyes darting from side to side? Hell, Howie was dyslexic and couldn't even fill out a credit card application without her help. And, above all, Howie needed an audience. Despite his paranoia about surveillance cameras, he suffered, she knew, from a far deeper fear: the fear that no one was watching. "Eat *that*, Bank of America!" he'd say to the Web site, but it was really to her.

Charlene surveyed the Prof's address book one more time,

then, with a sullen click, logged out. She wondered what it must feel like to know all those people, be known by them. Her imagination failed her, came up blank as the screen. She could see nothing but her own reflection in the darkened glass.

Frankly, Charlene thought, she was getting a little bored with this game, plus, after all those beers, she really needed to pee. But first—an idea struck her—she would go back on-line. Not into the AOL account, but to another favorite, IMM—IN-STANT MORTGAGE MALL!®. Our Prof, with everything else she had to attend to, had most likely neglected one simple task: that of refinancing her apartment. A lamentable oversight, in Charlene's view—on Manhattan real estate, yet. Especially as IMM made it all so simple, everything on-line, no arduous paperwork. *Borrow up to 100% of your home's equity! No home appraisal or insurance required! No application fee!* Charlene would guesstimate such matters as income, savings, and so on; Vera would apply for the max. Why not? As Dr. Laura was always reminding her callers, it never hurts to ask.

13

B UT HOW IS THAT POSSIBLE?" Vera asked, her voice
shriller than a grown-up's should be. "How?"

"Well, obviously you must have given your password
to someone." The Tech Support person spoke in a monotone,
sounding massively bored. He also sounded about twelve. Vera
hated these conversations at the best of times—the life-sapping,
will-sapping minutes on hold, the apathetic voice on the other
end, invariably male, invariably patronizing, and more often
than not delivered through a mouthful of pizza or muffin, depending on the hour in Washington State. And this was not the
best of times. Someone had gained access to her AOL account
and changed her password.

"Well, obviously, I did not," she snapped back.

"People always think they didn't. Then they remember that
they did." She pictured him shrugging and shooting aliens on
his screen.

"Well, I didn't. Trust me. I'm not stupid." It annoyed her that
she always found herself insisting on this. How much do you
know about gerunds, geek-boy? she wanted to ask. But gerunds
didn't run the world. Zeros and ones did. C++ did. Microchips.

"Or you must have stuck it on your computer, on a Post-it.
People always do that." He said "people" as if it were a term of
abuse, people meaning civilians, baffled like chimps before their
magic boxes.

"No I did not," she said. "I'm not a complete idiot. Anyway," she added, "I live alone, so even if I had, who would have seen it?" As she said this, a sudden, queasy certainty seized her: Colin. Who else? Why hadn't she thought of that right away? A hacker's idea of a joke. A little object lesson in computer security. She was going to kill the fucker, she was going to strangle him with the power cord on her Mac.

Her first impulse had been to call Tech Support at AOL, rather than Colin, whose mild, unthinking derision she feared more than the impersonal contempt of Support Boy. Like most civilians, she assumed that if her computer went on the blink, it must be her fault. Some archaic part of her brain insisted on attributing the actions of her Mac to a malicious homunculus behind the screen, a pissed-off pixie of the pixels.

But now she understood that she should have called Colin first, that Colin was to blame. I need a grown-up, she thought, as she had thought so many times before, a grown-up, not a superannuated adolescent. Especially right now. I just lost my damn job, she thought bitterly, I don't need my supposed boyfriend jerking around in my cyberspace, keeping me out, scent-marking it as his territory, boy territory.

"You fucker," she said, when she finally reached him, about half an hour later, in his office at Lucid.

"Say what?" That stopped the multitasking, for once. His keyboard went quiet.

"You fucker," she repeated. "It's not funny. I had a terrible day to begin with, and this was the last thing I needed. Not funny, OK?"

"Vera," he said, calmly, "I have no idea what you're talking about."

"Oh, cut it out. You've made your point. I'll choose a better password next time. But just stay out of my fucking computer, OK? Stay out of my face."

"What the hell are you talking about?" She heard his voice rise, atypically, with annoyance.

"My AOL account."

"Yes? What about it?"

"You know very well what about it."

"Look, Vera, I don't appreciate being accused of something that I haven't done. That I don't even know what it is." She had rarely heard such indignation in his voice. When he was angry or upset, he usually shut down, closed off all channels, one by one, like TV stations signing off for the night. Static and snow, until the signal resumed.

Perhaps, Vera thought, with a prickle of doubt, it really hadn't been him. This didn't sound like play-acting, like the hacker's barely concealed swagger. This sounded like someone who was actually aggrieved.

"You mean you didn't . . . ?"

"Didn't what?"

"Didn't go into my AOL account and change my password?"

"Of course I didn't. Why would I do that?"

"I dunno. Because you can?"

"Well, sure, I could. It would be trivial." Trivial was hacker-speak for something so simple to do that it wasn't worth doing.

"Well, somebody did." All of a sudden, she realized she was about to cry. At least I didn't cry in front of Support Boy, she thought—meaning in his telepresence, an oxymoron if ever there was one. But now I'm going to cry in front of Colin. And I haven't even told him about the job. The ex-job.

"What do you mean?"

"I can't get in. It won't authenticate me."

Colin was at his best when there was a problem to solve, as long as it wasn't an icky emotional one. As soon as he heard Vera's voice crack, he deployed Strategy A (avoidance) so that he could successfully deploy Strategy B (problem-solving).

"Listen," he said. "You stay right where you are. I'll get the next train, I'll be there in an hour or so. Then we'll take a look at your Mac and figure out what's going on."

He assumed, of course, that she'd done something stupid. Well, probably she had. It was only four in the afternoon and she felt like crawling into bed. In fact, she thought, why the hell not? Surely she'd earned the right to behave like a depressed person. Her daily dose of Prozac certainly wasn't doing the job. It was only the prospect of Colin's arrival that kept her clothed and propped up in her chair, staring glumly out of the window over a multiply dog-eared *New Yorker,* impersonating an adult.

"By the way," she said, as soon as he arrived, all business, unlacing his boots, "the board decided."

"Board?" She could see he was thinking computers, circuit boards, logic boards.

"The board of Metropolitan U. I'm out of a job come September."

"Hmmmnnn," he said. This was Colin's all-purpose signifier, meaning, she'd learned, I'm taking that in, I'm pondering that. I'm taking it on board.

"*Hmmmnnn* is right," she said.

"*Hmmmnnn,*" he repeated, with greater emphasis. "That's not good."

Such was Colin's notion of emotional support, she thought. But what would she prefer? *Don't worry darling, you'll get another job*? Or *Come here, poor baby, and let me make it all better*? Frankly (secretly), yes.

He was firing up her Mac. That was how he was going to make it all better.

"OK," he said. "Enter your AOL password."

"I've done that. About a million times." She'd even tried a few more times while waiting for Colin, never mind that she knew it had been changed. Such was the force of her magical thinking.

"Do it again, so I can see what happens." She did. He watched, not her fingers on the keyboard as she typed over his shoulder, but the row of bullets on the screen.

"Only four characters?" he asked.

"Is that bad?"

He shrugged.

"See, there it is," she said, as the indefatigable little box sprang up. *"User authentication failed. Check your user name and password and try again."*

"It's a name, isn't it?" he asked, swiveling around on her desk chair to face her.

"Well, yes . . ."

"That's what people always do." She noticed that he said "people" in the same tone as Support Boy, "people" as a synonym for mindless, benighted civilians. "A name. Which is the easiest to guess, if you know the person, and the easiest to crack, if you don't."

"Crack, how?"

"OK, so if I'm trying to get your password, I can't do it just by brute force. Well, in theory I could, but it wouldn't be practical."

"What's brute force? You mean, like physically breaking into the machine?"

"No, no. Trying every single possible combination of letters. If you just try all the lowercase letters on the keyboard, there are, you know, like, two hundred billion combinations."

"You're making that up."

"I'm not. And if you also use numbers, symbols, uppercase, the whole shebang, then it's, like, fifty-three trillion possibilities."

"You're making those numbers up. I mean, how could you just *know* them like that?"

"I do," he said. Meaning: any hacker does.

"It's Lulu," she blurted, tears suddenly stinging her eyes. "I mean, she's *dead*. So how could anyone guess?"

"Word list. All names. Usually one for male and one for female. It's the first thing I'd try."

Vera felt, all of a sudden, very, very tired. Taking five paces from the desk, she slumped into her big old armchair, a substitute embrace. Even now, she noticed, there were still a few tabby hairs woven into the warp of it. Or was it the woof.

"But why?" she asked. "Why would someone do that?"

"That," Colin said, "I don't know."

Who hated her? she wondered. Plenty of people, probably, but who hated her enough, resented her enough, to go in and mess with her AOL account? She felt suddenly exposed, unsafe, had a strong urge to draw the curtains. She surveyed her students in her mind, tried to come up with a suspect, someone to whom she'd given a bad grade, said something harsh, chastised for being late. Some quiet little psycho, just cocked to go off.

"Must be a student," she said. "I mean, who else?"

"Could be," Colin shrugged. "Could also just be random—someone who needs some IP addresses to pull some other shit. Or some script kiddie in Yugoslavia, nothing better to do."

You are networked to millions of people, millions of strangers, Vera thought. And any one of them could meddle with you—your virtual self, your proxy self—at any time. Your virtual self gets around a lot more than you do: in most transactions, you are present only as an absent body: you are where it's @. Part of a global community—without people. And Vera shivered, actual gooseflesh on her actual arm.

"No," she said suddenly, decisively. "It's not random."

"How do you know?"

"I just know." And then she realized how she did know. "The credit card thing. A few weeks ago my Visa card, now my AOL account. It's too much of a coincidence." A sense of profound dismay traveled through her body, from the inside out, as if alarm signals were overloading the system, causing the layers of her skin to come unstuck. "Man," she said, "what the fuck else is going to happen to me?"

"Wait a moment," Colin said. "Let's not get paranoid."

"Not get paranoid? Someone's out there using my credit card, someone's out there using my e-mail, and I shouldn't be paranoid?" She was becoming shrill. She felt transparent, legible, the Visible Woman. With microcircuitry where her veins should be.

"Let's think this through," he said. He swiveled a few more degrees so that he was facing her where she sat clenched in the armchair. He stretched out his long legs. He folded his arms. "OK, so person X goes into Vera's AOL account. Logs in, changes password. Vera logs in, gets Sorry, wrong password. What should Vera do now?"

"Cancel the account. Call the fucking cops."

"The cops? They'd laugh at you. It's not clear that a crime has been committed. I mean, how have you been harmed? What's been stolen from you?"

"My password. My, I don't know, access."

"Access to what? Your e-mail? It's not as if there's classified information in there. And you're always free to open another account. See what I mean—the question is, what harm has actually been done?"

"You mean, pretending to be me isn't a crime? Somebody steals my password, they're pretending to be me." The idea galled her, appalled her. Some adolescent prankster inhabiting her name, parading through cyberspace cross-dressed as vdesica, strapping on her identity like a freaky prosthesis.

"Not necessarily." Colin, she could see, was processing this as a technical question—the unbundling of identity on the Internet—rather than as the affront she felt it to be, creepy and insidious and unsettling. "If I use someone's password, I'm not necessarily claiming to be them. I'm merely establishing that I know something that only they're supposed to know."

"Oh Colin, for Chrissake, stop splitting hairs. How would you like it if I went on-line and pretended to be you, changed your password, screwed around with your life?"

"You couldn't do that, with the system we have at Lucid. Except maybe under some kind of targeted scrutiny." Once again Vera was struck by his literal-mindedness. That was the nature of the beast, she supposed, the very quality that made him so successful with machines. But the nature of the beast, she was beginning to think, was beastly.

She sprang out of the chair in a single, anxious spasm. "Well, I'm not going to spend the afternoon having a philosophical discussion with you. I've got to get back on the phone to AOL and tell them to close the account."

"Well, you could do that," Colin said, musing.

"*Could* do that? What the hell else would I do?"

"If it were me, I'd try to track this cracker down. Try to get AOL to look at their Web server logs and see the IP address."

"IP address?"

"That was used to make the Web hits that changed the password."

"Would they do that?"

"They should. They could, in theory, try to trace it back as far as possible. That's what the FBI does when a virus hits the Web. Whether they will or not is another question."

With great difficulty, Vera resisted the urge to beg Colin to get on the phone and intervene, on her behalf, with AOL. She knew that someone who was (a) male, and (b) technologically savvy would get a more respectful hearing from the confederacy of Tech Boys. But she would handle this herself. She was, allegedly, an adult. It was, allegedly, the twenty-first century.

Fuck, she thought, as she dialed the 800 number, dread and resentment like mercury in her veins, this has been one hell of a day.

"Do me a favor," she said, covering the mouthpiece even though she was on hold, "and open us up a bottle of red. I have a feeling I'm going to need it."

She should know better—did know better—than to drink on an empty stomach. An hour later or so, after two glasses of shiraz, she felt worse—headachy, wired, and borderline weepy.

"I don't understand any of this," she bleated to Colin, or, more precisely, to the back of Colin's head. He was attacking her Mac, as usual, with furious typing, but she couldn't tell whether he was cybersleuthing or simply posting to the Riley bulletin board, ClassicCar-nection, where, she'd gathered, he enjoyed enormous on-line *cojones* and unlimited flaming rights.

She did not understand why she, Vera de Sica, fee-paying netizen, didn't have the right to inspect the logs of her own on-line activity. Purported on-line activity. No way, the AOL rep had said. No mail server will do this for you, he helpfully pointed out, it's no different on Hotmail or Earthlink or whatever. If you want to get those logs, then you have to subpoena. And to subpoena you have to have some kind of court case brought by you, or against you, that's, like, relevant, you know? Otherwise, lady, you're out of luck.

You went through life, she realized, leaving a trail of data behind you—a data spoor, a data doppelgänger. Somewhere out there was a body of data, a data body, linked to you, the meat body, by a name. And that body, the data body, didn't belong to you. It belonged to somebody else, various somebodies, lived in a data bank, was bought and sold. It had, Vera realized, a life of its own, a separate career. You "owned" it no more—and no less—than you owned anyone else's.

"OK, then, can you change the password back again?" she'd asked AOL Boy.

"No problem, lady. We'd be happy to do that. Um, if . . ."

"If what?"

"If you can prove that you're you."

Vera paused. "And how would I do that?"

"Social Security number, mother's maiden name."

"But how was the password changed in the first place?"

"Um . . . Social Security number, mother's maiden name."

That's why it's called the Net, she thought, despairingly, the Web: no way out.

Not knowing what else to do, Vera went ahead and opened a new account, deepcover2. (There already was a deepcover and a deepcover1). She felt she should have boycotted AOL for its shoddy policies and crappy attitude, should have taken her business to another, more enlightened server, but in her current depleted state, lacked the stamina. Nor could she imagine being disconnected, however temporarily, from the Net. At Colin's suggestion—his insistence, really—she'd kept the vdesica account open as well. For a day or two, at least. Just to see what would happen. She was afraid of what might happen—from a hard-drive crash to an apocalyptic virus to, somehow, serious bodily harm—but, weakly, she acquiesced. Colin regarded the situation as an insult, if not to Vera, then to the on-line ethos and the hacker code of honor. Also as an interesting technical problem.

Machines are at their most interesting when they fail, he told her—when they respond to situations or information they're not designed to handle. Like people, she thought, but didn't say. Except a machine can always be rebooted.

What if, Colin speculated, he wrote a virus himself—a targeted virus or Trojan horse—and sent it to vdesica?

"That would be me," Vera said uneasily.

"Not anymore, sorry."

"Let's go get something to eat." She stood up, light-headed and dry-mouthed. "I feel as if, otherwise, I might puke."

There was something to be said for food, she thought, and, later, sex. Flesh on flesh, skin on skin, nothing on earth—or in cyberspace—remotely like it. Lying in Colin's arms, she was grateful, and, for a moment, at peace. Grateful for his body, her own: the frail, sad, lonely, superannuated human body, the outmoded, mortal, bipedal model with its fatal design flaws. There was something to be said for the body, more even for two.

Later, her night was restless and dream-riddled—a head full of worms, a suitcase that wouldn't stay packed—and Colin crept out at 6:00 to make a meeting in Madison by 8:00. She tried to go back to sleep, tried to cocoon under the covers, but buckets of bright May sunshine splashed in around the curtains, creating Rothko effects on her retina and activating the anxiety center of her brain.

Reflexively, she began running a checklist of everything she had to do that day, but it came up empty. The semester was over, she remembered, as was—ah yes—her livelihood. She'd be paid, according to contract, through August 31. There was nothing any board could do about that. But, as of this morning, she realized, she had nothing to do—no exams to mark, no meetings to attend, no students to see. No professional exoskeleton to shelter inside for a while. Nothing to do but job-seek and "network."

Network. There was another thing. A crackle of nervous energy jolted her into action, like Galvani's frog. She'd better get straight out of bed and dial up. Who knew what vdesica had been up to while Vera's brain had been off-line?

Coffee, that morning, was fear in a cup. Nevertheless, she sucked it down. No need to dress or wash because, hey, where was she going? In cyberspace nobody knows you're a dog. Or an unwashed woman in Old Navy pajama pants and a decrepit T.

Deepcover2 already had plenty of spam, offering her, among other things, free shipping, people-finding, and hot-and-heavy girl-on-girl action. The most powerful medium we hominids have yet invented, Vera thought, and what do we use it for? Mainly to shop, to lie, and to jerk off. In that sense, cyberspace scarcely differed from "meatspace."

There was also a message from cdevans@lucid.com, in his usual terse e-mailese: *might want to check this out,* it read, *incase perfidious person is same.* As what? she wondered, frustrated, as always, by Colin's verbal parsimony. There was a link, which, when she clicked on it, touted *Your easy-to-read* Credit Report *in seconds! Starting at $9.95! Now you can view your on-line* Credit Report *before making major purchases and see exactly what information is available to potential lenders and employers! Minimize your risk!! Be Automatically Notified of* Credit *Rating changes!*

Oh fuck, she thought, I should have done this a month ago. It was the first thing you were supposed to do, even Helena knew that. But she hadn't wanted to do it then. And, she thought, I don't want to do it now. It was deeply irrational, she knew, this reluctance to confront the realities of her financial life. To confront the debt, modest as it was, the meager resources, the impulse purchases, the as yet unnamed crimes against immigrant thrift. She wasn't a big spender, but neither had she accumulated anything. Making it to the end of each month had been her main financial goal.

And yet almost anyone who wanted to—landlords, employers, department stores, banks, credit card companies, hell, for all she knew, the mom-and-pop grocers down the block—could take a look, find out everything there was to know, down to the last, embarrassing cent. In fact, she thought, in a bolt of caffeine-fueled paranoia, *I'm probably the only person on the planet who hasn't seen my credit report.* It's like having a rap sheet that, unbeknownst to you, determines your options in life. What you can do, buy, own. Where you can live. How much freedom you have. Who, in other words, you are.

OK, she thought, time to find out. Since she didn't have a clue, she might as well see who Experian, TransUnion, and Equifax thought she was. The Vera defined by what she owed —by what she *didn't* have—suddenly seemed more concrete than the jobless, careerless, childless (and, she thought, amping it up, virtually friendless and penniless) person taking up space on the planet. Fishing out her credit card, for the $9.95, and taking a deep swig from the dregs in her cup, she clicked on the garish green splash. *Yes!* she clicked: *I would like to receive my report (choose one) instantly!*

14

VERA DE SICA, Charlene reflected, was a disappointing-looking woman. She had a round, fat face with, in the unbecoming light of the Department of Motor Vehicles, a distinct double chin. Her nose was flat and broad, one eye curiously slittier than the other. Her eyebrows, Charlene could see, were over-plucked, and her hair, a nondescript puff, over-permed. Somebody should tell her that, at jaw length, her "do" was a "don't," merely accentuating the width of her face. And those frown lines—girl, they added a decade right there. She, Charlene, could teach the DMV a thing or two about lighting. Did your driver's license really have to make you look like one of America's Most Wanted?

She looked so much better in the pinkish glow of the Oriole mirror. I guess that's why they call it makeup, she thought, not for the first time. She'd hoped at least for a decent photo, one worthy of Her Vera-ness, the professor, the New Yorker, the confident, independent woman with the SoHo loft, the penchant for Thai food, the assignations with Roberto in the park. With, Charlene imagined, the full complement of Italian shoes and La Perla lingerie, like she'd seen in *Vogue*. With Simone Foucault, M.D., of the Upper West Side, at her weekly beck and call. And with, of course, top-of-the-line veterinary care for Lulu the cat, not that it had saved her furry ass (nine pounds, shorthaired domestic, kidney failure).

Well, at least she had the diamond, Charlene thought, extending her hand and wriggling her fingers so that the Princess caught the light. And now she had the driver's license. Her face, her address, Vera's name and SSN. It was a start.

She'd come, she realized, to a dawdling halt in the crowded lobby of the DMV, where her fellow Californians, ever polite, diverted themselves around her, as if she were a stalled car on the freeway. Outside of the power-walking, Charlene had rarely seen a mob of Angelenos move so fast, but she, at that moment, had nowhere to go and nothing to do. She'd taken the afternoon off work—"personal time," it was called, which she had wisely invested in upgrading her persona, diversifying it, as you were supposed to do with your portfolio. OK, so every minute she'd spent in line at the DMV had cost her money in commissions: this week they were supposed to push the Microfiber MegaMascara, never mind that it flaked off in a kind of colorless dandruff, really gross. But the few bucks she would have made convincing her quota of Valley Girls to gum up their lashes was nothing compared to the rewards she would soon reap by being Vera de Sica.

With the driver's license, she could open a bank account. With the bank account, she could write lots of checks. Lots and lots of checks. Paperhanging was risky, she knew—cameras everywhere—but if you timed things right and kept on moving on, they would never catch up with you. And the banks made it so easy for you to open an account, almost as if they wanted you to rip them off. You never even needed to show your face. Or anyone's face: you could do it all on-line, ten to fifteen minutes max.

They even asked, on the application form, if you were planning to move soon—which Vera was. To Culver City, California. She just didn't know it yet. And then, perhaps, moving on, moving out. Howie didn't know that yet. But Vera needed her space.

Vera was very particular about things like that. No way would she endure living with such a slob.

Santa Monica, Charlene thought dreamily, or the Marina. A new apartment, still smelling faintly of paint. Fresh air, and a wide-open view.

"Hey, Charlene!" a voice called from across the hall, causing Charlene to start, then unstart, assuming that, as so often before, she'd imagined it: someone calling her name. Sometimes she even heard it in the water pipes, or coming from the TV.

"Hey you," the voice repeated, louder this time. "Charlene Cummins!"

In her hand, Charlene held a small, laminated card affirming, with all the authority of the state, that she was Vera de Sica. So who, then, would be calling "Charlene," yelling out the wrong name at the DMV? A high-voltage shock went through her, like the time her hair dryer had sizzled and died in her hand. Could this be it then, at last? Right here, right now, in front of all these people: *busted*?

She could, at that moment, think of no other explanation. Busted. Unmasked — as she'd always known that, sooner or later, she would be.

But how the fuck, Charlene wondered, could this've happened? As she knew firsthand, the Department of Motor Vehicles didn't give a damn who you really were. They cared only that you had a document verifying — or Vera-fying — your identity. Check its authenticity? Please! Those overworked peons barely had time to pee. They checked merely that no current license or identity card had been issued in California under that name — which it hadn't — and that the National Driver Register of motorists with suspended or revoked licenses didn't cough it up — which it hadn't. A split second in the Gorgon eye of the DMV and your face was digitally, which is to say eternally, affixed to that name.

And the document of Vera-fication? A Certified Birth Certificate from Birthcertificates-R-Us.com, one of many such online services, but the one Howie favored because they didn't nitpick if you accidentally skipped certain lines on the form, and they delivered to P.O. boxes, no questions asked. For $29.99, Charlene had been reborn (in cyberspace) as Vera. So—as far as officialdom was concerned—she *was* Vera de Sica.

"Hey," the voice repeated, and this time—relief mingling with dread—she recognized Cindy, from the Revlon counter, ambling amiably towards her, dog leash in hand.

"Where's the dog?" Charlene asked, idiotically. She felt that if she didn't say something she might collapse, sink weakly to the ground.

"Oh, I had to leave him in the car. No pets."

"You off today?" Charlene stammered. Cindy, as usual, was makeup free, and Charlene, as usual, would've loved to slap a big dollop of concealer on those sun-damaged spots.

"Nope," Cindy said. "On my way. Just had to stop off here for the eye exam." She made an exaggerated squinting gesture, over clenched fists, like a little old lady behind the wheel. "And you?"

"New driver's license," Charlene blurted, before thinking.

"Oh let's see," Cindy said, with the slightly lascivious expression people assume when seeing, or anticipating seeing, an unflattering photo.

"Oh no," Charlene said, mock-coy—horribly aware, as Cindy must be, that she was holding the item in question face-up in her hand.

"Come on," Cindy said, reaching over and tugging it, playfully.

"No, I can't," Charlene replied, grinning goofily, shaking her head. Then, realizing that Cindy, with her big strong physical-therapy hands, would probably tug the license right out of her grasp, she proffered it bashfully, at a distance, keeping her thumb lodged dead center, where the name was. People tended to look at the picture, Charlene had discovered, rarely the name —but her heart was squirming anyway, flopping in her chest.

"Hmm," Cindy said, scrutinizing the image with a professional eye. "I'd say that's definitely a 'before.'"

A "before"? Charlene found herself, despite the situation, obscurely offended. She'd been hoping somehow that this new ID would be the beginning of the "after."

"Surprised they don't offer digital editing services at the DMV," Cindy continued, brightly. "You'd think in LA, of all places—"

"You'd think," Charlene assented, yanking the card away and stuffing it deep into her bag, before Cindy took it upon herself to offer any more professional opinions. "Anyway," she said, gesturing with her free hand towards the parking lot, "have to run, shitload of errands. Say hi to the pooch for me!" And with an actressy wave of the hand, she ran for the door.

In the Brontosaurus, with fifteen minutes still on the meter, she sat in a sea of ticking SUVs and waited for her heart rate to return to normal. That had been close. Very close. Cindy was strange, unreadable: sometimes so cagey, sometimes Charlene's new best friend. Always wanting to poke her (unpowdered) nose into things. But this time, Charlene thought, she'd come through—had stood up for herself, thought on her feet, as Vera would've done. The Prof would be proud.

Pity the picture was so unflattering, that was all. Vera might need more than a makeover, Charlene thought, scrutinizing her face. Botox wouldn't hurt. A little eye-lift. Liposuction, even. God knows, she could afford it. And she deserved it. She deserved, Vera did, everything that money could buy. She owed it to herself to look her best—to make the most of herself, maximize her assets. Which was, in fact, what Charlene habitually told her clients: "Invest in yourself, honey," she would say, slapping Sheer Bronzing Shimmer over their nonexistent cheekbones. "Because you're worth it!"

Backing the Brontosaurus out of the DMV lot, Charlene glanced at the clock on the dashboard, which was wrong, because Howie never bothered to reset it for daylight-saving time, but she could no longer remember whether it was an hour ahead or an hour behind. The bottom had dropped out of her "Cartier" watch and shortly thereafter, the works. Thus all she knew was that it was somewhere between two and four in the afternoon. Plenty of time—but for what? A movie, perhaps? Something with Julia Roberts, with the lips and the hair and, nowadays, the tits?

As she negotiated the stream of Hummers on Sunset, bearing down on the Brontosaurus like those, what were they called, really big motherfuckers from *Jurassic Park,* Charlene couldn't help noticing—today—how almost every corner mall sported a Botox "clinic." Just like a tanning salon or a Taco Bell: plenty of parking, stop on by, girls, and have some poison injected in your face. Hell, she wouldn't be surprised to find a drive-through Botox station, this being LA. There was a price war going on, judging by the Day-Glo banners in each storefront, some promising A NEW YOU in ten minutes, others in nine—for 99 bucks, or 98.99, or 99.99. YOUR LIFE IS WAITING! one banner said. IF YOU'RE BETWEEN THE AGES OF 18 TO 65, AND WANT TO BE THE BEST THAT YOU CAN BE, THEN BOTOX IS FOR YOU!

And didn't she just, Charlene thought, swinging the Chevy, on impulse, across two slow-moving lanes of traffic. Vera wouldn't have frown lines, worry lines, because, let's face it, what did she have to worry about? Her brow would be smooth and serene, the brow of a woman whose glabellar muscles were underemployed. As, Charlene decided, hers would be, even if that did require subjecting herself to small doses of deadly toxin. What doesn't kill me makes me stronger, Howie was always saying. He'd got that from some action flick. Fishing in her purse for one of her new credit cards, Charlene wondered why Vera hadn't done this for herself a long time ago.

15

CLEARLY, VERA THOUGHT, staring at the columns of text, this was a mistake. A huge, horrific mistake. If it wasn't a mistake, the tiny rodent of anxiety already gnawing at her innards would become an infestation, rat-panic swarming through her body. But it had to be a mistake: the credit bureau must have her records mixed up with somebody else's, that was all.

She scrolled back to the top of the screen, trying to concentrate, trying to behave like a rational human being, rather than one whose circuits were swamped with epinephrine. All right, she asked herself, in the voice of her inner schoolmarm, what do we have here? Much of the information—"CONSUMER REPORT FOR: DE SICA, VERA M."—was accurate: Social Security number, birth date, address, phone. Former addresses, accurate (the tenement on Rivington, the studio in Hell's Kitchen, the raw loft space on Canal, all long since gentrified and sold out from under her). *You have been in our files since: 04/87*, the document informed her. The wording chilled her: you have *been* in our files, as if that's where she had existed. As if her other existence, her existence out in the world with other bodies, her own body with all its effluents and excitations and obscure impulses, were the simulacrum and where she'd really been living all along was in their files. *Our* files. Whose?

People she would never know, but whose business it was, apparently, to know her. Data "miners," who amassed information, like wealth, in data banks. Who bought it and sold it, brokered it. Who delivered it *instantly!* for $9.95. A portrait of You the Consumer, rendered in bits: credit or debit, plus or minus, yes or no. But why then, Vera wondered, defaulting to panic mode, did this Consumer de Sica resemble her so little, a data body patched together from unrecognizable parts?

She could find pieces of herself in there—the header information, her Citibank account—but all the rest, everything that came next, under *Your Credit Information*—five pages, no, six, seven—was gobbledygook, gibberish, a spew of misinformation, names and numbers and dates that had nothing to do with her. Cities she had never visited, stores she had never set foot in, accounts she had never opened, purchases she had never made, terrifying sums of money she apparently owed. She wondered, for a second, if she could have suffered some kind of breakdown, entered into a fugue state and embarked on a three-month, multistate spending spree without knowing it. She could almost imagine it, too—the prudent daughter of penny-pinching Neapolitans, dissociating big-time, rampaging across the West with a full load of plastic, randomly disgorging rounds of money she didn't have, the way someone else might empty an Uzi into a shopping mall. But, she reflected, others would probably have noticed if she'd gone Sybil, not to mention the lack of storage space in her apartment for all those goods. And she couldn't have missed that much work without being fired. But, wait, she thought—I *have* been fired.

I'm done for, she thought, I'm screwed, I'm dead meat. I'll never be able to clear up this mess. A wave of exhaustion and despair crashed over her, presentiment of the deluge to come—the hours to be spent wrangling with banks, credit bureaus, department stores, bill collectors, lawyers, police, Social Security,

Visa, MasterCard, American Express, the IRS, the DMV, AT&T, the whole horrible alphabet soup of them. Words she only vaguely understood flickered through her mind: lien, court order, garnishment, repossession, Chapter 13. The debtor's prison, about which she and Helena had joked so often, over so many drinks.

Wait a minute, she wanted to yell, tapping the screen: I'm right here! Here! Not there! Not in your files, wherever they are: that's not me, that cybercreature you've cobbled together from those bits. Mistake, Mr. Big Brother. Big, big mistake on your part.

But denial, Vera knew, was a strategy with a short shelf life, and her current brand of it—Only a Mistake—was expiring before her eyes. No way around it: this wasn't an error, a computer glitch, a garbled file, a bungled tri-merge. This was part of a pattern, a series, which had begun with the diverted Visa card in March—why, in the name of fiscal responsibility, hadn't she checked her credit report then?—and re-upped only yesterday with the stolen password. Somebody was out to get her. To get "her." But who exactly was that "her," and where was she to be found? She, Vera de Sica, was sitting right here, on the island of Manhattan, at her desk, in front of her Mac, wearing the T-shirt she had slept in, which (she sniffed) smelled faintly of her, her body, animal, human. But there was another Vera de Sica out there somewhere—but where: is cyberspace a place?—a Vera de Sica constituted solely by a string of identifiers: name, address, phone number, Social Security number, date of birth, and so on. Until this moment, the identifiers had accurately identified some body: one body. Until this moment, the two Veras—data de Sica and meat de Sica—had coincided. Now, apparently, they did not.

She was replicating, like a virus. But who or what was the host?

And why her? This was the part she couldn't fathom. Who would want her identity, anyway, shabby and threadbare as it was? Surely, if you went shopping for an identity—a used identity, in good condition—you would pick a well-upholstered one, a solid and substantial self? A big fat identity that could show you a good time? Whereas hers, she felt, was meager and anemic, dressed in hand-me-downs and held together with safety pins and Scotch tape. A makeshift identity, a fixer-upper, that had, by default, been doing the job. The job of being Vera de Sica.

Until now.

This couldn't just be random, Vera thought, queasily. This must be someone who knew her and hated her and wanted to harm her. Otherwise it made no sense.

For some reason, again, she thought of Colin. But that was ridiculous. Why would he set out to harm her in this way? And, more to the point, why was it that—feeling her identity usurped, undermined—she immediately thought of him?

At that moment the phone rang, so loudly that she started and, like a gothic heroine, clutched her hand to her heart. So he knew. He knew what she was thinking, could sense, from New Jersey, the paranoid clamor of her thoughts. Otherwise, why would he call at this early hour, normally consecrated to a good rousing bout of alpha-mailing on ClassicCar-nection.com?

So convinced was she that the call was from Colin that it took her a few seconds, a Marcel Marceau double take, to recognize the voice on the line. Simone almost never called her at home, either. What on earth was going on? All the parameters of her life seemed to be collapsing.

"Hi Vera," Simone was saying, brisk and to the point as usual, "hope it's not too early to call, but I did just want to check in with you."

"No, no . . . it's fine. Uh, what's up? Need to reschedule?"

"No, not at all," said Simone. "In fact I'm very much hoping to see you at the usual time this afternoon."

"Um—sure," Vera replied, though she had in fact completely forgotten their 4:00 appointment. But how could Simone have known that? And Vera would have remembered it at some point, anyway—she always did.

"That's good," Simone said, firmly. "Because I was just a little concerned about you."

"About me? But how—?"

"I have to say, Vera, that I feel a little confused about how to respond to your e-mail."

"My e-mail?" Vera frantically searched her memory, coming up blank.

"I'm assuming it's some kind of joke, but even as a joke, it strikes me as a little . . . inappropriate."

"Um, I—"

"And if it's not a joke, then I need to know that too. Perhaps we're being a little passive-aggressive about this?"

Vera found herself at a loss, even for a suitable sound—phatic communication, it was called in the ESL biz, indicating that the channel was still open. Simone almost never used shrink-speak, so Vera knew the situation must be dire. She just couldn't understand why.

"Vera? You still there? I'm just a little concerned, that's all. It seemed out of character, you know, not your usual style? So I just wanted to check that everything's OK, whether perhaps you're having a hard time or something . . . ?"

"Well actually," Vera managed to say, "I *am* having a hard time. I'm having a really hard time." Her voice sounded strange, strangled. Oh no, she thought, I'm going to cry.

Somehow she managed to get through an abbreviated,

though not particularly coherent, account: someone had gone on a major spending spree in her name, oh, and someone had also hijacked her AOL address, which would account for whatever wacko e-mail Simone might have received, she hated to think. She didn't know who was out there or why they were doing this to her. She was fucked, she concluded, she was well and truly screwed, she didn't even know where to begin. And then she cried.

She could hear Simone's evaluative, empathetic silence on the other end, could almost hear her trying to determine whether this represented a psychotic break on Vera's part, with dissociative features and paranoid ideation, or whether Vera had just had some rotten luck. Fortunately, Simone went with the latter interpretation and marshaled her professional skills to talk Vera down.

"Identity theft," she concluded. "It happens a lot these days, from what I hear. It happened to a friend of mine in Colorado, somebody stole her wallet at a restaurant, and it took her months to sort it out. So I would suggest that you get in touch with the police right away. They'll tell you what you need to do."

Even in her distraught, drama-queen condition, Vera couldn't help feeling that it made more sense to report the theft of her identity to a psychiatrist than to a cop. What was she going to say, anyway—Excuse me, officer, my identity's on the lam? My identity's gone AWOL, can you put out an all-points bulletin, armed (with plastic) and dangerous?

"Will do," she said dutifully. "And I'll see you at four."

Was this an emergency, she wondered, should she call 911? Probably not—the dispatcher would dismiss her as a nut, and she didn't really see how it would help to have some emergency vehicle zooming to her door—but she had no idea how else to contact the police. A few anxious minutes with the phone book

—the yellow pages, no, the blue pages, damn, which precinct was she in, anyway?—and she found a number to call, which led to several bumbling, misdirected, and redirected conversations, which in turn led to further calls, which in turn led Vera to a profound and immediate grasp of the nature of a Catch-22 (which, she vaguely and irrelevantly recalled, Heller had originally entitled Catch-18—not quite as catchy).

Desk Sergeant A informed her that it was not really a police matter, that what she needed to do was to file a fraud alert with the three national credit bureaus. OK, she said, thank you very much. Customer service serfs X, Y, and Z at Equifax, Experian, and TransUnion told her, serially, that, no, they needed a police report before they could process a fraud complaint. OK then, she'd get right back to them. Desk Sergeant B (Desk Sergeant A having apparently knocked off for lunch at 10:00 A.M.) reiterated that, no, ma'am, the police could not file a report because, technically speaking, the fraud was against the credit card agencies, not against her. Not to mention the question of jurisdiction. Where had the actual crime, the actual theft, taken place? She didn't know? Well, he was sorry, he couldn't help her then. What she needed to do was file a fraud alert with the three national credit bureaus.

Perhaps, Vera thought, this was what happened when your identity was stolen: you became a bureaucratic paradox, an impossible being, an entity both multiple and absent, shuttling forlornly in a zone of existential invalidation. Or perhaps—a more likely explanation—the dickheads at the NYPD knew nothing and cared less.

Gnawing off a good chunk of fingernail, tasting blood, tasting tears at the back of her throat, Vera decided that what she needed was information. That was why—in addition to shopping, porn, and identity tourism—Man had created the Internet. And why, presumably, Bureaucratic Man had created the Federal Trade Commission. So that the Federal Trade Commission could create a Web site called "When Bad Things Happen to Your Good Name."

Our economy generates an enormous amount of data, it informed her. Her tax dollars at work, stating the obvious. You paid twice for what you bought, she now understood: first with money, and then with information that was worth money. A grand bazaar of information about you was conducted daily, without your knowledge or participation. What had formerly existed only in paranoid fantasy—the notion of constant surveillance—had become simple, quotidian fact. Not only in cyberspace but in New York City: to venture into public these days was to appear on TV (some three thousand surveillance cameras in Manhattan alone, she knew, courtesy of the ACLU). And netheads trained their own Webcams on themselves twenty-four hours a day—because if no one was watching, how would they know they existed?

Vera glanced, involuntarily, over her shoulder, scanned the row of tenement windows across the street (a white cat and a sports trophy looked back), then, with some effort, redirected her attention to "When Bad Things Happen." The good news was that something called the Truth in Lending Act limited her liability for unauthorized charges to $50 per card. (But that's still a lot of $50s, the impecunious part of her brain niggled, unless I can convince them to waive it in each case.) Something else called the Fair Credit Billing Act established procedures—a hellish paper trail of procedures—for resolving billing errors, including fraudulent charges, on credit card accounts. So she wouldn't actually have to repay any of this small fortune that had been spent in her name—a policy that made little sense to her but that she was in no mood to contest. She would, however, have to pay—and pay, and pay—with her time, writing and telephoning and logging and copying and filing and documenting and re-documenting, until doomsday or the collapse of the global consumer economy, whichever came first. And she would soon be cornering the market in certified mail at her local post office, where a single semicomatose worker tended to long queues of the underclass in need of money orders and one stamp.

Take action! the FTC Web site exhorted her. Take immediate action! The site was illustrated, for some reason, with cartoons of little red birds energetically repairing their credit, as if it were a nest. Weakness and willlessness washed over her; the only action she could imagine taking at that moment was sinking, bleating, to the floor. Instead, summoning every last scrap of her working-class work ethic, she scrolled dutifully down.

If you suspect that your personal information has been misused to commit fraud or theft, take action immediately, and keep a detailed record of your conversations and correspondence. You may wish to use the form "Chart Your Course of Action" on page 14. However, three basic actions are appropriate in almost every case.

Your First Three Steps.

First, contact the fraud department of each of the three major credit bureaus. Tell them that you're an identity theft victim.

Please note: Fraud alerts and victim statements are voluntary services provided by the credit bureaus. Creditors do not have to consider them when granting credit. In addition, fraud alerts and victim statements expire. You need to renew them periodically. Ask each bureau about its policy.

Second, close the accounts that you know or believe have been tampered with or opened fraudulently.

Third, file a police report with your local police or the police in the community where the identity theft took place.

It was, Vera could see, going to be a very long day. She put her face in her hands, trying, with the heels of her hands, to give herself a short-term face-lift, stretching the crumpled skin of her brow and applying acupressure to her temples, which were beginning to throb with dull insistence.

Local authorities may tell you that they can't take a report. Stress the importance of a police report: many creditors require one to resolve your dispute. Also remind them that under their voluntary "Police Report Initiative," credit bureaus will automatically block the fraudulent accounts and bad debts from appearing on your credit report, but only if *you can give them a copy of the police report. If you can't get the local police to take a report, try the county police. If that doesn't work, try your state police. If you're told that identity theft is not a crime under your state law, ask to file a Miscellaneous Incident Report instead.*

Guess what happened to me, she imagined telling Colin or Helena: a miscellaneous incident.

The phone rang again, shrilly, and, again, in her compromised condition, Vera felt sure that she had conjured Colin or Helena simply by thinking of them. A man's voice at the other end, hence, surely, Colin. Well, she had a story for him. An incident report.

"Ms. de Sica?" he asked. "How are you this morning? This is Hugo from Carlson Travel. Just wanted to check whether someone will be around to receive your tickets if I messenger them over in an hour or two."

"Tickets?"

"To Bali, first class on Qantas, as you requested. Departing JFK Monday, twenty nights confirmed at the Four Seasons Resort at Jimbaran Bay. Lucky you! Have a fabulous trip!"

16

CHARLENE WAS HAVING a hard time keeping the Brontosaurus in its lane, what with all the little peeks she kept taking at herself in the rearview mirror, a procedure that required her to rise to a semi-squatting position in the driver's seat, not really conducive to highway safety. But great for the quads.

Her brow felt kind of tingly, but she couldn't tell if that was from the ice pack the "doctor" (some Korean woman in a lab coat, doctor my ass) had applied, the four or five tiny pinpricks she had received, or the presence of the *Clostridium botulinum* toxin in her tissues. The doc had authorized her to resume normal activity immediately, though not to "invert": Did Charlene really strike her as the type who would be proceeding forthwith to yoga class? Charlene had assumed that the results would be immediate and dramatic, that she would leave the clinic looking beatific, "youthened" by twenty years. (Not that she'd looked beatific at eighteen, she had to admit: she drank too much, even then, and had been smoking her mother's cigarettes since the age of nine.) But, though her forehead looked a little pinker and a little puffier than usual, the scowl (she checked again) was firmly in place. Perhaps she had been ripped off, big-time, and the Korean had injected sugar water or puppy pee into her face. Or perhaps, as promised, she would notice a "marked improvement" within days. She might also experience nausea, headache, flu-like symptoms, and temporary eyelid droop, the doc had said. Great, Charlene had wanted to respond—I needed to pay you a hundred bucks for that? I could get the same results myself, with a bottle of Jack.

Rising once more in her seat to scan for signs of beatification, Charlene almost sideswiped a black BMW SUV, and, in a defibrillating adrenaline surge, yanked the Brontosaurus, just barely, back into its lane. The driver of the BMW—your basic LA blonde with the stuffed animal on the dash—leaned long and hard on the horn, lip-gloss writhing as she sped past. Charlene gave her the finger. "Fuck you!" she yelled, belatedly. "Fuck you, in your F.U.V.!"

That's it, she thought, that's it, right there. No way am I going to drive this piece of crap anymore, Howie's piece of crap. It may make him feel big and important, but I need something more elegant, more maneuverable. She pictured herself zipping along the Pacific Coast Highway in something sporty, something silver gray—something that would seat two people max, two people, moreover, with well-toned butts. As opposed to the Brontosaurus, which routinely accommodated not only lard-ass Howie and lard-ass Charlene and their assorted debris, but giant boxes of stuff they were returning to Electro City—TVs, satellite dishes, computers, stereos, home entertainment centers —or shipping to eBay bidders (Louis Vuitton luggage, Burberry handbags, Calvin Klein bedclothes, videocams, laptops, and Palm Pilots by the dozen).

Vera wouldn't be seen dead in a 1985 Monte Carlo, Charlene knew. Vera would insist on—well, Charlene could hardly imagine what Vera would insist on in the automotive department, but she had picked up a few pointers from Howie and Ray's chop-shop chatter: heated seats, CD changer, moon roof, turbo-everything, and, oh yes, GPS. The kind that talked you to your destination like a helpful passenger, informing you, in tones of deep regret, when you had missed your turn — then instantly re-calculated your route.

It was too early to go home, anyway; Charlene didn't want Howie to know she'd taken the afternoon off work — or why. She could already hear his slurred contempt: "Botox? Botox ain't going to do it, babe. Try a total face transplant instead." Never mind that he had gone and got hair plugs on the cheap, and they hadn't taken.

She had time to kill, and money to burn. She'd maxed out Vera's new credit cards, collecting cash advances on every un-spent cent and depositing the (not insubstantial) amount in a couple of bank accounts in Vera's name. As of today, our Prof was sitting on a nice little nest egg in Santa Monica — except she didn't know it. So even when the Prof wised up and shut the credit lines down, Dr. Charlene would still have cash to spend and checks to write. And quickly, too: paperhanging was an art, all in the timing, unless you were ready to blow town, which Charlene wasn't, just yet. She realized that she actually liked LA, the strip malls and open skies and valet parking, the year-round sunshine and the Santa Ana winds; she even sort of liked the Revco job, for the structure, something to do. Maybe she'd stay there for a while, go part-time so she could study some-thing — interior decorating, or Color Me Beautiful, something creative anyway. Start over, do it right, but with a little capital this time.

So she, Charlene, was under a lot of pressure to spend money. Right now. Turn cash into assets, before her nest egg went out the window, or fell out of the nest, or whatever it was that happened to nest eggs if you didn't act smart. Or if you al-lowed Howie to get his itchy little fingers on them. Not that he would because, in Charlene's opinion, Vera's banking arrangements were none of Howie's business. He knew, vaguely, that they'd burned through her credit—so, as far as Howie was concerned, Vera was toast. But, Charlene thought, why shouldn't a girl have a little caviar with her toast?

Exiting suddenly and decisively onto Wilshire, Charlene decided to cruise through Beverly Hills and see which of the many luxury car dealerships caught her eye, which she would even have the nerve to drive the Brontosaurus into. Maybe she wouldn't do that: she'd park on a side street somewhere, stroll in instead. But then she'd have to get new shoes. These flip-flops just weren't going to cut it.

Manolo Blahniks weren't really designed for people with broad, bunion-y feet, she soon discovered—no "toe cleavage" for this girl—so she settled for a pair of alligator sandals instead, which looked kind of orthopedic to her but which the saleswoman assured her were French, incomparably comfortable, and extremely chic. Charlene went with fire-engine red, a fashion statement. Thus armed—she also bought a pair of sunglasses that said Armani in no uncertain terms—she sauntered, feigning nonchalance, into the nearest BMW dealer. There was one, it seemed, on every block.

She recognized the look on the salesman's face immediately (and he was a salesman, however much he might see himself, in his own mind, as Richard Gere in *American Gigolo*). It was the same look that crept across Ray's face when some lowlife wandered into the establishment, and Ray, in a single, dismissive scan, appraised the walk-in's net worth. The same look, come to think of it, that she herself gave the teenagers who came in on Saturday afternoons for a free makeover and bought nothing, not so much as a blemish stick. Well, let Mr. Fake Tan look her over with that pained air: she would show him.

"Good afternoon," she said, in her grandest voice. "I'm here to spend some money!"

He flinched slightly, but he was, after all, a salesman. Who depended on commissions to keep himself in Italian suits and those soft black loafers that looked like bedroom slippers. For all he knew, Charlene could be a Lotto millionaire, or Britney Spears's long-lost aunt. Or the trailer-trash first wife of some game show producer. Hollywood was full of people like that.

"Well," he said with a practiced wink, which avoided any unsightly screwing-up of the facial muscles, "we're here to help you do just that, young lady." He took her ever so lightly by the elbow and guided her, in a courtly manner, towards the merchandise, displayed not on some crowded back lot but in sparkling vitrines.

The BMW Z8, she soon gathered, was top of the line: aluminum frame (not that she cared), every technological gizmo imaginable (not that she really cared about that either), heart-stoppingly expensive, and, the clincher, limited edition. But, her new pal Richard Gere confided, for an extra 20K up front, for a preferred client such as herself, he could arrange to have one delivered within the month.

"That settles it," she said, with a shrug. "Let's do it then—let's sign on the dotted line." Arching his immaculate eyebrows, her coconspirator named a terrifying amount—and that was just the down payment. She shrugged again, less convincingly. With what she hoped was insouciance, Charlene produced one of her new checkbooks, scribbled flamboyantly, and peeled off a check —Vera's name, Charlene's street address, and a design of clouds and rainbows, just to add class.

The salesman looked stunned, jubilant, and dubious all at once, inspected the document with an experienced eye, then disappeared for a long time, where, Charlene knew, he was checking and rechecking her bona fides with the bank. Fishing for her sunglasses and turning her back on what she suspected was a two-way mirror, she feigned sudden, compelling interest in the promotional video repeating itself on multiple screens across the room. She didn't want Richard Gere to see the light mustache of sweat that had just broken out on her upper lip.

The money was in the bank, she knew—all those cash advances were, after all, cash—but there was still so much that could go wrong. Mr. Gere might take it upon himself to do a little extracurricular investigation. Or someone at the bank might, for once, have half a brain. But the window of opportunity was so narrow, barely wide enough for Charlene to squeeze her ass through. By tomorrow, for all she knew, Vera might have instituted one of those annoying fraud alerts, which—if every lowly functionary at every financial institution did his job—could put an abrupt end to the shopping spree. So, Charlene thought, blotting her lip discreetly on her sleeve, Carpe Diem (the name of a discontinued sunscreen from Oriole).

As she waited, Charlene studied the "literature" the salesman had given her, paying no attention to the specs but lingering over the high-gloss images. She really liked the way the Z8 looked, zippy and svelte with its pointy nose and small rear—rather, she imagined, as Vera herself might look. She pictured herself in the driver's seat, opulently ensconced. She pictured the top down, the CD player blasting, and her hand tapping impatiently on the steering wheel as she tailgated some lumbering SUV. Howie, she noted, was not in the car.

"We're all set," the salesman announced, emerging at last from his lair. "I do apologize for the delay. And, of course, as soon as your vehicle arrives, one of our Customer Concierges will be in touch to arrange delivery."

Charlene made a gesture of indifference, as if to say, Have your minions talk to my minions.

"A pleasure," he said, proffering his fingertips in limp fare-well. "Now, will the young lady be requiring a limo from here?"

"Mine's just around the corner," Charlene lied.

On the way home to Culver City, tingling with relief—or was it just the Botox?—Charlene tuned in, as usual, to Dr. Laura, feeling, obscurely, that the doc would be proud of her. Like the doc, Charlene had taken charge of her life. Judging by her pub-licity shots, Dr. Laura had had a little "work" done herself, and Charlene knew for a fact that the doctor never left the house in anything but a stretch Caddy. So surely she would applaud the steps Charlene had taken to actualize her potential, would per-haps even encourage her to take more.

"I want you to commit to action right *now*," Dr. Laura was saying to a caller who was bellyaching about how she could never lose weight. "Who's in charge of your life, you or the cup-cake?"

The cupcake, Charlene thought guiltily, or rather, the Ho Ho. This was not, she knew, the answer that Dr. Laura was looking for. Dr. Laura wanted the caller to realize that she was in control of her own destiny, that she could discard her old fat self when-ever she wanted to. "*Healthy* and *successful* people," said the doc-tor, with disdain, "*manage* their identities. Manage *multiple* identities, as conditions change."

Conditions were certainly changing, Charlene thought. The Z8, for instance—where was she going to park it when it ar-rived? On the street, in Culver City, right next to the Filipinos' rust-bucket? Where the pigeons could take a flying crap at it? She didn't think so, thank you very much.

As Charlene pulled the Brontosaurus (soon to be history, soon to be extinct) into the carport, she noted, with relief, that the Lincoln was gone, which meant that Howie was out on some unnamed errand. That meant she'd have the run of the place for a while, could drink her beers in peace, watch *Survivor* or *Who*

Wants to Be a Millionaire if she frigging felt like it. Also check out her horoscope on the Internet—her birthday was coming up, and she had this really good feeling, like the stars were all lining up, finally, on her side. And, while she was about it, she'd take a look at Vera's in box too, see if Roberto had slipped something juicy in there while she'd been out.

Charlene was surprised to see that the AOL account was still active—surprised, and a little disappointed. She'd counted on Vera to take immediate action. Didn't Vera know how stupid it was not to cancel the compromised account, how risky, with all those hackers and viruses and who knew what else out there? Even Howie ran a virus checker, when he remembered, knew how to disable cookies (except on porn sites, which wouldn't let him), and was considering a firewall. One would really expect a Prof to be smarter about such things. Perhaps Vera was busy and distracted; perhaps she had a big deadline coming up for one of her scholarly papers ("Language, Identity, and the 'Self': The Sequel"); perhaps she was out of town. But this really wasn't like her, this lack of attention to detail. She owed it to herself to be more careful.

There was some spam in Vera's box, not much, mostly solicitations to GET OUT OF DEBT NOW: WE'LL SHOW YOU HOW. An invitation to a poetry reading to benefit political prisoners in some country Charlene had never heard of, nor gave a rat's ass about. AMAZING YOUTH REGAINED, yeah right. Nothing from Roberto, oddly. And—oh, Vera—an e-mail from Citi Bank, marked URGENT: IMMEDIATE ATTENTION REQUIRED. No message, when Charlene clicked on it, just an attachment: HERE IS THE CONFIDENTIAL BANKING INFORMATION YOU REQUESTED.

17

IT'S UNBELIEVABLE," Vera said. "It's . . . overwhelming."
She gazed at Simone's Navajo rug, noting that it hadn't been
vacuumed in a while, then gestured with upturned palms,
grasping for words. "It's like . . . falling off a cliff."

Simone nodded thoughtfully from her black leather chair,
across from Vera. She was a small, neatly constructed woman
with a shiny, dark, no-nonsense bob. Her face, in professional
mode, was humorous and composed, but Vera liked to watch
her elbows and knees, which kept up a constant animated com-
mentary, like subtitles. She sipped her iced coffee, looked empathetic, waited for more.

"It's not just, you know, the hassle, the endless phone calls
and red tape and all the letters you have to write . . ." Vera's eyes
stung, unexpectedly, with tears. "It's—"

"The sense of violation?" Simone supplied, experimentally,
after a few seconds.

"Well, yeah, sure, the sense of violation, but not just that."
The sense of violation, Vera thought, is the least of my worries.
"It's not even all the fucking time it takes out of your life—the
guy at Experian told me it costs the average 'victim'—that
would be me—hundreds of hours, literally, and hundreds of
bucks to deal with the mess: get your records straightened out,
cancel everything, get new cards, new IDs, create a paper trail,

follow up, the whole damn thing. And then you can never be sure that they won't use your information again some time in the future. Or resell it."

"They?"

"The thief. Thieves. Whoever."

"So basically it's this sense that you might never feel safe again? In the way you did before?"

Simone was being unusually shrink-y this afternoon, Vera thought, with a prickle of irritation, dropping her gaze to the rug again, tracing a particular orange zigzag that she tended to zone in on, idly, while thinking. Yes, doc, clearly one wouldn't feel too safe when one's identity had been hijacked, one's credit rating ruined, and one's privacy dismantled. Nor would one necessarily take comfort in knowing that one was a mere statistic, one of some 10 million (and growing) whose identity went AWOL every year in the U.S. One could still feel, Vera thought, furious, foolish, and curiously ashamed—like the victim of a con, which was why, she understood, so few cons were ever reported. This line of thought resonated somewhere in the back of her mind, evoked an elusive unease, which she didn't pause to examine. She looked back up at Simone.

"It's more like . . . ," Vera said, "the whole house of cards has come toppling down. The job thing, then this. It's almost as if I've been expecting it my whole life." Almost, she thought, but didn't say, as if someone had finally been proved right—her parents, Ernesto, the nuns at Sacred Heart, her teachers at UMass, hell, even the Puerto Ricans on the subway who asked her point-blank what she was, meaning what ethnicity. Everyone, Vera thought, who'd ingrained in her the idea that the daughter of immigrants, scion of De Sica Cleaners & Expert Alterations, could impersonate a middle-class person for only so long. Could, in other words, seek to invent a life—and a self to go with it—for only so long. Before the jig was up, her cover was blown, the entire flimsy edifice of identity collapsed.

Could you steal something, Vera wondered, that—in her case—didn't really exist? An impostor posing as an impostor: it made no sense, it made her head swim.

"Not to mention," she added, electing to steer the discussion from the cliff-edge of existential vertigo, "this constant pounding headache I've developed."

"Well," said Simone, with a grave nod and an almost imperceptible glance at the clock, "we'll want to spend more time on all of this next week."

Sleepwalking out of Simone's office, Vera realized, after a few blocks, that she had somnambulated right past her subway stop. Since it was a mild, incipiently sultry June day, and since she had—ha!—nowhere in particular to go, she decided to keep walking down Broadway to the next stop, Seventy-ninth Street, dodging the phalanx of baby strollers on the sidewalk—dark-skinned nannies with light-skinned babies, or Caucasian mothers with Chinese babies, but seldom a matched set.

Her mind was roiling, partly with rage and anxiety, but also with a more troubling emotion, a kind of appalled, titillated valence towards, well, Vera, this other Vera, this brazen, reckless spender, this go-for-broke patron of high-end department stores and state-of-the-art electronics, this overreacher who, compared to her dull and humble self—Vera the first, the dusty and outdated floor model—evidently lived an audacious, complicated, and well-appointed life. With, one could only assume, schadenfreude as the drug of choice. Vera imagined this Vera dripping with diamonds, driving a flashy car, flaunting the latest in crippling footwear, and pecking away at her Palm Pilot with manicured precision. She probably owned a couple of furs, too, the unethical bitch—all on Vera's dime.

She wanted to kill her. No, she wanted to *be* her. No, she wanted, somehow, both.

More grist, Vera thought, for the mill of Simone. It was more than she—one person, or was she now two?—could wrap her mind around.

Absently swiping her Metrocard at the Seventy-ninth Street entrance, Vera was stopped short by a painful bump to the hipbone. The turnstile, instead of turning, barred her entrance and upbraided her with a stern INSUFFICIENT FARE. At that moment, the last frail joist of Vera's composure gave way. This, she felt, was more than she could bear. She wanted to collapse right there on the grimy, spitty floor, wail and beat her fists on the ground. Even her Metrocard was null and void, even the Metropolitan Transportation Authority had invalidated her existence. As she fumbled for cash to refill the card, she realized that she was sobbing, vigorously though without sound. The pinstriped man next to her at the Metrocard machine registered this briefly, then resumed the required urban mask of disregard. Just another crazy lady at the subway station.

When, later, she recounted this incident on the phone to Helena, it was as the punch line of life's latest little joke against her, the Case of the Missing Identity. Helena was suitably aghast, though distracted—Vera deduced from the clattering and slooshing sounds on her end—by something she was cooking.

"It's a good thing I'm effectively unemployed," Vera said, "because, from what I hear, dealing with this is going to be a full-time job. I went to this Web site that tells you what to do when your identity's been stolen, and the first thing it says is 'Get Comfortable.'"

"Get Comfortable?" Helena asked. "Oops, shit, I dropped the tofu."

"Get Comfortable, because you're going to be sitting in that chair, making phone calls and writing letters, for a long, long time."

"It's unbelievable," Helena said. "You're the third person I know that this has happened to. Hey, it's *The Net!*"

"The net?"

"Yeah, you're Sandra Bullock in *The Net!*"

"Never saw it."

"Same thing happens to her, her ID is stolen, all her passwords are changed, she becomes a non-person, because . . . I forget why, some bad guys want information or something."

"Well, I don't know what these bad guys want," Vera said, "but I'm assuming it's money. Credit. Though why the fuck they didn't go after someone who actually *has* some money beats me."

"Doesn't matter, apparently, as long as your credit is good. Then they burn through that and go on to the next person."

"Yes, but this can seriously ruin your life. I mean, for ever. The Fraud Unit rep at Experian was telling me these horror stories about what can happen—how these guys can lease cell phones and cars and God knows what else in your name, and then *you* keep getting dunned for the bills. Or they get arrested for some crime, drunk driving or whatever, and they're carrying your ID. So the next time you get pulled over for so much as a broken taillight, it's off to the pokey with you. Or let's say—"

"Hey, enough, enough with the worst-case scenarios. Think positive, think damage control."

"Damage control? An asteroid hits your life, you're not thinking damage control. You're thinking, am I ever going to get out of this crater alive?"

"Honey, it's not an asteroid," Helena said, chopping something. "It's just a pain in the ass."

Easy for you to say, Vera thought, a concept she expressed

with a snort. But she realized that, if the same thing had happened to Helena, Helena would have just dealt; hell, she'd have paid someone to deal with it for her, so as not to interrupt her work.

"Just do what you have to do to make it go away," Helena continued, and Vera could almost hear the shrug. "Problemsolve. You're Sandra Bullock, remember? You've got to stay perky and spunky for the whole movie."

"I hate perky and spunky," Vera said, trying to be perky and spunky.

"Mmm, well, let's have a late lunch tomorrow at Second Nature, OK? My noodles are boiling over. And I'm leaving for Seattle again next week."

Vera hated Second Nature, too, but, since it was organic and vegan, Helena never felt guilty about anything she ate there. So it was worth the occasional gummy veggie burger to get her friend's undivided attention.

Both Helena and Colin had been underwhelmed by her news, Vera thought petulantly, deeming her situation worrisome but manageable—a massive inconvenience, a bureaucratic nightmare, a cautionary tale, sure, but hardly the existential black hole Vera was making it out to be. Colin had even taken to humming "There'll never be another you" under his breath when the subject came up. So perhaps it wasn't an existential black hole after all. Perhaps she was simply failing to be sufficiently postmodern, was still clinging to some antiquated notion of the self when she should instead be celebrating the mutability and multiplicity of identity in cyberspace, and so on.

The current academic line, she knew, was that the body—the carbon-based support system for consciousness—was obsolete, that users of the Internet "perform" their bodies as texts, and that this was, somehow, a good thing. She'd like to see how

Guillermo Mendoza ("and Lacan") would react if someone performed *his* body as a text.

Besides, she wasn't an academic. She wasn't even a teacher anymore. She was an unemployed person with a missing identity and a massive headache.

And, she wondered, whose head was it, anyway?

When Colin showed up later that evening—bursting hyperkinetically through the door, not even pausing, as usual, to unlace his boots—Vera was lying on the sofa with the lights out, practicing autohypnosis to make her headache go away, and longing for Lulu, for the cat's warm purring weight on her heart.

"Guess what," he said. "I've solved the problem."

"What problem?" she asked. The soundtrack that began running through her mind, as it so often did in Colin's presence, was Percy Sledge, "Try a Little Tenderness." On really bad days, she heard Elvis—"I'm so lonesome I could cry," which she persistently misremembered as "die." At Brooklyn Multi it was the Animals ("We Gotta Get Out of This Place"). And, leaving Simone's office, the whole Grand Ole Opry.

"Come on," he said, exuberantly. "I'll take you out for a drink and explain it." He was, she could see, on a performance high, feeling his oats the way he did when he'd written some kick-ass code, or rejiggered some widget for his Riley, or flamed some know-nothing on ClassicCar-nection. And why not? she thought. He's young, he's super-smart, and this ebullient single-mindedness is what drew me to him in the first place. Isn't it?

"Baby," she said, wheedling, "I have the worst headache. Couldn't I just lie here and feel sorry for myself instead? Couldn't you just minister to me with hot compresses or cold compresses or whatever kind of compresses would make my identity come back? And my credit rating too?" She'd aimed for a self-mocking tone but feared she might actually have come across as a whiner.

"No, really, Vera, I've solved the problem. Come on, let me take you to St. Dymphna's and we can sit out in the courtyard and I'll explain it to you. It's pretty neat." His long arms wind-milled as he talked, and he poked her playfully in the ribs. "C'mon!" Translation, Vera thought: Colin was in the mood for a Guinness and for exercising his bragging rights.

Perhaps a good bracing shot of alcohol was just what she needed, she thought, half an hour later, ordering a gin and tonic from the busty Irish hip-hopper who tended bar at Dymphna's.

"G and T?" asked Colin, waiting patiently for the head of his Guinness to settle, or whatever it was that the head of a Guinness had to do. "That's not like you."

"I'm not feeling quite myself, somehow."

They found themselves a table in the corner of the courtyard, whose décor consisted of assorted beer cans and an orange plastic net overhead for those occasions when St. Dymphna's out-raged neighbors began hurling household objects at her late-night acolytes.

"OK," he said, "so here's the story."

She sipped her G and T. It felt tart and tingly on her tongue, the best thing that had happened to her all day. This is how peo-ple become alcoholics, she thought.

"I got in there." Vera recognized not only Colin's tone — high-testosterone — but also the extent to which it was tamped down to the requisite degree of hacker cool.

"In where?"

"He fell for it. He clicked on the attachment."

"Honey chile," she said, channeling Nina Simone, "I have no idea what you are talking about."

"I told you — the Trojan. Well, because I didn't have so much time, a back door. So I can go in later and do whatever I want."

Gradually, Vera persuaded Colin to translate. He had, she gathered, written a kind of targeted virus—a Trojan horse—and sent it to Vera. More precisely, to Vera's AOL account.

"The vdesica account?" Vera felt an irrational twinge of panic, as if she herself had been targeted, since she was, wasn't she—hadn't she been—vdesica? Even though vdesica was, she knew, simply a string of characters, an "access device" to an e-mail account, not a person, not a body—not her. But perhaps her body wasn't "her" anymore: perhaps nobody's body was. Perhaps whoever had taken over the account had *become*, in some sense, vdesica—the virtual entity, the identity constituted by that access? It was all too bewildering, too dizzying, especially in conjunction with gin.

Yes, Colin said impatiently, that account—the hijacked one. But here was the point: the trick was always to get the target to open the attachment. And Colin had pulled it off, he'd succeeded: the crook had clicked, the "back door" had been installed.

"So what exactly does this mean?" Vera asked. "Not to be dense or anything, but . . . I don't get it."

"It means," Colin said, "I can get back into that machine any time I want, install whatever spyware or snoopware I want, keep track of this guy."

"You mean, like, find out where he lives? Who he actually is?"

"Well, not necessarily. I can find out the IP address of the computer when it's connected, which might tell me which part of the country he's in. But the IP address is just a number, so obviously it's not going to deliver up his name and street address plus a map of how to get to his house."

"Then what's the point?"

"Because, Vera, there are all kinds of ways of finding out who somebody is. Think about it: I can set it up so that it sends me information every time the machine's on-line—mail logs, history folder, usernames or passwords, whatever. Go in, take a look around. Or do some keystroke sniffing, see every character he types." Colin, Vera could tell, was highly adrenalized by the situation, by this extremely interesting technical problem. By the challenge to his ingenuity, the possibility of diabolical solutions. She realized she'd rarely seen him so alive, that most of the time he spent with her he was, relatively speaking, in power-saving mode.

"But what happens when I shut down the AOL account? Because I'm not leaving it open indefinitely, that's for sure. That vdesica has got to go. She's sending wacko e-mails to half the people I know." Even as she said this, a bolt of panic surged through her, a strong urge to run home and log on. The e-mails, she thought, were even more insidious than the other forms of theft, eating away at her already tenuous connections with other people. Roberto, for instance, had just express-mailed her a copy of the University's fifty-page *Policy on Sexual Harassment,* without so much as a note. She cringed, she burned to think of it.

Colin struggled to compose his expression into one of benign rather than incredulous condescension. "It has nothing to do with AOL, Vera. Even when the mail account dies, the back door will still be there. I just need to know the IP address and then I can get back in, if it's switched on and connected to the Internet."

"But won't he be able to tell . . . ?"

"Nope. At most he might notice that some days the computer's a little slow. Which he probably is too, so he won't give it another thought."

"But Colin . . . isn't this . . . illegal?"

This time, he didn't even try to mask his incredulity. "Vera, excuse me, who are we talking about here? Some crook, correct? Does he worry about what's legal when he steals your identity to make a quick buck?"

"I know but . . ." She shook her head rapidly, like a cat centrifuging water off its fur. "I don't know. I don't know what I think. I think I need another gin and tonic, that's what I think."

By the time she got back to the table with her second G and T, and, as an afterthought, another Guinness for Colin, he was smoothing out a wad of crumpled pages, still curved and compacted from his back pocket.

"Thanks," he said, craning his head to sip from the full pint, then pushing the wad across the table at her. "Check these out, I printed them for you. So you can see what's out there. Commercially."

"OK," she said, taking them absently, "but you know what I'm wondering, I'm wondering why we're always assuming this guy is a 'he.' Surely it would have to be a woman, to pretend to be me?"

"Not if he does everything on-line," Colin said impatiently. "There's no gender in cyberspace. Go on, take a look."

She rifled through the printouts with an initial queasiness—gin or existential vertigo, one of the two—which, after a few pages, developed into full-blown psychic seasickness, a sense of the world shifting treacherously around her.

"You've got to be kidding, Colin," she said, weakly. "I mean . . ."

"Nifty, huh? And they're not that hard to write, if you know what you're doing."

"But this?" She read aloud:

"*SpyBuddy is the ultimate solution for monitoring spouses, children, coworkers, or anyone else! SpyBuddy allows you to monitor all areas of your PC, tracking every action down to the last key-*

stroke pressed! SpyBuddy has the ability to log all chat conversations, all Web sites visited, all windows opened and interacted with, every application executed, every document printed, all text and images sent to the clipboard, and even every keystroke, including system keys! All this for only $49.99!! With SpyBuddy you no longer have to wonder who's doing what on your computer when you're not around! SpyBuddy is ideal for home, education institutions, or work!

"Education institutions or *work*?" she repeated. "So how do I know that there isn't already something like this on my computer at the Multitech?"

"You don't. Except they probably can't afford it."

She rummaged in her memory to see if, over the years, she'd ever keystroked anything compromising on the bulky, sticky antique that the college provided in the adjuncts' office. Did looking for another job count? she wondered. Did those heat-of-the-moment salvos calling the board a cabal of geriatric cocksuckers count? If she hadn't already been fired, she might be worried. E-mails never die, that she knew—hitting "Delete" simply inters them in a virtual graveyard, a parking place for potential revenants.

"But this is the one," Colin said, jiggling his knee. "This is the one I really want you to see—"

"MyLittleEye is the FIRST remote-install software product offered anywhere! You will simply not find this software anywhere else! MyLittleEye offers you the ability to remotely install the spy software from any location and view the logs from anywhere in the world! Chats, conversations in REAL TIME, keystrokes, passwords, e-mail. Remotely view the desktop and MORE!"

"It costs $79.99," Colin said, reaching across the table and tapping on the logo, which bore some resemblance to the irradiated eyeball on a dollar bill. "But if it does what it says it does, it could save us huge amounts of time. Viewing the desktop remotely—that's pretty neat, as if you were looking over the person's shoulder all day. We could see anything we wanted to, catch him in the act. Worth a try, wouldn't you say?"

"Shit, Colin," Vera said, "I don't know. I don't know anything anymore. Let me think about it, OK?" She gazed helplessly around her, at the orange netting, at the bar's neon sign. St. Dymphna, she suddenly recalled, was the patron saint of the insane.

18

Howie, charlene could tell from the back of his head, was in a foul mood. There was a certain scrunching of his shoulders that she'd learned to recognize, a certain, almost simian retraction of the neck. The Gateway screen had gone dark, with the hard drive whirling mournfully, which suggested that he'd been rifling through the desk drawer in that furious and exaggerated manner for some fifteen minutes. Next to the mousepad, in imminent danger of being upset, was a tumbler half full of Jack Daniel's, straight up. Not a good sign, Charlene knew, especially—she checked her new Swatch—at this early hour.

It was just after 6:00, which meant that a good—i.e., bad—five hours of drinking lay ahead. And her feet hurt like hell, after a particularly excremental Tuesday at the Revco. She considered turning around, getting back in the Brontosaurus, and driving to the mall, but Howie had already heard her come in, had turned his head with an exasperated "Hey!"

Really, Charlene thought, she was just not in the mood to deal with Howie's crap tonight. She'd had a long and unrewarding afternoon with a group of giggling Japanese housewives—didn't they get that Oriole just didn't cater to their skin tones?—traffic had been backed up for miles on the 405 because some Fiat had decided to go up in flames, and her newest shoes—

a pair of high, beaded mules that had looked much better in the store—were rubbing her raw. Now Howie and his little tantrum.

"What's up?" she asked. Though, from the way he was tossing stuff out of the drawer—birth certificates, drivers' licenses, gift certificates, boxes of checks—she could take a wild guess. Howie was looking for something and he couldn't find it, and it was somehow her fault. He had what his Special Ed teacher in the fifth grade had diagnosed as a "low threshold" for frustration.

"Where's Marc Gibson?" he asked. "What the fuck happened to Marc Gibson?"

"How would I know, Howie?" That was his department, not hers, the constant stream of new marks, mostly from *Who's Who*. Some also from the rental car scam. And the occasional night of dumpster-diving outside the offices of large corporations, though Howie usually didn't care to exert himself that much.

"I can't find Marc, what's-his-face, Gibson, for Chrissake."

"Well, I don't have him. Which state?"

"Fucked if I remember. Maryland, maybe?" He shuffled a small stack of drivers' licenses like a hand of cards. "Franz, Kriseova, Massard, White—I'm still not seeing Gibson."

Most of the licenses had Howie's face on them—the averted gaze, the puffy eyelids, the oddly full and slack lower lip—but some still bore the original images, strangers looking startled to find themselves in such company, a multiplicity of Howies.

"What do you need Gibson for anyway?" Charlene asked, picking up some of the birth certificates Howie had so wantonly scattered on the rug—hey, they'd paid good money for them—but otherwise trying to stay out of his way, arm's length at least. "Use someone else."

"I got a little problem with his Visa card. The machine ate it."

"Machine?"

"At the track today. When I went to get a cash advance."

"I thought Gibson was all used up," said Charlene, trying to remember. "Didn't we cash him out couple of months ago? Wasn't that Gibson, the one with the beard?"

"Maybe, but I still had his Visa in my wallet. Thought I'd give it one more go."

That's Howie for you, Charlene thought, in a nutshell: he uses up Gibson months ago, knows not to try Gibson again because it'll set off alarm bells all over town, loses big on the horses one afternoon, and does it anyway.

"Fuck, Howie." She didn't need to spell out the implications: the bank machine seizes the card because there's a fraud alert on it, the videocam seizes Howie's image.

"Fuck *you*, Charlene. Anyone can make a mistake."

"Make a mistake? Push your luck, you mean."

He swiveled around in the desk chair, gestured menacingly, and none too elegantly, with his tumbler of Jack. Some slopped out onto the shag rug, which fortunately was much the same shade already.

"Hey, I'm a gambler at heart. Win some, lose some, what can you do?"

What can you do? Charlene thought. Act smart, for once.

"But you know what really sucks?" Howie asked, taking a long, deep, contemplative swig, head back, almost upending the glass into his mouth.

You do, Charlene thought. When Howie was on a roll like this, her side of the conversation had to take place mostly in her own head. It was safer there, freer. Anything she said out loud —or, for that matter, expressed on her face—could become grounds for corporal punishment. The main thing was to shut up and stay out of reach.

"What does?" she asked, demurely.

"I got a ticket too. Same fuckin' afternoon, just wasn't my day."

"Parking ticket?"

"In the lot at Santa Ana. Handicapped space. I mean, what's up with that, do you see a whole bunch of guys in wheelchairs going to the races every day? Me neither."

This time Howie didn't need to spell out the implications. The Lincoln was registered in his own name, Howard J. Hoffner —probably the only thing they possessed that was. It had been his first major acquisition, the one thing he had really wanted from day one, this wedding-cake pimpmobile with the red interior. The Chevy, by comparison, was your basic chop-shop job, registered under the name of Max Fisch or Frisch, something like that, and Howie didn't care if Charlene drove it into the ground, if it got booted and towed and turned into a Campbell's soup can. But the Lincoln was his.

Howard J. Hoffner's car ticketed in the parking lot. Howard J. Hoffner's face captured and date-stamped on the security cam. Could be dangerous, if anyone was paying attention. If anyone was trying to put one and one together to make one.

"Fuck, Howie," she said again, her dismay slipping past the border police of her vigilance.

"Stop telling me fuck, Charlene, I'm telling you, stop." He half rose from the chair, thought better of it, slumped back unsteadily. Took advantage of this moment of relative equilibrium to drain his glass.

"But fuck," she repeated, despite herself. "You know what that means. Why don't you just go hand-deliver your name and address to the LAPD? And mine too, while you're at it?"

"The LAPD?" Howie asked, with grandiose scorn. "You really think anyone at the LAPD is pulling overtime going through

ATM tapes and parking tickets? Give me a break, Charlene—those guys don't want to know. The banks write off the losses, the cops get on with the important stuff. Taking graft, beating on wetbacks, and such."

He had a point, she knew. "Enterprises" such as Howie's were almost never investigated. You had to be the Russian Mafia, manufacturing Visa cards en masse, before anyone took you seriously.

"And meanwhile I make a living," Howie continued, with an expansive gesture, "so everyone's happy." He tried to take another sip, sucked only air.

"Except me," Charlene muttered. "Don't know why I don't just get my ass out of here, go while the going's good."

"Get your ass out of here?" he sneered, his voice rising to a taunting monotone. "Not sure it would fit through the door, babe. Anyway I know you'd never have the guts. Gutless Charlene." He raised his tumbler in a mock-salute. "Where would she go, anyway?" He peered in mock-puzzlement into the empty glass.

"Gimme that," Charlene said. "I'll get you a refill." Howie was less of a hazard if he stayed in one place, didn't try to move around too much. And she'd probably gone too far this time, threatening to leave—that was, after all, his prerogative. The key, she understood, was not to threaten, just to leave. But would she, in fact, ever have the nerve? She closed her eyes, tried to imagine, came up blank.

When she returned with his glass—having prudently pre-filled it with ice, though she knew he'd object—Howie had sunk into a kind of glazed trance, which she recognized as his heroic struggle with ratiocination.

"Know what?" he asked, sucking deeply on his fresh drink, then adding, almost spluttering, "Shit, Charlene, you know, no ice!" She retreated to a judicious distance, and, in the absence of any other seating, eased herself onto a giant Panasonic box, hoping the merchandise would withstand her weight.

"Know what?" he repeated. "Know what I'm thinking? It was getting time to leave anyway."

"Leave?"

"California. This state." He gestured vaguely, and loopily, towards the walls. "Fuckin' La-La Land. Fruitcake Central. Time to move on."

"Move on where?" Charlene asked, carefully. She'd been anticipating this, just not so soon.

"Wherever. Midwest, Northeast. Someplace we haven't been yet. There are fifty-one fuckin' states in the US of A, Charlene!"

"Fifty," she responded automatically, the good student of geography.

He lurched to his feet and she saw that she had blown it. Howie didn't like to be corrected, and he could still stand up. His face was livid and blotchy, his torso angled with intent. It was too late, Charlene knew, to head for the door. There was no one to call. And the Filipinos upstairs had developed this really bad habit of turning deaf after 6:00 P.M.

"Howie, no," she said quietly.

"*Howie, no*," he mimicked, in a mean falsetto. "Howie, yes," he repeated, shoving her hard. She lost her balance, toppled off the carton. The corner gave her a good, sharp poke on the way down, and she hoped, weirdly, that she hadn't damaged the goods. The shag carpet was scratchy against her face, and smelled of dog, though they didn't have one. On instinct, she covered her head with her hands.

"Fifty *states, Howie*," he continued, in that same fake voice, going for her ribs. She willed herself to go numb, play dead, the way she'd learned around Ma as a kid. Luckily Howie wasn't wearing shoes, and his aim was impaired. He managed to land a few kicks in the kidney region. Her right shoulder got one, then he stumbled, grabbed at her hair. She could smell him now, the same oniony tang as when he'd pulled a job. He lost his footing again, yanked out some hair. The air felt strange on that part of her scalp, scalding and cold. He kicked at her knuckles till her clasped hands came apart. She squirmed deeper into the rug, dog smell and dust. She just prayed he'd fall over before he went for her face.

19

COLLECTING HER MAIL had become a daily ordeal, the mailbox itself a portal into a parallel universe where, without ever leaving Manhattan, Vera de Sica was on the lam. A trail of dunning letters marked her trajectory across a Southern California landscape—Vera pictured it bruise-colored and neon-lit—of strip malls, Electro Citys, car dealerships, racetracks, and, what was this now? Botox clinics. While she, Vera—meat Vera, flesh-and-blood Vera—was growing more haggard by the day. She'd taken to doing her Dorothy Parker impression en route to the mailbox, muttering aloud, in a toneless drawl, "*What fresh hell is this?*" After all, she reasoned, this was New York, where people were permitted to be crazy, and most of her neighbors were crazy—or geriatric—themselves. "*What fresh hell is this?*" she asked the ancient Ukrainian lady from 5G, who smiled vaguely and relocked her box with a trembling hand, departing with a CVS circular and a dollar-off coupon for Domino's pizza.

Nobody used the U.S. mail anymore, Vera thought—noting, from the lack of echo as she inserted the key, that her box was stuffed again—except financial institutions, department stores, and purveyors of consumer goods who had been massively defrauded. Then their computers generated a small landfill's worth of correspondence, all of which had to be promptly acknowledged and responded to, with another landfill's worth of forms and affidavits, duly duplicated, notarized, and dispatched via certified mail. Which, in turn, generated another avalanche of paper. And so on, apparently, until not a tree remained.

This will never end, Vera thought, glumly, unwedging the wad from the overstuffed box and picturing herself running screaming into the street, wild-eyed, like a character in a Koren cartoon. She wondered, again, how someone she'd never met, who lived, for all she knew, in Novosibirsk or Tierra del Fuego, could cause such disruption—could in fact teach her, as no philosophy professor had managed to do, precisely what her existence consisted of: not Being, not Nothingness (as she had, in middle age, begun to fear), but a massive database.

Shuffling through the stack as she began her dispirited trudge back to the third floor, she spotted an envelope that wasn't regulation business size, that didn't sport a return address from Maryland or Delaware or Nebraska—places, she could only assume, that offered low overheads and lower wages to the financial services industry. This one was large and square, buttercup yellow, with Vera's name and address printed in shaky capitals, like the script of an elderly person. Not her mother's old-fashioned hand. No return address. A "Love" stamp, Vera's second least favorite, after the flag.

Somewhere between the first and second floors, curious, she ripped the envelope open. Then, in her confusion, dropped all the others. She had a sudden strong urge to sit down, which she did, right there on the stairs, avoiding, with a New Yorker's semiconscious radar, a clot of compacted chewing gum. Her heart, she discovered, was racing, a strange icy tingling mounting to her head.

Inside the envelope was a brightly colored Hallmark card, a staged photograph showing a Shar-Pei seated at a table, fork in paw, wearing a pointed paper hat and gazing lugubriously at a wedge of cake. Within, the caption read: *A few more wrinkles? Who cares?! You'll always be Top Dog to me! Have a paw-fectly Happy Birthday!*

"To Vera," it said. Signed, simply, "Yours, Vera."

She checked the date on her watch, noting, as she did so, how her hand was shaking. It was, yes, June 9, the day before her birthday—which she had completely forgotten, as, apparently, had Colin (who didn't believe in such conventional observances anyway). Normally, she'd expect a call from her parents in the morning, 10:00 A.M. sharp, but they'd gone on a cruise with their bingo group. Her brother, who'd been strangely silent of late, might also call, if his wife reminded him. Helena—well, Helena could barely keep track of lunch dates and hair appointments, let alone the circuit of the earth around the sun. And anyway she was in Seattle, installing her "Body (Re)Membered."

But "Vera" had paid attention.

Whoever or wherever she was, Vera was keeping track. Of her. But why? And how? The yellow envelope was postmarked LAX, Los Angeles International Airport—which could mean anything, or nothing. Someone who was traveling. Who was en route. Though she knew the stairwell was deserted, Vera felt a sudden crawling sensation on the back of her neck, a sensation so powerful that she had to turn around, abruptly, to check.

"Hey, can I come out to your place this evening?" she asked Colin, when, after several tries, she reached him by phone at Lucid. Her voice, she could hear, was high and unsteady, someone else's voice.

"Um, sure," he said, keyboard clacking. "Sure, why not." He sounded taken aback, unsurprisingly, given that Vera usually balked at the idea of displacing herself to New Jersey, ostensibly because there was nothing to do there (except have sex, which they could do more comfortably in her bed than on Colin's funky-smelling futon) but really because, Manhattanite that she was, the idea of boarding a train to Jersey was, well, mortifying. At that moment, though, she craved to be where no one could find her, where no one would even think of looking—at the picnic table in Colin's overgrown back yard, under the enormous elm, surveying, over an alcoholic beverage, the drivewayscape of dismembered Rileys.

"Why not?" she repeated, trying to sound playful, light. "Hey, it's summer, I'm sick of the city. Sometimes a girl just needs to get away." And then, without intending to, she added: "I just don't feel safe here."

"Hmmmnnn," Colin said, incurious as ever. "OK, then. How about the . . ."—rapid clacking sounds—"four-twelve train?"

When, at last, she was installed, sipping her G and T and batting away blood-sucking New Jersey mosquitoes in the toxic dusk, she told Colin about the birthday card. She was afraid that he might laugh; she also found herself hoping, in some deep, shameful place, that he'd confess he hadn't forgotten her birthday after all and produce some wonderful surprise. He did neither. He stopped what he was doing—rubbing some small greasy metal object with a rag full of solvent—and took a sip of his Pale Ale.

"Hmmmnnn," he said, "that's cheeky. Very cheeky." His interest, she could see, was piqued; he even laid the gizmo aside.

"Cheeky?" she said. "Scary. Fucking sicko, if you ask me. I called the cops again, told them about it, told them I had it in a Ziploc bag, so they could do forensic tests on it."

"On a birthday card?" Colin's habitual expression, when processing information from other humans—"wetware"—resembled a smirk (eyebrows raised, lips quizzically pursed), so Vera couldn't tell in this instance whether he was actually smirking or not.

"Why not? I was thinking, you know, saliva, DNA, finger-prints, postmark, handwriting analysis . . ." Her voice trailed off; she felt stupid, naive. "That's what they do on TV, anyway."

"Did they laugh?" he asked, not unkindly.

"Basically, yes," she admitted. "They think I'm a nut."

He made a face, as if to telegraph, broadly, "Not without cause."

"Each time I have to deal with a different person down at the precinct house," she continued indignantly, "tell them my tale of woe from the beginning, while they keep putting me on hold for people who have 'real' problems. They say they'll get back to me, but they never do. And I'm still waiting for a case number, let alone a copy of the Incident Report. Which I'll probably never get."

"Did you bring it?" Colin asked.

"Bring what?"

"The card? In its Ziploc baggie?"

"Of course. But I don't want you getting your greasy finger-prints all over it."

She showed it to him, handling it gingerly at the edges, Ex-hibit A.

"Cheeky," he repeated, shaking his head, not entirely in disap-probation. "Doesn't really tell us much, except that he's cheeky."

"She," Vera said.

"He, more likely. Statistically speaking. Most crimes are com-mitted by men, especially on the Internet."

"She," she insisted.

"How can you be so sure?"

"The card. The choice of card. I can't really explain it but I know."

"I doubt it," he said, "but never mind."

Had he always been so arrogant, Vera wondered, studying his young, chiseled face, so mobile, so intelligent, and so doubt-free. And if so, why had it never bothered her this much before?

"Well, I'd say this definitely gives us carte blanche," Colin said, concluding aloud some private line of thought. "No pun intended," he added, with a sudden grin. Lit up like that, Vera thought, he looked boyish, disarming, not arrogant at all. He looked, in fact, adorable. Therein lay the problem.

"Carte blanche?"

"To respond. In kind."

"In kind? As in, send a birthday card back?" Vera asked, deliberately obtuse. She could tell, from Colin's newfound animation, where this was heading.

"As in, install the remote spyware. The fucker's asking for it."

"Could you really do that? I mean, for real?"

"Try me. I've already tested out a few ideas, on the dirty machine." The dirty machine was one of four computers Colin kept at home, one that could be—and often was—compromised with impunity. There was a lot of stuff he wouldn't dream of doing from Lucid or from the altar consecrated to ClassicCarnection.com.

The idea, Vera thought, should be liberating, empowering—the idea of spying on the spy. The idea of regaining some purchase on her own existence, of worming her way into the privacy and anonymity of someone who had reduced her own to a termite heap. Of controlling, rather than being controlled by, the machine. Of amassing information, also known—these days—as power.

Why, then, instead of the adrenaline that was so clearly driving Colin, did she feel a sluggish dread? A visceral reluctance, a reluctance of the body—an unsettled sensation in her throat, a slow return of the ache in her head?

"I don't know," she said, thinking aloud. "I'm just not sure I can do that."

"You're right," Colin said.

"I'm right?"

"You *can't* do it. You don't have the know-how. I'll be the one doing it for you."

"Oh for God's sake. Always so literal-minded. You know what I mean."

"No, actually, I'm not sure that I do." His face was beginning to set along stubborn, truculent lines. She recognized the expression, along with the slightly heightened color along the cheekbones.

"I mean, I just don't know."

"What don't you know? We have the technology. The guy's a crook. He's taunting us. It's a no-brainer."

"True, but . . ."

"But what?"

"But . . ."

"Look, the police don't want to know. The credit card companies have already written it off. No one out there is going to help you. If you want to know who this guy is, this is the only way to find out."

Do I want to know who this guy is? she wondered. Woman. Person. Actual physical body sitting at a computer somewhere? The idea was more sinister, and yet more banal, than the idea of a virtual entity operating like a prion in cyberspace, wreaking virtual havoc on her virtual self. Or was it actual havoc on her actual self? She could no longer tell.

"I don't know, Colin. It just seems—dangerous. Stupid, somehow. Asking for trouble."

"Stupid?" She could see that she had insulted his hacker pride. "Stupid? You think you can go install a back door or a keyboard sniffer or a RAT if you're stupid?"

"Rat?"

"Remote Access Trojan, but that's not the point. The point is, we're smarter than he is, this . . . whoever he is, random person, script kiddie."

"I'm sure we are, but I'm not sure *that's* the point either." For Colin, Vera realized, all questions ultimately came down to this: who was smarter, who could devise the more ingenious solution. Even, she realized, the question of desire—hence his unselfconscious, almost instrumental approach to sex.

"Then what is?" He drained his Pale Ale in one long gulp, picked up the gunky metal object again, and began worrying at it with the rag. Eye contact was not an option when he was annoyed.

"Um," she said.

He raised one eyebrow, fastidiously de-gunking the fine metal thread, as if to say "I'm waiting."

"Um, OK, let's think this through," Vera continued. "Let's say we—you—go in there, remotely. What do we find out?"

"What do we find out? Whatever we want to."

"Well, what do we want to find out? Real name, address, if we can even get that, so I can put the cops on them—but what else? I'm not sure I really care who this person is. Who she 'really' is. I just want to make her go away."

"In order to make her go away, you have to find out who she is," Colin said, as if solving for *x*. "Because right now, unfortunately, she's Vera de Sica, and that's the cause of all your problems."

"Not *all* my problems," she rejoined. "Some of my problems, unfortunately, are caused by the fact that *I'm* Vera de Sica."

Even Colin, it appeared, couldn't refute this. He shrugged, as if to concede a technicality.

"Look, we can find out pretty much anything we want to," he repeated. "About this person. Via his hard drive. It's like looking into someone's brain. Looking into someone's computer is like looking into their brain."

"I'm not so sure I really want to look into someone else's brain," Vera said. For instance, she thought: yours. Right now.

"Oh come on!" Colin said. "Of course you do. That's power, right there."

"Ugly shit in there," she continued, thinking aloud. "Other people's brains."

"Yes but that's what makes it interesting."

"Maybe. But maybe it's better if that stuff stays under wraps. Private. The way it's meant to be."

"*Meant* to be?" His tone derided the very notion of intentionality as a factor in the Universe. His universe, where all that distinguished human beings from the higher apes was technology and, possibly—as a concession to Vera—syntax.

"Well, I mean . . . I don't mean '*meant* to be,' as in some grand scheme of things. I just think we probably need a fair amount of privacy to survive. As a species." And as individuals, she thought. Particularly me. Particularly now. "That's why we have skin," she improvised. "That's why we have skulls. That's why we can lie."

Colin gave the gadget one final wipe and put it aside. "*You have zero privacy anyway,*" he parroted. "*Get over it.*"

He was right, Vera knew. She just didn't know if she should get over it. On the other hand, why persist as if human beings were still—if they ever had been—the windowless monads of the seventeenth century? These days we all have Windows, she thought. We're jacked into a distributed system, a circuit of information rather than matter, a system where the self is a rumor. We've told our machines to talk among themselves—and they have. About us.

Birth certificates, school records, medical records, voter registration, drivers' licenses, car insurance, motor vehicle registration, parking tickets, passports, academic records, student loans, library records, video store records, bank accounts, ATM cards, credit cards, debit cards, employment benefits, tax returns, marriage licenses, court records, divorce decrees, child support payments, unemployment benefits, bankruptcies, liens, arrest records, rental agreements, change-of-address forms, mortgage information, electricity bills, gas bills, phone bills, cell phone logs, property taxes, homeowners' insurance, campaign contributions, stock holdings, charitable donations, Social Security records, food stamps, pension, disability, death. All stored in public and private databases, machine-readable and network-linked.

Not to mention the rest of it, the personal debris, the data droppings that end up on everyone's hard drive—the e-mails, the travel itineraries, the on-line purchases, the porn, the bad poetry, the drunken 3:00 A.M. chatroom postings. The Friendsters, the Fakesters, and the Fraudsters. The Web site devoted to one's hamster. The personal ads, with their tone of suave desperation. The bookmarked sites—the panicky research into Creutzfeldt-Jacob, that short-lived fascination with Furries, those red satin tap pants that you really wanted. If someone knew everything about your on-line self, would they know you? All of you? And would you know that they knew?

How much, Vera wondered helplessly, should we know about each other?

20

SHIT, CHARLENE THOUGHT, Little White Lie really wasn't doing the job. She leaned closer into the mirror and saw, under its thick paste of concealer, the reddish-purple flush under her left eye, right where her cheekbone would be if she had one. So much for "This concealer covers up all sins, honey—trust me, it should really be called the Big Lie!" So much for her attempts to dot on and blend with damp sponge, so much too for her efforts to comb her hair forward. And hence, probably, Cindy's odd, solicitous expression as she'd inquired, while setting up, about Charlene's sudden "rosacea."

"Yup," she'd said, with a shrug. "Just came on like that."

Cindy, unconvinced, had recommended a Revlon product—but from the Deep Cover rather than the skin care line. She'd also, which Charlene thought was really weird, handed her a business card (CINDY SHERMAN, VISAGISTE), with her cell phone number penciled in.

"I don't have a card," Charlene said, trying to keep it light, "'cause Oriole's too cheap. And that sucks because, if a client comes back, she never remembers what you look like. She's always looking at the product, not at you. Or at her own friggin' face." And with that she moved away, to sanitize the tips of the testers. Today was Saturday, which meant lots of teenagers, which meant lots of black eyeliner and gooey lip-gloss. And that gross sparkly stuff—What Cheek!—that they loved to shoplift.

So Charlene was busy, had to get her show on the road. No time for schmoozing or for girlish confidences. No time for that whole sisterhood routine.

Nonetheless, she had to admit, as she sharpened the lip pencils, she was touched. In fact—though she wouldn't—she wanted to weep. Weeping had ceased to be an option years ago. It took her a moment to recognize the feeling, that helpless swelling sensation at the base of the throat.

She palpated her cheekbone gingerly. It hurt, tender and puffy to the touch. This wasn't the first time. But she knew, suddenly, that it would be the last. A decision had been taken somewhere inside her on her behalf. She—Vera—was simply not going to live like this anymore.

As that ad said—for Paxil or Prozac—*your life is waiting.* And as Dr. Laura always said, the time is *now.* Well, not right now, because Charlene had makeovers to do, New You exfoliant to flog, but tomorrow, once Howie had cruised off in the Lincoln, Vera would get on the phone. She'd been studying apartment listings until her wrists ached (she'd once given herself carpal tunnel syndrome on Match.com), and now she was ready to act. She would make the calls, set up the appointments, drive around Santa Monica and the Marina with high-end agents. She'd wear the French sandals, the giant Armani sunglasses, the Swatch watch that said "class." And she'd have cash in hand, scads of cash in hand, for up-front expenses, plus a little something extra for the agent's efforts. If anyone asked, she'd say that she and her "husband" had decided to separate, that she needed her own space. She was leaving, she'd confide, to become her own person.

Right now, though, she had to look sharp. A roving pack of adolescents—with name-brand nose jobs, belly shirts and navel rings, with candy-colored cell phones and Daddy's credit card in their Hello Kitty clutches—had entered the store. The surveillance camera showed them in a suspicious cluster in the hairspray aisle. It was, she could tell, going to be one hell of a day.

On the way home, slumped behind the wheel of the Brontosaurus, she fantasized about inflicting bodily harm on those brats, giving one of them a nice poke in the eye—or rather, in the sky-blue contact lens—with the mascara wand. "Oh my," she imagined herself saying, "my hand must have slipped." Luckily the early-evening traffic on the 405 wasn't moving anyway, since she barely had the energy to hold down the gas pedal. Her feet throbbed, her shoulder ached, and she'd developed this weird headache, on the "rosy" side, which seemed to emanate from her ear. Inching through the insane mass of stalled metal—headlights surreal and dreamlike against the lavish dusk—Charlene practiced creative visualization, picturing, down to the last icy bead of sweat, the six-pack chilling in the vegetable compartment. That kept her going, along with the imminent prospect of elevating her feet and the sincere hope that Howie would not be home.

But he was. Or at least the Lincoln was, the bull's-eye of its blunt rear end mooning her from the carport. A dull, familiar sensation came over her, a sensation that she now recognized as dread.

It was so unfair: *Extreme Makeover* was on, and she was eager to see the unveiling of Caroline, dog groomer from Carson City (though how anyone could need fat injections to the face, not to mention chin and jowl implants, beat the shit out of Charlene). Now, instead, it was going to be an evening of QVC, Howie's holding forth, and the long slow countdown to pass-out. But tonight, Charlene thought—thereby motivating herself to kill the engine and exit the car—would be the season finale for this particular programming. There just wasn't enough action to attract an audience, and the "star" had definitely slipped in the ratings —not to mention the violence quotient, which was way too high. As she turned her key in the lock, Charlene imagined herself on Dr. Laura, saying in a strong, wry voice for all of Southern California to hear, "After tonight—it's *hasta la vista,* Howie!"

To her surprise, though QVC was burbling softly, Howie wasn't installed in front of it, was in fact neglecting one of his favorites: the lingerie-clad babe-ette pleasuring herself with the Pedicure Bubbler. A fried odor emanated from the kitchen area, as did loud rustling sounds, as if a large bird were building a nest. Mystified, Charlene peered over the partition, to the wholly unprecedented sight of Howie disengaging, from its circusy packaging, bucketsful of the Colonel's finest, Charlene's snack of choice. Odder still, Howie appeared to be attempting to arrange these comestibles on a plate.

Charlene hadn't even known they *had* plates. Of course, they had all kinds of household objects, intermittently, but it was hard to keep track of what was "theirs" and what was destined for eBay.

"Hey," she said, startled. "What's up?"

"Dinner," Howie said, with his self-deprecating smirk. "For you, babe. And," he continued, extricating a Bud from the refrigerator's icy heart, "your cocktail, madame."

He's a con artist, Charlene reminded herself. He can be charming when he needs to be. That's how he gets people to hand over their car keys.

She popped her Bud warily.

"Get a load off," Howie suggested, gesturing towards the La-Z-Boy, "put your feet up and I'll bring you your wings."

"Howie," she said cautiously, "I'm bushed. I wanna drink my beers, watch *Extreme Makeover,* and go to bed. OK?"

Howie shrugged, palms open as if to say, But of course. As if Charlene ever had any say in what they would do or what they would watch—except, possibly, the last time he had slugged her. A year ago? Six months? She'd lost track.

As Howie busied himself with the plates and the wings and the beers, like a small anxious rodent, Charlene tilted herself cosmonaut-style into the recliner and tried not to feel sorry for him. With his nervous scurrying, his narrow shoulders sloped and tensed as if anticipating a blow, he resembled—give or take a bald spot—the skinny adolescent she imagined him to have been, fixing popcorn and pizza for himself while his mother worked the night shift. She'd been a nurse's aide with chronic back pain and a martyred air; his father, a truck driver, had driven off one day into the sunset, or, rather, the evil yellow glow that had usurped the sunset in Detroit.

So how could Charlene just walk out on him too? It didn't seem fair, and besides, she knew that—despite his flawed sense of how best to express this—Howie needed her. He needed someone there, like a studio audience, to witness his small triumphs, his screw-you's to the system, his jabs at the behemoths of banking and credit, his successful entrepreneurship—the entire project, in other words, of becoming somebody. Somebody else, most of the time, but still somebody. Without her, his enterprise would crumble; he'd become, she foresaw, a drunk living in his car. A petty crook—a buckler, a criddler, a dumpster diver. A cirrhosis case.

It would be so easy to stay and look after him. He'd be fine for the next few weeks, she knew, sheepish and contrite, buying her things, offering her amateurish foot rubs, installing that Webcam that had been sitting in its box since May. She couldn't really imagine leaving him in that condition, needy and goofy as a chastened child.

"Grub's up," he said, presenting her with a plate, while he retired to the couch to gnaw on a thigh. What movie was that from? she wondered irritably, which of the late-night war movies that had served as young Howie's babysitter, speech coach, and etiquette guide? But Charlene was famished, in no mood to question her dinner or its presentation, so she tore right into it—the Honey BBQ Pieces, the Tender Roast Sandwich, the Hot and Spicy Chicken Breast, the Extra Crispy Thigh, even the Colonel's Crispy Strips, which she usually didn't care for. A few more beers, even some coleslaw, for the vitamin C. Howie, she had to admit, had gone all out—including, for dessert, the Fudge Brownie Parfait, which he never let her order, because, in his oft-stated opinion, it went straight to her ass.

She knew what would happen next, and it did. A bucket of spicy chicken was Howie's notion of foreplay, the dinner and the movie and the late-night drink at the romantic bar all rolled into one. But nobody had touched her in so long that it almost felt good, Howie's damp, tentative hands on her feet. He crouched at the foot of the recliner, as if in penance, manhandling her bunions with his fried-smelling hands. "A little R and R?" he suggested, with an odd, ingratiating leer. "After a rough day?"

R and R? she thought. Lying there upended, as if in the dentist's chair, discreetly enduring Howie's valiant efforts to get it up, Howie's struggle to stay focused and find the right spot—this was hardly her notion of R and R. More like S and M, she thought, without the toys. But Charlene, hungry for touch, had evolved a strategy over the years: she made it through the event —fifteen minutes max and increasingly rare—by being Liz in *Cleopatra*, Liz Taylor in that shimmery gold bra thing, with the major eye makeup, giving imperious, if unspoken, commands to the grubby, grunting slave she'd capriciously chosen to service her. (The next day, of course, he'd be beheaded.)

"Relax, babe," Howie whispered. "You know you want it." His

breath was hot and beery in her ear; one of his hands wandered tarantula-like up her thigh. Oh shit, Charlene thought, when did she last wax? But then, almost immediately, she eighty-sixed that thought—did Howie ever shave, or even take a shower, for her? And, more to the point, would Vera be lying there, with a man at her feet, worrying about how smooth her legs were? Hell no, Charlene thought. She'd be seizing the moment—seizing the man, in fact, and piloting various parts of his body where she wanted them to go.

"That tickles, Howie," she said, redirecting his hand. He paused, resumed his fumbling, but in a less annoying spot. Wow, Charlene thought, that wasn't so hard. A woman like Vera knew how to get what she wanted, in bed as in life. So tonight, Charlene suddenly decided, she'd be Vera—Vera instead of Liz, Vera with the great ass and the Julia Roberts hair, the sexy lingerie and the un-shy hands. And Howie—well, Howie would have to be Roberto, Vera's Latin lover. Not that he really had the technique, or the finesse, for the role, but still, Charlene thought, all that porn viewing had to be good for something. And anyway, this could be Vera's last time with Roberto—why not? Yes, that was it: Vera had already cast him off, given him his marching orders, except he didn't know it yet. The poor sucker was on his way out, and he had no idea. *Ciao*, Roberto, she thought, *ciao;* the very word turned her on, made her feel glam.

"Not so fast," she mumbled, adding "Roberto" in her head. Slow down, Roberto, unbutton me, peel off Vera's lingerie, languorously, appreciatively, the silky thigh-highs, the satin tap pants, the lace-up bustier with Vera's creamy pale cleavage spilling over the top. Kiss me there, Roberto, and there, for once in your life. Without thinking, she arched her back like a cat. And oddly enough, Howie seemed to respond, seemed to apply himself more ardently to his task.

He has no idea who he's dealing with, Charlene thought.

He doesn't know who he's fucking, she thought, and the idea made her hot—hotter, she thought, than she'd felt in years—drowned out the usual static, Charlene's static, stray thoughts about money and flab and bad smells. He thinks he's fucking Charlene, she thought, but Charlene has gone. Howie's fucking Vera—no, Vera's fucking him—and, *ciao,* Howie, for the very last time.

21

S HE'D BEEN HAVING that dream again, the one that left her soaked with cold sweat under her breasts, behind her knees, in the curve of her back. Trembling, she opened her eyes, pushed a mass of damp hair off her face. The morning sun was blazing through Colin's uncurtained attic windows—it was going to be another stifling day—but even its harsh light couldn't dispel the smoky air of her dream.

Always the same situation, with minor variations—the barricaded street, the somber, masked policemen, the military jets screaming overhead.

"We need to see some ID, ma'am," the officer demanded, barring her way politely but firmly with a large firearm. "Only people with ID allowed below Fourteenth Street."

"But I live here," she'd protest, searching desperately through her empty pockets, her empty bag. "I do, I swear I do. Right there"—pointing down the abandoned avenue, where no life was visible, no people, no buildings, just dense drifts of smoke.

"ID, please," he'd repeat, tonelessly, already looking past her, as if she no longer existed.

Vera didn't need Simone to interpret the dream for her. In fact, she was beginning to think, she no longer needed Simone for anything. Whatever problems she was having with her identity—and they were legion—no longer struck Vera as psychological. If they weren't bureaucratic—badgering the NYPD for a police report, filing for a new Social Security number—they seemed, for lack of a better word, metaphysical. Reality just wasn't what it used to be. The first law of thermodynamics had apparently been repealed, at least where identity was concerned.

And the dream? September 11, almost a literal replay of her experience, except for the missing ID. She'd had her ID then, a driver's license, which she'd duly produced at the barricade, conscious, even then, of the futility of the gesture, the improvised rituals of surveillance. What she most strongly recalled —and re-experienced in the dream—was the sense of stunned disorientation, of a suddenly disordered universe in which anything was possible, and nothing was safe.

"Colin?" she called out, still queasy with fear.

"Down here," he yelled, from two flights below—the laundry room. She'd been afraid, for a moment, that he might have left.

Later, returning to Manhattan with the slightly cored-out feeling she always had after a night with Colin—a sense of mild depersonalization, akin to jet lag—Vera re-entered her own life like a prison sentence. As she emerged from the subway, the air was already thick and muggy, smelling of asphalt and sulfur, with base notes of garbage bag. Near the front door of her building, where her *New York Times* had been carelessly tossed, a mob of pigeons jostled one another to peck at dog shit. I don't have to live like this, came the fleeting, traitorous thought: I don't have to live in this city. But where, then? Her mind spun blankly around the globe. That's why she was still there, she realized: New York was the ideal place for someone who no longer knew where to live, or how.

The phone was shrilling as she entered her apartment and, though she needed to pee, she dumped her mail on the desk and picked up right away, a recently acquired reflex. If you didn't talk to the collection agencies, they hounded you day and night.

"Well hello," said a man's voice, "it's the big fat loser."

"Uh—who is that, please?"

"The big fat loser," he repeated, "to wish you happy birthday." In that instant, she recognized her brother's voice, and, then, in the background, his wife's chiding "Oh, Ernie!"

"Hey Ern," Vera said, mildly confused, "thanks for remembering." She began to riffle idly through the stack of mail. "But what's this about big fat loser?"

"I don't know," he said, and his voice was chilly. She pictured him inspecting his immaculate hands, pale and powdery from their latex gloves. "I would have to ask *you* that." She and Ernesto had never been close—six years, two hundred miles, and approximately 200K in annual income stood between them—but they were usually civil, approaching each other warily, like members of different but non-hostile species.

"Me? Why?"

"Well, maybe that e-mail was your idea of a joke, some wacky New York thing—"

"E-mail?" Vera said. "Oh shit." Now she was going to have to tell him the whole story, the whole humiliating saga, which would immediately be added to Ernesto's dossier against her—further evidence, if any were required, of his younger sister's unfitness for adult life. "Listen Ern . . . ," she said, then faltered.

As she tried to formulate her next sentence—"That wasn't me, that was the *other* Vera de Sica"?—her hands, in semiconscious multitasking, began to deal with her mail. Tossing most of it aside, she used her house key to slit open the sole misfit among the gaudy overdue notices, a plain white envelope from an institution she didn't recognize. With half an ear on what her brother was saying—"Just out of the blue like that?"—she scanned the opening lines and then felt something like an icy explosion in her head, a starburst that sent white spots skittering across her vision. "Oh my fucking God," she interrupted.

"Vera?"

"Oh my fucking God," she repeated, "Ern, I have to go right now. I have to make a call, I'll call you back—"

"Vera?" he repeated, alarm beating out annoyance in his voice. "You OK? Is everything OK?"

But she had already hung up. Then immediately she realized she shouldn't have—Ernesto was precisely the person she needed to speak to, someone well versed in money and property and mortgages, as befitted a grown-up person living in Newton, Mass., with 2.2 children and 2 SUVs. She dialed his number with shaky jabs, her eyes jittering in disbelief over the paper in her hand.

"Ern? It's me again, look, I'm sorry, I need to ask you something."

"Vera? What on earth is going on? First that stupid e-mail, now this crazy—"

She spoke over him, panicking. "OK, say somebody takes out a loan against their . . . your, your apartment, your home . . . and then defaults, then what?"

"What's going on, Vera? Have you got yourself into some kind of mess?"

"Me? Not exactly . . . just tell me, Ern, what would happen?"

"What would happen? What do you *think* would happen? Worst-case scenario, you stand to lose the property." Just hearing those words—"lose" and "property"—sent her into an instant, irrational tailspin, a vortex of dread that, like a black hole, admitted no light.

She'd never been one for bag lady fantasies (her parents had had them, diligently, on her behalf), had always believed, Micawber-like, that something would turn up. But nothing had. And now she saw how easily it could happen, how one could indeed lose everything all at once—through, if nothing else, a refusal to deal: a kind of cowardly hubris, a lifetime's worth of willful inattention.

That's it, she thought. That woman—whoever she is—has gone too far. She's going to suffer for this, she's going to pay. She's going to be punished, if I do it myself, with my own hands. Vera had a quick, violent flash of ripping someone's head off (someone with her own curly hair), which alarmed her, pacifist that she was. Then, she couldn't help it, she imagined stamping on that someone's face, repeatedly, with her hiking boots, flattening the features to a bloody pulp. She was scaring herself, her heart racing, high-octane chemicals raging through her. There was no way she could phone Instant Mortgage Mall right now, have a coherent conversation with a Credit Product Specialist about the document she'd just received. They'd think she was a psycho. "*I'm* not the fucking psycho!" she imagined herself yelling, in a psychotic roar.

Instead, she called Colin. As soon as he picked up, she blurted, "OK, that's it. Just go ahead and do it."

"Do what? And—top o' the morning to you too, my dear!"

"Do whatever you want. Open season."

" 'Open season'?"

"She needs to die."

"Do I take it," he asked, after a pause, "that we are alluding to Vera de Sica the Second?" He seemed in an unusually good mood, not even—as far as Vera could tell—keystroking away.

"She's applied for this, this . . . horrendous loan against my apartment. If that letter hadn't come here, I could have lost the whole thing! My apartment!"

"I thought you hated that apartment."

"I do," Vera admitted, "but it's mine. I own it!"

"Well," Colin said, "technically speaking, the bank owns it, but I get your point."

"Colin, this psycho is trying to mortgage *my* home! Out from under me! Don't you get it?"

"Yes, I get it—Not Good."

"Not good? It's all I have, all I own, all I fucking have to show for myself! And it could be taken away from me, just like that! Tomorrow I wake up to find myself unemployed, with nowhere to live, in this hellhole of a city, and all you can say is *not good*?"

"It takes at least six months to evict someone in New York, Vera," he said, reasonably (which, under the circumstances, struck her as maddeningly unreasonable). "And you could always move into my place for a while."

"*Your* place? You must be kidding." She hadn't really intended to screech like that, like a demented parrot.

"OK, OK," he said, hastily. "Bad idea. Sorry. Let's back up a little, get the whole picture." And gradually, with unwonted delicacy, Colin coaxed the details out of her. Vera de Sica, SSN So-and-So, had been turned down for an Express Equity Loan (for reason 16A—please refer to key on back), but, pursuant to provision 29B, would be granted a revolving line of credit for a maximum of $25,000.

"Which is peanuts!" Vera expostulated. "She could blow through that in an afternoon! Then she defaults, and I lose my apartment."

"Probably not," said Colin, "because you've already filed the fraud alert, and they should have picked up on that, but, in theory, yes."

"And I would never have known, except, apparently, IMM doesn't correspond with P.O. boxes. So they sent it here."

"You'd think he would have known that. The crook."

"You'd think. Lucky he didn't. *She!* I'm telling you, Colin, it's a she."

"Well," he said, "we'll soon find out."

She hesitated, her scruples now on the scrap heap. "How soon?"

"Well," he said jauntily, and she could almost see the immodest smirk, "just as soon as somebody wakes up on the West Coast."

"What do you mean?" But she already knew.

"It's done. As soon as you left this morning—I tested the software, went in the back door, deployed it. Took me under an hour, all told. Nice hack, if I do say so myself."

Vera paused. So Colin had, once again, acted unilaterally. In whose interests? Not necessarily hers—Colin, she knew, was capable of doing almost anything for the technical challenge alone. Nor did she know whether to be annoyed that he'd ignored her qualms and forged ahead, or grateful that he'd anticipated her change of heart. So she decided to be neither, to accept the situation as a *fait accompli.* After all, she could always tell herself, she hadn't actually given him the go-ahead.

Colin regarded the on-line world as a realm separate from the embodied world, a game with its own rules. She, on the other hand, couldn't help seeing it as an extension of the "real," governed by the same rules of conduct. Who, she wondered, had the better case? Or had the question, de facto, become moot? ("You see," she heard her mother's voice, "you *should* have gone to law school!")

"So as soon as someone goes on-line on that machine . . . ?" Vera asked, in her own, shaky voice.

"We have a really good shot at finding out who he is."

The idea was exhilarating, yet alarming, as if something had come adrift in the world, something had buckled in the space-time continuum. She was about to confront a logical impossibility: an embodied virtuality, herself—Vera de Sica—both *here* and *there* at the same time. Herself as another—an idea, she had to admit, not without appeal.

"Oh, and," Colin said, "happy birthday!"

"Oh yeah," she said. "That."

"Look out for a package from Bibliophile.com—I found you a little something you might like. Nineteen fifty-five edition, mint condition," he added, with studied nonchalance. The keyboard started up, then stopped.

This came as almost as great a shock to Vera as the tidings from IMM.

"Thanks, hum," she stammered, "I mean, hon."

She was ready to turn around and get right back on the train to New Jersey—a personal best, twice in as many days—but Colin convinced her that there was no point in doing so until the spyware started sending out data files.

"To you?" she asked, nervously.

"Ah—no." Vera pictured the raised eyebrows, the mild incredulity. "To an address that I set up specifically for this purpose."

Actually, Colin said, there was no reason for her to come to New Jersey at all. He could forward her the data, though she probably wouldn't be able to make much sense of it.

"No," she said firmly. "I want to see this. In real time. I want to see this with my own eyes."

Some two hours later—most of which Vera had spent on the phone in a harrowing and ultimately unproductive wrangle with IMM (they wanted to see a copy of the police report, which of course she didn't have), the phone trilled again. Anticipating, as always, some fresh hell, she was relieved to hear Colin's voice, brusque though it was.

"Come on out here," he said, without preamble. "We have a live one!"

Seldom—no, never—had Vera set about transporting herself with such alacrity to Basking Ridge, New Jersey. But as soon as the train left Penn Station, she slumped into a heavy doze, feeling suddenly drained, bereft of affect, as if, after weeks of arduous preparation, boarding a long flight for a foreign country. She would have slept right through her station, slept all the way to Gladstone, if the conductor hadn't nudged her kindly with his clippers. She stumbled off, confused, to find Colin sprawled over one of the Lilliputian green benches on the platform, his long legs jiggling with impatience.

"C'mon," he said, all but dragging her towards the car (a beat-up brown Mercedes diesel that he drove for its unparalleled economy and efficiency). "Loads of good stuff already!"

"Enough to . . . you know, identify her?" Vera asked, feeling obscurely afraid.

"Sure!" Colin said. "Positive ID: name's Vera de Sica!"

"Not funny," Vera said, shaking her head. "I don't know why, but this whole thing . . . this spy thing . . . I'm finding it a bit . . . scary."

"Why on earth?"

"Dunno. Just feel as if we've crossed a line here."

"'Line'? No 'lines' in cyberspace. Hyperrelational environment."

"Whatever," she said. "It just feels weird."

"But you still want to do it," he said—a statement, not a question. "You still want to know."

"Hell yes!"

As he drove through the leafy green streets, past the McMansions with their obsessively maintained lawns, Colin explained what he'd already managed to download—essentially, a copy of the infected computer's file system. Including, of course, all deleted files and image files. "Those are cool because they tend to be porn," he added. "You can have yourself a little slide show as the machine leafs through them automatically."

"Colin, I'm not really that interested in looking at porn right now. I'm interested in finding out who this asshole is."

"You will. We will."

"But how exactly?"

"Well, I go through the files at my leisure and see what's there. Which can be pretty tedious sometimes, especially the e-mail. And the kids' homework." Here he made a gagging noise. "Not to mention Napster! You wouldn't believe some people's taste in music!"

"I don't see how Napster's going to help us. Like if we know this guy's a huge Billy Joel fan or something—"

"It isn't. But you can still have a good time ridiculing his taste."

"Colin, I'm serious. How are we going to find a name? A real name?"

"Well, take your pick. Word documents are good, a letter or something, Yours Truly, Joe Blow. E-mails, address books, Win-Fax if they have it. Quicken, TurboTax, whatever—assuming that criminals keep financial records, which I very much doubt. Also all the Internet stuff—bookmarks, cookies, browser history, and so on, where they've been lately. Most on-line apps will have their passwords 'remembered'—you launch them, off they go and connect. Luckily for us, humans are stupid and lazy. They have trouble remembering a few passwords, but the computer remembers everything. Trust me, it's all there. Somewhere."

"I'm a human," said Vera, quietly.

"What?"

"Nothing."

"But," he said, barreling ahead, "I've saved the piece de resistance for when you're here."

"*Pièce de résistance,*" Vera said, automatically, correcting his pronunciation.

"Hey," Colin said, riled, "I'm not one of your students. In point of fact, if I'm not mistaken, you don't even *have* any students anymore." Then—registering that this had hurt—he added, in an exaggerated and placating manner: "*Pee-ess de ray-sis-tance.*"

"Sorry," she said. "Reflex by now. What is it? The *pee-ess de ray-sis-tance,* I mean?"

He gave her a cocky, sidelong glance as he turned the Merc into his driveway, which, much to his neighbors' distress, looked like the lair of a white-trash auto mechanic, complete with the occasional chassis on blocks.

"That's when," he said, killing the engine with a flourish, "we turn on the Webcam, remotely, and we see his face."

The idea stunned Vera into silence. There was something so creepy about it, so transgressive, that she felt a physical sense of dread. She—Vera de Sica—would be staring unseen at the face of a stranger—a.k.a. Vera de Sica—while the stranger stared unseeing into the screen, at Vera, as if the screen truly were a portal through space. Through matter. Matter doesn't matter anymore, Colin was always saying—but maybe it did.

One body, one identity: the idea had been so simple, so convenient. She was nostalgic for it already.

"Yikes," she said.

Colin took this as a compliment. "Pretty neat," he assented.

"But—isn't that going a bit far? I don't really feel the need to get, you know, up close and personal with him. *Her.*"

"You aren't," Colin said pedantically. "The Net is basically a means whereby one computer communicates with another. If anyone's getting up close and personal, it's them."

"Who?"

"The machines."

This was, she gathered, supposed to make her feel better.

"OK," she said, opening the car door and pinning up her thick, sweaty hair with a chopstick she'd found in the glove compartment, "let's go do the dirty deed."

"Hey," Colin asked, as he bounded ahead, kicking a coil of fan-belt rubber out of the way, "who was it who hotfooted it out from Manhattan for precisely that purpose?"

"Um—me?"

The "dirty machine" was, for some reason, installed in the laundry room, a pleasant, airy space about half the size of Vera's apartment. The much-abused, jury-rigged pile of components sat on a counter next to a heap of Colin's unwashed clothes, which were, by and large, indistinguishable from his washed ones. Dense blocks of code, indecipherable to Vera, were unreeling themselves across the screen.

"See?" Colin said. "There he is!"

"Where?"

"On-line right now." Colin pulled up a stool, with an awful scraping sound of metal against tile. Then, with his long limbs at odd angles, he began typing furiously. "Hmmmmnnn . . . ," he said, happily—full-power mode, all plugged in.

"Hmmmmnn what?" asked Vera, pulling up a second stool, with the same agonized screech.

"Hmmmmnnn . . . he's been a busy guy."

"What's he been doing?"

"You mean, where's he been?"

Vera had assumed, naively, that he, whoever "he" was, had been at his keyboard, but she corrected herself. "Yeah, where's he been?"

"Well," Colin said, "just this morning, he's been to Citibank, Chase, um, Victoria's Secret, eBay about a million times, don't know why he doesn't just write a script to check automatically for him, MasterMoney, what's this, on-line blackjack, voter registration for the state of Ohio, and, *ay caramba!* it seems our guy has a thing for Hot Asian Babes. Must be running up quite a tab there."

"Is he still there?" Vera asked. "Cause I'm not sure I really want to see his face while he's . . . you know." *Her* face, she thought, stubbornly, still unwilling to renounce her belief that this second Vera, Vera the Con, was female. She could be a woman who liked to look at other women, Vera rationalized — why not? Plenty of those around. In cyberspace as in meatspace. In laundry rooms as on-line.

"No," said Colin, "right now he's on . . . what's this, Lincoln-Mania.com."

"More porn?"

"No, cars."

She shrugged. Some women were into cars, too.

"So," Colin asked, pushing the stool abruptly back from the counter, legs extended, hands interlaced behind his head, "you ready? He could log off any minute."

"I guess," said Vera.

"You *guess?*"

"I'm ready."

"OK," he said, "let's go." Whatever juices were surging through his circuits — adrenaline, testosterone, norepinephrine — were now speeding through Vera's as well, so that for once (outside of bed) their body chemistry was synchronized, both systems intent on the same task, high on mastery. If it were always like this, she caught herself thinking, I'd stay with him forever. I'd become a hacker myself.

"OK," he said, typing with taut concentration, "I've basically captured the executive functions of the system, so I should be able to make it do whatever I want it to. And right now, I want it to . . ."—long pause—"turn on the Webcam."

Nothing happened for several seconds. Colin and Vera stared Uri Geller–like at the display, willing it to change. It didn't. Then it did. The screen cleared, flickered, staged a brief shower of digital snow, cleared again, and then, all at once, crisp as the nightly news, a face appeared.

They both gasped.

"There's our guy!" Colin crowed, leaping to his feet. "There he is!"

"That can't be right," Vera said, at the same moment, collapsing back.

The face was in extreme, distorted close-up. It was the face of a stranger—a stranger with slack features and the empty, fixed stare of a leatherback turtle—yet at the same time obscurely familiar. Vera stared. The face stared back, barely moving, barely blinking. The more she looked at it, the less it looked like anybody she knew.

"That can't be right," she repeated, almost whispering. "That can't be me."

22

CHARLENE WASN'T SURE she liked her new Mac — she kept trying to close the windows from the wrong side, and she was having major hand-eye coordination problems with the touch pad — but if an iBook was good enough for Vera, then it was good enough for her. And she did like its slenderness, its luminous, almost otherworldly quality, so different from the bulky Gateway that had served her and Howie's purposes for so long. Plus, it was elegant, unobtrusive — something that could be slipped into an Oriole free-gift tote bag and brought home without attracting undue attention.

All things considered, it had been a highly successful afternoon, though Howie, perversely, had taken his own sweet time getting out of the house. Usually on a Sunday he was in a big hurry — hangover permitting — to drive off in the Lincoln, reap the biweekly harvest from the mailboxes, and then do whatever it was that he did the rest of the day (hanging out at the shop with Ray, mostly) to avoid excessive face time with Charlene. But today, no. Today he had to diddle around on the Internet for hours, until Charlene was ready to wheel him to the front door in his desk chair and tip him out. Finally, though — languorously — he'd roused himself and readied himself for the outdoors, pausing uncharacteristically to ask Charlene if she'd like to "tag along."

Hell, no, she'd thought, watching the back of his head disappear from her life.

Fifteen minutes later, having applied a new coat of Double Trouble and fluffed up her perm, her brow as blank as a Barbie doll's, Charlene, too, had set sail—not to return until Vera de Sica, Ph.D., with her bold, curlicued new signature, was the proud leaseholder on a new condo in a "singles" complex in the Marina. With wet bar, Jacuzzi, and gym. And an air-conditioned garage for the Z8, when it arrived. The condo's owner, a "munitions expert," had been posted at very short notice to Abu Dhabi and, though Charlene had hoped for immediate occupancy, the best he could offer was July 1. He needed a couple of weeks to "get his affairs in order," he'd said vaguely, gesturing at the plastic-sheathed furnishings.

"That makes two of us," she'd responded, with a conspiratorial wink. He looked gay to her, with all that jewelry, but you never knew, and anyway she needed to update her flirting skills, which had expired of inanition under Howie's regime.

So that left a "couple of weeks"—it was actually closer to three—before Vera could assume occupancy. Charlene was afraid that if she stayed with Howie in the interim, she'd lose her nerve, or some of her teeth, or both. Besides, hadn't she committed to immediate action? And wasn't the time *now*? Hence the reservation she'd just made at the Shutters Hotel in Santa Monica, for a Professor de Sica, arriving June 10—that very night—departing July 1. Hence, too, the hasty purchase of some personal items that the Prof, disporting herself in her Ocean View Royal Suite, would surely require—a brand-new iBook and some diamond drop earrings, to wear to dinner, if she fucking well felt like it.

But as soon as she'd made the reservation, Charlene was stricken with anxious misgivings, second thoughts. Would

Shutters, with its discreet, cloistered ambience, be acceptable to Vera, accustomed as she was to the Old World opulence of the Biltmore? Perhaps she should have picked something with a bit more pizzazz—the Mondrian, perhaps? But Shutters was hellishly expensive, plus Charlene had it on the best authority (*People* magazine) that the stars went there to recuperate after major facial surgery, so how bad could it be? Anyway, Charlene wanted, for once in her life, to be right on the beach—she pictured herself, impossibly lean and golden, power-walking along the lacy surf—so if Vera had any issues with her accommodation, she'd just have to get over them.

As Charlene was packing all her new shoes into a shiny black garbage bag—they'd sold every last piece of Louis Vuitton luggage on eBay—the phone rang, an unusual enough occurrence that she started, as if someone had fired a shot. Thinking that, for some unimaginable reason, it must be Howie (who else had the number?), she picked up at once, picturing, not without pleasure, some horrible emergency—the Lincoln skidded into a drainage ditch, Howie, purple with anoxia, in the final convulsive throes of a heart attack.

"Howard J. Hoffner, please," said the voice on the other end, all business.

This wasn't good. In fact, it was catastrophic. In the six or seven years that Charlene had lived with Howie, nobody—to her knowledge—had ever called his house and asked for him by his (real) full name. Even Ray, who knew him only as "Howie" or "Mr. Cash," always called Howie on his cell, though Mr. Cash was a poor conversationalist, mumbling unintelligibly for fear of being overheard on a police scanner.

"Pardon?" said Charlene, stalling for time. She wondered if she should adopt a Polish accent, like Janusz the janitor at the Revco, and pretend to understand nothing.

"Is that the residence of Howard J. Hoffner?"

It had to be a cop. Only cops actually said "residence" (and "incident" and "responded"). Charlene's heart began to pound, a live toad in her chest. She felt a head-rush like a hit of crystal meth.

"Who's calling, please?"

"This is Detective Carver from the LAPD Fraud Unit. I'm trying to locate a Mr. Howard J. Hoffner. Our records show a white 1985 Lincoln Continental, tag number HJH-LOL, registered to him at this address."

"Um—not here. Nobody's here. I'm the maid," she said, clicking Off with a tremulous thumb.

How long, she wondered, until they showed up?

She checked the time on her iBook, 5:28 P.M. She gave them half an hour, max. No time for the thoughtful triage of her worldly goods, no time for deciding what, from Charlene's life, Vera might conceivably need. She'd take the shoes, since they were already packed, the iBook, her cosmetics kit (no sense in wasting good product), a week's worth of clothes, plus tooth-paste, deodorant, and hair gel. Oh, and her favorite Versace knockoff (the orange Lycra minidress), the Gucci jeans, and the last remaining photo of her mother, aged thirty-three, with sunken cheeks and vacant stare. Charlene—Vera—was already wearing the diamonds and the ultrathin Swatch, she had a thick envelope of cash and a walletful of bank cards. All Vera's IDs. The rest she would leave behind—for Howie. Or the cops. Or whoever might care about the accumulated crap that was the sole, abject issue of their lives together.

After she'd hastily bundled these items into the back of the Brontosaurus—she'd dump it at the airport, a mere fifteen min-utes away, and swan on down to Shutters in a cab—she paused to reflect. Anything else? She'd left nothing, she knew, with her name on it, or Vera's—just a few chain-store clothes that could have been anyone's. Let the cops paw through them, wonder if Howie had been, among other things, a cross-dresser.

Her heart was still jumping, her breathing ragged from exertion. Was the time really *now?* Was she really going to leave it all behind, all those IDs and birth certificates, all those mailbox contracts, bank checks, marriage licenses, charge cards, all those personal organizers and plasma TVs, all of it purchased with the credit—the misplaced trust—of others? Was she really going to let Howie come home to the cops like a pig to the slaughter?

She'd do him one last favor. And then she'd be on her way.

Outside the back door was a brand-new thirty-gallon plastic garbage can that Howie had acquired for who knew what purpose (they simply tossed their trash in the building's communal dumpster, which emitted nightly scrabbling noises). Hauling the blue bin inside by the scruff of its neck, she placed it upright in the bathtub. Then, in a controlled frenzy, breathing as if in the final stages of a triathlon, Charlene began gathering armfuls of paper from Howie's "office," documents, checkbooks, IDs, whatever she could find, heaving them into the bin until it was full. Matches—where the fuck? did they have any matches? oh yes—the booklet she'd snagged from TGIF's. In her handbag. By the door.

But were these cheapo matches going to do the job? Charlene looked doubtfully at them, like a row of bad teeth, and then at the trash can, densely packed with paper and plastic, with imaginary people and illusory funds, with passwords and user IDs, patterns and codes, identifiers and credit, the unreal coin of the unreal realm. None of it existed, yet it would take more than a match or two to make it disappear.

She needed a . . . what was it called, an accelerant? Something flammable. Or did she mean inflammable? She suddenly recalled how, during slow stretches at work, glazed with boredom, she'd stare at the product labels, the way you'd read the back of the cereal box at breakfast, idly pondering the difference between "jumbo" and "extra-large," or "flammable" and "inflammable"—a line of thought that led her directly to the medicine chest and the Jumbo Economy bottle of nail polish remover that lived there (Oriole's Clean Slate). She opened it and upended it, dousing the bin's contents with clear fluid. It smelled—she wasn't sure why—like dead things, like hospitals, like the morgue. Then, doing the thing you were never supposed to do, she struck all the matches at once on her platform sole. Tossed the fireball, ran for the door. From deep within came a muted roar.

As she backed the Brontosaurus out of the carport, tires squealing à la *Thelma and Louise,* she noticed that the Filipinos' Toyota was parked in the street, which meant they were home. Oh well, she'd just have to hope their smoke detector was working.

23

VERA HAD ADOPTED the face as her screensaver, a mug shot courtesy of Colin. So every time she turned on her Mac, there he was, staring somewhere over her right shoulder with his lizardlike gaze. And each time he reappeared —several times a day, in living color—her sense of outrage rebooted itself. Surely, Vera thought, a crook owed it to his victims to look a little more imposing?

What bothered her most about the face was its banality—the puffy eyelids, the retreating hairline, the blotchy skin badly shaved, even the tuft of nostril hair the Webcam had picked up. Mr. de Sica, it appeared, hadn't been ready for his close-up. But, as Vera pored over the image like a dissatisfied client, something else kept nagging at her—the creeping sensation that she'd seen that face before. But where? And when?

As a prompt to her memory, she'd had Colin steal time on the state-of-the-art scientific printer at Lucid to produce a hyperrealist portrait on photographic paper, which she'd taped above her desk like a household saint. And as she went about her business beneath this mundane icon—mostly undoing the damage that the 1400 cc of gray matter inside that unprepossessing cranium had caused her—she hoped that one day, in a flash, her brain would do what brains do and suddenly, obliquely, make a connection. Pattern recognition, she told

Colin—it was something humans did well. He'd shrugged and continued his massive data mining of the diverted information —something, he told her, that computers did well.

"Why, then," Vera asked, ungratefully, "hasn't it done it already? It's been four days, nearly five, and we don't even have a name."

"You want names? I'll give you names," Colin had said. Oh, he had names all right, names galore, names to spare—hundreds of documents in scores of names. Including, of course, the name of Vera de Sica. Did that mean, then, that she was the guilty party? There was no way of knowing—yet—which, if any, was the miscreant's "real" name. Was he, for instance, Marc Gibson, Karl Franz, James Massard, Stephen Massie, Howard Cash, Holland Hefner, E. D. Kriseova, or Ed Peters, in all of whose names, among others, he'd obtained credit? Or was he none of the above? Was he hiding in plain sight amidst a throng of aliases, or was his "real" name the sole string of signifiers that he never used?

"I don't know," Vera replied wearily, "and I don't care. Just find me a name that I can take to the cops."

"The cops don't give a damn," Colin pointed out, somewhat ungallantly. "They haven't even assigned you a case number yet, you're such small potatoes."

"I know," she admitted. "But I just want to know. For myself." (Make that, she thought, "my" "self.")

"I'm working on it," Colin had said curtly. He didn't like being told what to do, and he'd already explained the problem.

The problem, as so often with machines, was not a dearth of information but an overabundance: the scarce resource turned out not to be raw data but human time and attention to make sense of it. Watching the code unreel relentlessly across Colin's screen that first day, Vera had been seized with queasiness, a kind of information sickness—and that had been just a few minutes' worth. Within hours, Colin had downloaded more files than he, or his data-mining routines, could keep up with. Fortunately, for some reason, Our Guy hadn't been back on-line since then, so, after an initial burst of frenzied hyperactivity, Colin was slogging through the backlog. Colin was great on Proof of Concept, Vera thought, but not so big on follow-through—once he'd shown that something could be done, he tended to lose interest, leaving the grunt work to others while he sprinted ahead.

Come to think of it, Vera reflected, that was how he approached human relationships—theirs, for instance. Proof of Concept: they were together. Follow-through: someone else's job. She had to admit, though, that, in cyberspace at least, his concepts usually proved workable, even inspired.

Faced—almost literally—with the evidence, Vera had grudgingly conceded that the crook was not only male but presumably a pro, part of a larger fraud ring that gave as little thought to the flesh-and-blood reality of its victims as workers at an abattoir. Somehow, this idea rankled more than her earlier, more paranoid conjectures: paranoia had at least provided a plot, had made her an actor in her own drama. Randomness, arbitrariness—the fact that her life could be ransacked for no particular reason—were harder to swallow. She wanted a name. She wanted a motive. She wanted to know who this person "really" was.

There was, she realized, a growing list of words that she could no longer use, even in her own mind, without quotation marks— "who," "person," "really," and "was," for starters. Not to mention "own" and "mind." She could see herself becoming one of those people who used air quotes compulsively, like a tic.

How on earth, she wondered, would she ever get a new job,

ticcing like that? Not that she'd made much of an effort in weeks, halfheartedly checking the Metropolitan U listserv when she thought of it, which was about as often as she went to the gym. Like the irrational creature she'd apparently become, she was channeling all her energy into this obsessive pursuit. And what for? She'd be on welfare before she knew it, she'd be out on the street without any help from a crook.

Head in hand, she breathed deeply (as instructed by Simone) and pictured herself on a remote mountaintop in the Andes, where no one would ever be able to find her. She could pretend to be a deaf-mute. Or amnesiac. She would wear colorful embroidered blouses and live on avocados. Tend llamas. Pay cash— or barter—for everything.

At that moment, back in Alphabet City, the phone rang, and she forgot how to breathe again. Glancing at her watch, she saw that it was just past noon, 9:00 A.M. on the West Coast. It figured. The calls would continue until eight, without let-up.

This time—she gradually ascertained—it was a BMW dealer from Beverly Hills, incoherent with rage, railing about some convertible that had been leased in her name and that his driver had been unable to deliver on the appointed day. The address had turned out to be fallacious, "right next to some crummy building with crime-scene tape," he'd added, indignantly, as if that had been the final straw. He wanted Vera to do something about it. *Now.* He wanted her to pay. *In full.* He was sending someone right over to break her legs.

After wrangling for half an hour with the incensed purveyor of luxury vehicles (who'd apparently never heard of identity theft), trying to convince him that yes, she was Vera de Sica, SSN such and such, but no, she'd never ordered a Z8, whatever that was, nor had she ever resided in Culver City, wherever that was, Vera hung up and glared venomously at the face on her wall. She felt a now familiar surge of rage—she pictured herself clubbing Old Droopy Eyes right on the bald spot—but what she mainly felt, as she did so much of the time, was exhaustion. A bone-deep weariness, a near paralysis of the will—just as, she imagined, a battered wife must feel, never knowing when, or from which quarter, the next blow would fall.

Andes. Mountaintop. Crisp air, brilliant light. Utter silence, except for the cry of the yak. Llama. Whatever it was.

She tried to breathe, as instructed, failed, tried again, succeeded this time. Then, as the oxygen hit her brain, so did an idea: *hey,* she typed rapidly to cdevans@lucid.com, *see if any of those naems have address in culver city.*

why, he typed back, almost immediately. Colin always seemed to answer his e-mail in real time, regardless of what else he might be doing.

just bcasue

ok (?)

That was better. She even felt somewhat—as Simone would say—empowered. So, Vera thought, she should seize the moment, the fleeting charge, and attack some of the more aversive tasks on her list. First she had to produce the necessary stack of documentation for the BMW dealership, the credit agencies, and the bank in question, testifying that she, Vera de Sica, was in fact herself, and that she, herself, had never signed a lease agreement on a BMW in Beverly Hills, California, so help her God (not to mention that she didn't even own a fucking car). Then, noting the date, she realized it was time to pay some bills—real-life bills, bills that this Vera, Vera the Poor, had actually incurred. Gas, electricity, fun stuff like that. First, though—to avert disaster—she'd better check her balance.

As soon as she logged on to her bank account she could see that something was horribly, ludicrously wrong.

Her available balance, which just yesterday had stood at several hundred dollars, now stood at tens of thousands—almost double, in fact, her annual income.

She logged out immediately, then logged back in, to see if that would correct the error. The same hilarious, entirely imaginary amount. Under other circumstances, Vera might have experienced a tiny thrill, however transient, at seeing such sums, however phantasmagorical, credited to her account. But, as it was, she groaned, despair weighing her down like an extra g-force. Not again, she thought, not again—I just can't deal with this anymore.

She couldn't imagine what had happened, but she knew it couldn't be good. Most people, finding an unexpected bonanza in their bank account, might allow themselves a few moments of optimism, a flutter of fantasy. Not Vera. She'd been conditioned by now to expect the worst. Nothing good had happened to her since . . . well, she couldn't remember when.

Within minutes she'd changed into a clean black T-shirt, an almost clean pair of khakis, and her favorite sandals, the ones with thick, juicy soles like truck tires. She stuck a chopstick in her hair, powdered her nose (her skin was breaking out, she looked like shit), applied a ragged dash of Insouciance, and headed out, turning back at the door for her sunglasses, checkbook, and, why not, all her bank statements from the past year.

The only place Vera hated going more than the post office was the bank—Shittybank, as she called it, sometimes to its face. Every aspect of the Banking Experience, from the bunkerlike architecture to the best-friend ATM, seemed designed with a single purpose: that of preventing you, the customer, from ever interacting with a fellow human being. But today, Vera swore, she would prevail. She would—without the use of ski masks or anthrax threats—compel a bank employee (a) to acknowledge her existence, and (b) to address her problem, in person and in real time. She could picture it already, a rousing victory, a Rosa Parks moment, bringing hope and inspiration to oppressed bank patrons across the globe.

Otherwise . . . otherwise, what? What would it be called, she wondered, if someone "went postal" in a bank?

In the event, her mission was accomplished with anticlimactic ease. After a mere ten-minute wait, Vera was ushered into a cubicle of bulletproof glass, which, for all the privacy it afforded, might as well have been on the main floor of Macy's. But when she saw the bank employee fate had assigned her, Vera allowed herself some hope. She actually seemed alert and humorous, this young Nuyorican with the elaborate hair, elaborate nails, and glint of don't-bullshit-me intelligence in her eyes. Her name was Georgia, which didn't fit.

Deciding to give civility a whirl, Vera humbly explained her plight. An unexplained deposit had appeared in her account. She suspected an error, but she feared fraud.

"What kind of fraud?" Georgia asked. "Account takeover, or true-name fraud?"

True-name fraud. Yet another oxymoron to define her condition.

On her way over, and during her short wait, Vera had begun to elaborate a theory, drawing on her substantial exposure to cop shows. Check kiting, it had to be: the crook makes a (bogus) deposit into Account B using (bogus) checks from Account A, and then withdraws as much as he can before the bank wises up. All this, of course, in the name of poor Sucker B. Vera didn't really understand how this was possible—God knows, she had to wait long enough for her own (legitimate) deposits to clear— but she supposed it might be, if you knew how. And if large enough sums were involved.

Georgia looked skeptical, pursed her well-outlined lips and pulled them to one side, in that rubbery, expressive way of New York women. "Could be," she said, attacking the keyboard with her talons, "or could just be a computer error. Let's take a look what's going on."

Meekly, Vera wrote her account number on a purple Post-it, as requested. Then she watched Georgia tapping, pausing, tapping, trying to read her face.

"Hmmnn," she said, after a few seconds, just like Colin. "Here it is." She pointed at the screen, which Vera couldn't see, and copied down the amount. "Nice chunk of change."

"Would be," Vera said, shrugging, "if it were real. And if it were mine."

Georgia gave her a strange look, almost embarrassed. "I don't know what to tell you, ma'am. It's real all right."

"What do you mean, real?"

"See here," Georgia swiveled the monitor so Vera could see, and indicated a long string of block letters and digits, codes and acronyms, none of which meant anything to Vera. Then she tapped the screen with a salmon-colored tip. "This tells us that it was a wire transfer from a U.S. bank. Goes straight out of their account into yours. Equivalent of cash."

"Wait a minute," Vera said, "I don't get it." She felt sick all of a sudden, as if she'd been the butt of a practical joke. She almost expected a cameraman to leap out of the filing cabinet and reveal that the situation was a setup, staged for the amusement of TV viewers and airline passengers the world over.

"Somebody wired you this money, ma'am. Late yesterday. From"—and she pointed—"BOANASMCAORG90405."

"Um—and that would be?"

"Bank of America, Santa Monica. California. Here's the branch number, routing code, so on. Beneficiary—that would be you—VERADESICA2112STNYNY10009, correct?"

"Correct," she said weakly. She wanted, suddenly, to lie down on the floor.

"Sender," and here Georgia paused, screwing her face to one side again, "uh, VERADESICA1PICOBLSMCA90405. Family member?"

"Um," Vera said. She stared blankly at the young woman, at her lacquered, labor-intensive loops of hair. She stared at the poster above her head, a throng of ecstatic, multiracial loan recipients. She stared down at the desk—the teddy bear mug, the jokey memo pad, the moon-faced toddler in the heart-shaped frame. "Um," she repeated. "Sort of."

"There you go, then," Georgia said, swiveling the monitor back to face her and leaning at a jaunty angle in her chair. She steepled her fingers, absently appraising her manicure and her rings. "Mystery solved! If I was you, I'd get right on the phone and thank them. Nice surprise, huh?"

"Um," Vera said again, rising shakily to her feet. "I'll do that. Thanks." She gathered her possessions like a sleepwalker, dropping her sunglasses, then her pen, but, as she reached the exit, she gathered her wits sufficiently to ask: "Oh, and could you print out that information for me? All those codes and such? Just so I have a record?"

"But why?" Georgia asked disapprovingly. "Haven't you signed up yet for our on-line banking? It's free, it's convenient, and you have access to all your account information twenty-four/seven!"

"No, I have," Vera mumbled, making a gesture of appeasement. "I have. Signed up."

"Then you can print it out yourself when you get home! That's the beauty of on-line banking!"

The beauty of on-line banking, Vera thought, as she stumbled home, was that she could go on-line whenever she wanted —several times a day, if necessary—to make sure the money was still there. She had no clue where it came from, or what she was going to do. Nor had she any idea how the sudden transfusion of funds was related to the mug shot on her wall. She refused, in her gut, to believe that man, that face, was responsible. But if not him, then who? Once again, she realized, as she autopiloted across Fourteenth Street—risking death by little old lady with shopping cart—she was fresh out of ideas.

All she knew for sure was that she couldn't tell anyone, not even Colin. Especially not Colin, with his unpredictable sense of right and wrong—though didn't he himself engage almost daily in some form of electronic breaking and entering? Not that he ever called it that. Or ever admitted he might be operating in murky, as yet undefined areas of the law. Besides—she inquired of the absent Colin—what was she supposed to do, anyway? Hand the money over to the NYPD, who would barely give her the time of day? Return it? To whom? To some unknown person —some crook—who'd stolen it, in a sense, from Vera herself? To some multinational bank or credit card company, who'd already written it off as a loss against taxes? Vera thought not. After all she'd been through in the past few months—after all the, what did lawyers call it, mental anguish—she felt that she'd earned, many times over, the sum now sitting in her bank account. If she hadn't, who had? (And, with all these rhetorical questions, why *hadn't* she gone to law school?) Her argument, she realized, probably wouldn't stand up in a court of law, or at the Pearly Gates, but she didn't care. Nothing that was happening to her made sense anymore.

She, Vera de Sica, was about to commit a crime. A misdemeanor. Or perhaps not. She wasn't sure. She was no longer sure of anything—least of all who Vera was, what she wanted, and what she was going to do next.

With that much money in the bank, she thought, almost

tripping over a nodded out panhandler on the corner of St. Marks, she could leave New York—travel for a year or so, live somewhere cheap, South America perhaps. She could even—thinking the unthinkable, now that it had been thought for her—sell her apartment, never come back. See the rainforests and the glaciers, the polar ice caps, the mono titi and the parrotfish, before they disappeared. Why else, after all, had she studied Spanish and French and Italian, crammed linguistics for four years, sat through that tedious ESL certification? So she could go places, do things. And she hadn't been anywhere yet.

Wasn't this, she imagined Colin asking, the kind of thing one was supposed to do in one's twenties? Travel around, teach English in Costa Rica, that sort of thing? "My point exactly," she imagined retorting.

So what are you trying to do, "find yourself"? she saw him inquiring, complete with air quotes. Ah, no—she would say—*au contraire*: I'm all over the map as it is. There are too many of me out there already.

"This isn't a solution, Vera," he'd say, with a shake of his head (or was that her father talking?). "In the long term. It doesn't solve anything." I know, she'd reply, but what's the problem? The problem is that I'm me, and there's no solution to that.

Some people are dealt so few options, Vera thought, such a meager hand of cards. But she, in the great identity gamble, had been given more face cards than she could use. And what had she done with them? Like an audience member paralyzed before the magician's white-gloved hand, she'd remained frozen on-stage, unable to choose. She'd believed, vaguely, that the choice would make itself, that her "real" life would come along one day and kidnap her. But it hadn't, and her life was already half over; she'd become who she was, whoever Vera was, by default. "Default option," she thought despairingly. "User ID."

Wondering, once again, if she were losing her mind—if she were turning into one of those people, increasingly numerous in New York, who walked around conducting conversations with invisible interlocutors—she realized that, navigating from shady spot to shady spot along Avenue A, she'd arrived home. She triple-unlocked the door, kicked off her sandals, and, by force of habit, hit the remote (occupational hazard of living alone). As she washed the city grime off her hands and face, she could vaguely hear the TV babbling in the next room. "Identity theft!" she thought it said, but that was probably just her bad conscience.

Glancing through the open door as she dried her hands, she froze. Now, she was convinced, she really *was* losing her mind. There on National Network News—but why?—was a blurry face she recognized all too well, in medium close-up, crowned with a baseball cap, eyeballs darting nervously from side to side.

"*ATM surveillance tape,*" the caption said. "*ID thief Howard J. Hoffner in action! Is YOUR identity safe?*" Then came a logo—*NNN Special Report*—and a voiceover: "Details after the break! We'll show you last Sunday's dramatic arrest!" Vera sank, with a little bleating sound, into her chair. Her mind was a complete and perfect blank.

If this was Howard J. Hoffner, and he'd been arrested on Sunday, who, then, was Vera?

24

CHARLENE WAS CATCHING some rays—on her own private balcony with the white wooden railings and the nerve-racking chaise longue, so adjustable that she was afraid it would spontaneously adjust itself and eject her. If she didn't move around too much, reaching for her magazine and her Long Island Iced Tea, she could probably avoid actual bodily harm. She'd once sustained a knee injury falling out of a hammock in Oaxaca.

Maybe, she thought, blotting her brow, it was time to go indoors. She'd slathered her face and legs with Be Bad tan accelerator, intending to toast for a while, but, frankly, she was sweating like a pig. OK, so she probably didn't need the thick white hotel bathrobe over her bathing suit, but she wasn't about to reveal too much flesh, either. What if, say, some studly fellow guest —some lonely rich guy—should step out onto his balcony to gaze at the Pacific and should catch, instead, an eyeful of Charlene's flab?

As Charlene heaved herself, with trepidation, off the chaise and back inside, she wondered which of the suite's many accoutrements she should use to hose herself down: the marble whirlpool bath or the multiple-head shower massage. She hadn't really mastered the digital control panel of either and tended to get at least one nasty surprise—a fire-hose blast to the face, a mini-tsunami in the tub—per ablution. Perhaps she'd just stand at one of the twin marble basins and use a washcloth, like a French whore. Everything was unnecessarily complicated here, a source of stress.

First, she went from room to room turning on all the TVs—that, at least, she'd figured out how to do. There were four TVs in the suite, which she found comforting, a seamless cocoon of chatter as she moved from space to space, so she'd never have to face another moment of silence, of sheer panic—as she had when she'd first arrived, when, catching sight of herself in a mirror, she'd wondered who on earth she was and what on earth she was doing there.

Untying her robe, putting her newly "relaxed" hair into a sparkly barrette, lighting her aromatherapy candle, Charlene wasn't even aware that she was listening to the TV until a phrase caught her attention, repeating itself in the hyperinsistent manner of the top-of-the-hour tease. *Identity Theft!* she thought it said, but that might just be her paranoia. She stopped, tilted her head like a hunting dog. *Identity Theft!* it repeated. *The Crime of the New Millennium! Find out if YOU are at risk when NNN brings you exclusive coverage of an ID fraud ring cracked right HERE in Southern California! Right after the news at noon! Stay with us!*

Identity theft, she thought vaguely: that's what happened to me.

She couldn't, at that moment, have explained what she meant. It was as if she'd never heard the term before—though of course she had—and, hearing it, understood, at last, a malady that had afflicted her all her life.

It was not a term that she and Howie had ever used to describe their "operation." As far as Howie was concerned, his victims—if there were any—were the banks, huge impersonal concerns that kept write-off accounts for that express purpose. Just another cost of doing business, like paying high-priced accountants to cook the books. Besides, Howie always said, those suckers got exactly what they deserved. A sucker, by Howie's definition, was anyone who was willing to work for a living, or to accept another person—e.g., Howie—at face value.

Registering, subliminally, less chat from the TV, Charlene turned to glance at the screen behind her—and froze in disbelief. There, as part of the tease, with its own special logo— a little stick-bandit absconding with the "I" in "Identity"—was an image of her and Howie's apartment building, with yellow crime-scene tape across the entire first floor. A blue police barricade had also been erected across the driveway, where a uniformed cop loitered, doing nothing at all.

She'd always known the building was ugly, but on TV, it looked wretched as well—a shoddy mustard-colored box for hopeless shoddy lives. Charlene felt her heart contract, grow chill and quiet in her chest. She was afraid she might faint.

She pulled the robe around her tightly, took, in slow motion, the clasp from her hair. Gliding like a sleepwalker, she made it to the living room, where she sank into the sofa's voluptuous embrace. The news had come on—some war somewhere with Arabs getting killed, who cared—and she sat blindly through the weather, sports, and traffic. Commercials for Viagra, Volvo, Vagisil. And then, at last, the Special Report—*Is there another you??? Identity Theft: The Crime of the New Millennium!*

The report opened with dramatic footage of a man being hustled into a police cruiser, with fire trucks in the background, on a street Charlene recognized all too well. She even recognized some of the people gathered, abuzz with excitement, behind the barricade—people of the Filipino persuasion. The man, of course, was Howie. His hands were cuffed behind his back, he had his chin ducked down, which had the unfortunate result of foregrounding his bald spot, and a tall black cop was yanking him, with what looked like unnecessary force, into the car.

Charlene sat blankly, emptied of affect. It was too much to take in. Too much information, too much news. Her brain refused to process it. And Howie on TV—how could that be real?

Now she was looking at an oddly shaped blue thing, melted, bulging, Dali-esque. The color seemed familiar, but she couldn't think why. "And this," said the excessively lip-glossed Anchor Babe, sticking her face in front of the camera and pointing, "is the evidence!" Zoom in on the amorphous blue object, which— in a rush of icy fear—Charlene recognized at once.

"Inside this very trash can," the Anchor Babe said dramatically, "the thief tried to destroy all evidence of his multistate, million-dollar crime spree by setting it on fire, using a sophisticated chemical agent!"

Million-dollar? Charlene thought, numbly. That's news to me.

"But instead," the Babe continued, "in an act of poetic justice, this trusty container"—zoom in again—"miraculously melted in on itself, preserving the evidence!"

("How's that for an act of God, Chuck?" she said, in a faux-spontaneous aside to her sidekick, Anchor Beef. "Amazing," he replied, shaking his manly head.)

Indeed, Charlene saw, that was precisely what had happened. Sealed within that misshapen form, like a time capsule from an extinct civilization, smoldered all the documentation of Howie's crimes. Well, not *all* of them, she thought, remembering his fists.

Howie, she understood, was going to prison for a very long time. She wondered whether he would rat her out. Somehow she thought not, though she couldn't say why. She couldn't see how, even to his way of thinking, it would help him.

An immense sadness came over her, a sense of desolation, not for Howie — though, unexpectedly, she pitied him — but for herself. If that made her a bad person, well then, she was. She hardly had the stomach to watch the rest of the report, but she did, just in case it mentioned her — the suspected female confederate, the Bonnie to his Clyde. It didn't. She watched the brief interview with Detective Carver, a formerly handsome OJ type with overdeveloped biceps and deep grooves where his smile would be, if he ever smiled. He explained self-importantly how he and his partner had cracked the "ring": a fortuitous parking ticket at the track, an ATM surveillance tape of Mr. Hoffner here attempting to use a stolen card. Just your basic police work, ma'am.

So Howie had been right after all. About the cameras. Well, at least he had been right about something.

Charlene killed all the TVs with a single zap, stared shell-shocked at the blank screen. That was that, then. That part was over. The future, beginning that very moment, yawned at her feet, an enormous void.

So far, her — she counted them on her fingers — five days as Vera had brought her no joy. She'd taken two weeks off work — sick days, she'd explained to Cindy, and, in a sense, they had been: she'd felt rotten most of the time, anxious, lonely, and at loose ends. Charlene had thought that luxuriating in her new surroundings would be a full-time job — sleeping until noon under the Frette sheets, drinking Baileys Irish Cream for breakfast, scheduling massages twice a day if she damn well felt like it, summoning room service at all hours: room-service movies, room-service cocktails, room-service pedicures, room-service snacks. Maybe even — she was sure such things could be arranged — a room-service boy.

Instead, the Ocean View Royal Suite had begun to close in on her like a prison cell. It was hard work being alone all day, not knowing what to do with yourself from one moment to the next, not really understanding how anything worked. Of course, if you inquired, some bellhop or concierge would explain it to you, but, though the employees were impeccably polite, Charlene—a connoisseur—recognized disdain when she saw it.

Though she hated to admit it, she was actually looking forward to going back to work—back to the Revco, back to the Oriole counter, back, even, to eight hours on her feet doing makeovers. There were, after all, only so many Hip-Hop Yoga classes a person could take. Only so much porn a person could watch. And at least at work she had something to do and someone—Cindy—to talk to.

Plus, she now knew, she'd be needing the money. Sooner rather than later. Howie's prime-time appearance had been the second major shock in as many days: the first had been learning the Prof's true financial standing, her real net worth. Charlene had been operating under the assumption that, if you informed the Universe, loud and clear, of your aspirations, the Universe would cooperate. Instead, the Universe, like so many of its occupants, had stabbed her in the back.

The day before, not really knowing what to do with herself between *Oprah* and *Big Brother,* and wondering idly why her fat loan check hadn't shown up yet, Charlene had embarked on a flurry of phone calls to Instant Mortgage Mall, somewhere in cyberspace, a.k.a. "North Dakota." Through sheer persistence, not to mention a certain excess of time on her hands, she'd managed at last to reach a human being, who'd informed her, in an unmistakable Bangalore accent, that the loan "Vera" had applied for had been denied.

How could that be? Charlene had stared at the sleek, multifunction phone as if it, or its Italian designers, were somehow to blame. Equity loans were usually a no-brainer, so she knew something was up. She'd discovered precisely what when, by dint of a little social engineering—a call to Human Resources at Brooklyn Multi, the old IRS audit ploy—"Prof de Sica" had ascertained her actual income for the past five years.

"Could you repeat that, please?" she'd asked the Human Resources temp, dumbfounded.

"Sure, Professor. Got a pen handy this time?"

Charlene had stared at the five sums she'd scribbled down. Without exception, each was less than she, Charlene, had earned at the Revco, base pay plus commissions. This had to be—she could only think—a bad joke, a misplaced decimal. She re-checked the figures. Apparently not. Apparently this paltry salary was for real. Charlene's first impulse was to laugh, then to cry—or to laugh the way hysterical women do in the movies, peals of laughter morphing into sobs, until someone silences them with a slap.

There'd been no one there to slap her face. So she hadn't laughed and she hadn't cried. Instead she'd just felt sicker, more depressed. She'd betrayed Howie, delivered him to the cops on a skewer, and now she'd betrayed Vera, who could barely pay her bills. And what for? So she could loll disconsolately around a hotel suite, where the very showerheads conspired against her?

She'd gazed around her then, at the opulent, understated furnishings, the light-drenched balcony, the prized Ocean View—all procured with resources that didn't exist, by a person who didn't really exist either. And now that person had everything she could think of, right at hand. A closetful of new clothes, new blonde highlights, real leather on the couch. Two well-stocked bars. Four TVs, a VCR, a DVD player, a three-line phone, high-speed wireless Internet access, two data ports, and a fax machine—and yet, Charlene realized, she was utterly alone. She hadn't spoken for days to any living being—except Room Service, which didn't count. Nobody had touched her, except Charlene herself, imagining herself all the while to be another. Not one person on earth knew where she was. She could just evaporate, disappear, and no one would know—except Housekeeping, who'd have to come in eventually and change the sheets.

If she continued living like this, she'd end up in the psych ward, like her mother. She could, at that moment, imagine no other future for herself. She already had the drinking part down pat.

As she stared out at the slender curve of the shoreline— where she hadn't yet taken so much as a "power stroll"—something else had dawned on Charlene: that, during these five days, the only thing she'd truly savored had been the peace. The privacy, the absence of questions, demands, accusations. In other words, the absence of Howie—the end of the monologue that had drowned out all the other channels in her brain. The real luxury, it turned out, was being able to hear what was going on inside your own head, even if, admittedly, it wasn't much. Even if it was just a ping of distress, a black box after a plane wreck, waiting to be found.

25

A T THE AIRPORT, Vera had to present each index finger for digital analysis. She had to peer into a little machine to have her iris scanned. She had to take off her shoes and proceed through the metal detector barefoot, then remove her bra (in a secure cubicle, under the lascivious gaze of a female Fed) because the underwire was triggering a Code Orange. Between the curb and the gate, her hand luggage—all she'd brought with her—was X-rayed three times, and hand-examined once. She half expected to be ushered aside next for a Pap smear and a DNA swab.

At the gate, where she sank limply into a plastic chair with her bottled water, her *New York Times,* and her *Vanity Fair*—feeling, somehow, that she had got away with something—soldiers strolled by with automatic weapons and jumpy-looking dogs. One of the dogs, on a routine sniffing mission in a trash bin near Vera, showed signs of agitation, but the offending item turned out to be a half-eaten burger. And all this, she thought, is supposed to make us feel *safer*?

At last her flight was called—United, flight 121 to Los Angeles—and, after a final frisking at the mouth of the Jetway, she was on her way. Assuming, now, that no zealot attempted a takeover with a plastic fork, she had a good five hours ahead of her to gaze from her window seat at the miraculous clouds and ask herself, once again, just what she thought she was doing.

Colin thought she was flying out to LA for an interview — which, in a sense, she was. If she'd told him the truth, he would either have laughed out loud or recommended psychiatric intervention. So she hadn't. She'd begun to see that this was how deceit worked — like a mutant prion attacking the central nervous system of one's being, leaving spongy areas, no-go areas for self and others.

Guiltily she glanced down at the novel on her lap, a first edition, elegant, off white, with marbling like wood-grain. Her favorite author, favorite book. Which meant that Colin had actually been listening when she'd talked about books, instead of, as she'd assumed, thinking about Rileys or sex. The pages were thick and velvety to the touch, the endpapers a rich red. She leafed gently through, found the opening lines. "My sin, my soul," she read, then stared out at the sky.

She hated misleading — OK, deceiving — Colin, who admittedly was a tad distracted at the moment, an easy mark. He'd given up his data-mining operation in disgust — now that the culprit had been unmasked on national TV — and was working furiously instead to hack some eBay bidder who'd pulled a scam on a fellow Riley enthusiast. He'd been writing code for three days straight. But the two of them had made love the night before with such fierceness, such sweetness, that Vera had wondered, in awe, what their nights would be like if she were *really* leaving town. So far, all she'd done had been to raise, over dinner, her idea — it wasn't really a plan yet — to sell the apartment, take "the money" (source unspecified), and travel for a while.

"Seeing I'm unemployed and all," she'd said. "And seeing I hate this apartment anyway. As you know." And she'd gestured around her, at the dismal space. "Think of all the money I'd save on rent and Prozac!"

She'd watched Colin taking this information on board. He'd nodded thoughtfully, seemed to get it. He hadn't said any of the things his proxy had said inside her own head; he hadn't even said "hmmmnn." Instead, he'd looked at her for a long moment over his wineglass. Possibly because of the faded green T-shirt he was wearing, his eyes had turned a cloudy, arousing gray.

"I'd miss you," he'd said. This was the closest thing to a declaration of affection Vera had ever heard from Colin. It had rendered her dumbstruck for the rest of the evening—except in bed.

By morning, of course, both had reverted to type. She was rushing around trying to find some clean clothes, he'd remained couchant, hands behind head, studying the ceiling paint job.

"Know what?" he'd said, instead of, for instance, "Good morning."

"What?"

"What might be neat?"

"*What,* already." She was never at her best while packing, an activity which, to her mind, represented too great a commitment. How on earth was she supposed to know what she'd feel like wearing, or even fit into, two days hence?

"I could rig you up with a GPS transmitter. That way, I'd always know where you were, on your travels."

"Well, I could just tell you where I was, couldn't I . . . ?" Mimicking a phone call: "Hi Colin, guess where I am? Buenos Aires!"

"But this would be much more fun," he said. "I could map your precise coordinates at any moment. Think about it: twenty-four satellites in the system, and at least four can always find you, within a hundred meters."

"What if," she said, reconsidering the black T-shirt, putting it back, "I didn't want to be found, within a hundred meters or even a hundred miles?"

"Well then you could just turn it off," he said, reasonably. "And turn it back on when you wanted to." And here he mimicked data scrolling across a computer screen: "VDS at Position X, latitude thirty-five, longitude fifty-eight. Sun is shining, rum is strong. Come join me for a while!"

"Well, that might work," she'd said—and meant it. She could imagine finding Colin delicious in small doses, even imagine acquiescing to such a scheme.

Nevertheless, she'd misled him: there was no interview, at least in the sense he'd understood it. There was only some private, unfinished business. As the plane reached cruising altitude, Vera began to feel queasy—airsickness perhaps, not enough oxygen in the mix. Strapping on the banditlike sleep mask that she knew would leave red marks on her face, she tried, strenuously, to sleep but succeeded only in dozing most of the way, in a twitchy, twilight state.

What if, she thought, she just kept the money, said nothing to anyone, left the country on an extended trip? Did Brazil have an extradition agreement with the United States, she wondered uneasily, did Nicaragua, Chile, Belize? Did keeping a large sum of cash that had arrived without explanation in her bank account make her a crook, or merely an accessory after the fact? And if the latter, then who was the guilty party? Vera de Sica, presumably: it was "Vera de Sica" who had wired the funds. But could Vera be an accessory to herself, an accomplice in her own crime? And what, after all, was the crime?

Theft, she thought, repositioning the lumpy pillow behind her neck. Stop dancing around it; you know it's theft. That money, whatever its source, doesn't belong to you. Nor to "Vera de Sica," whoever she is. If you, Vera, ever find her, "Vera," you'll have to turn her in. For theft.

But theft of what, from whom? The dollars that had shown

up in her bank account weren't in the form of gold bullion or even paper currency; they were packets of electronic information that had been routed from one computer to another, pulses, bits. And bits didn't exist, as such; they were characteristics of a wire—on or off—at any given moment. Her virtual self had sent Vera virtual assets; why shouldn't she keep them, for real? Why shouldn't she, for once, grab hold of something that came her way? Do something she wanted to do, be a person, at last, who acts: who claims, hell, reclaims, what is rightfully hers? Perhaps even—in an imperfect world—wrongfully hers?

Suddenly nauseated, she asked the flight attendant for a flat Coke, no ice. Then, peeling off the mask, she demanded another, this time with a squeeze of lime. She began to feel better, but not much. Closing her eyes again, she concentrated, until the descent, on not throwing up.

As soon as the plane landed, she shouldered her way to the exit door, then hightailed it out of the terminal with her hand-luggage, leaving the other, missionless passengers in her wake. The hot, smoggy air struck her like a bad dream, the repetition compulsion at work. LAX, she realized, had unfortunate associations—but this time, like a true New Yorker, she summoned a cab.

"One Pico Boulevard," she told the driver. "In Santa Monica."

"You mean the restaurant?" he asked. "One Pico?"

"Um," she said, "dunno. Whatever's there. At One Pico Boulevard. Santa Monica."

He shrugged, though nowhere as expressively as a New York cabbie, and, flipping the meter on, pulled calmly and courteously away from the curb, actually checking over his left shoulder as he did so. Vera, in the back seat, bracing for death, was gobsmacked by this maneuver.

One Pico Boulevard turned out to be a large, ornate wooden structure, resembling, with its white wooden battlements, a fairy-tale fort. Or, Vera thought, tipping the cabdriver lavishly for getting her there alive, a country-club prison for corporate offenders.

"So what is this place, anyway?" she asked, struggling with the pop-up handle on her bag, which had decided, just then, not to pop up.

"Shutters," the driver replied, a shade defensively. "One Pico, like you asked."

Once inside, she gathered—from the haute beach-bungalow décor and the phalanx of eager, abnormally good-looking employees—that the place was a hotel. She approached the reception desk with some trepidation—not her usual muted class anxiety, but a keener sense of being, at that moment, in an absurd and impossible situation.

A young being of bionic perfection was eager to assist her.

"I'm looking for . . . ," Vera said, "Vera de Sica."

"Of course, ma'am. That's D-E, S-E-?"

"I," Vera said. "S-I."

"Of course. One moment, please." The miracle of carbon-based engineering consulted a miracle of silicon-based engineering, a slender screen that seemed to float, lily-like, in space. "Dr. de Sica expecting you?"

Doctor? Well, why the hell not. Under the circumstances, it seemed almost apt.

"Good question," Vera said.

"I'm sorry?"

"I mean, yes. Well, no. Probably not."

"Oh dear," the lovely creature said, "I see that the professor has already checked out."

"Hmmmnn," Vera responded, for lack of a better riposte.

Her spirits sank—all this way, after all, for nothing? for this bathetic dead end?—but what she mainly felt was an overwhelming, guilty relief. So there was to be no reckoning, no dénouement, no exposition—but, hey, she'd tried, hadn't she? She'd done all she could, taken pains, gone the extra mile—the extra three thousand miles in fact. Her *intentions* had been good—really, the best. So let the record show: she, Vera, had tried to do the right thing.

She nodded, shrugged, turned to leave, then hesitated. She would have been a terrible lawyer after all, unable even to convince that most pliable jury, herself.

"Um . . . did she . . . the professor . . . by any chance leave a forwarding address? Any contact info?"

The guardian of the screen gazed into it, gazed back at Vera, looked dubious.

"I'm a family member, see," Vera improvised, with a gesture she hoped was both expansive and disarming. "Just in LA for a couple of days, and I'd hate to miss her. Here, I can show you some ID, if you don't believe me!"

"No, that's OK." The exquisite almond eyes met hers, decided. "There *is* a number to call, it says here for document delivery—I guess she was expecting something to be delivered."

"That would be me!" Vera said, nonsensically. "I'm the delivery!"

It wasn't so hard after all, Vera saw—this business of abusing credit. The freely available credit of others.

She left the lobby on a wave of adrenaline, all but brandishing the number on its monogrammed message slip, then had to turn back, somewhat ignominiously, for her bag, which she'd left to one side.

There were no pay phones outside, on Pico or Ocean boulevards, nor, in fact, anywhere in sight. Every body in LA apparently now came complete with cell-phone prosthesis. So, retracing her steps, she ordered a $10 latte in the hotel café to earn, circuitously, the right to a local call.

What if, she wondered, Vera answered? What would Vera say? She had no plan of action, no script; her heart and lungs were not cooperating, both all of a sudden on the blink.

"Holiday Inn Santa Monica? How may I direct your call?"

Vera's first impulse, like a prank caller, was to hang up. Then she gathered what was left of her wits, and croaked, "Uh—where are you?"

"What's that?"

"Where is the hotel? Located?"

"One moment please." A recorded message clicked on, giving, at length, the establishment's exact coordinates, complete with driving directions from all points of the globe.

"Is this somewhere I could walk from here?" she asked the doorman, showing him the address.

"Walk?" he repeated, all but blanching in alarm. "Please allow me to get you a cab." The distance, as it turned out, was some four or five blocks.

The Holiday Inn, on Colorado, looked like any Holiday Inn anywhere, except, possibly, more bunkerlike, with its late-Sixties waffle façade. Disembarking from the cab, feeling the afternoon sun strong on her skin, Vera realized that she was wilting —crumpled and sweaty and sleep-deprived. What she most wanted at that moment was a shower and a nap, an ice-cold drink, but, like the insane person she'd apparently become, she perseverated in her task.

The second time, as with most transgressions, was easier than the first. The entire transaction—this time with an all too human, grumpy and multitasking Latina at Reception—consisted of four sentences:

"Vera de Sica, please."

"Who may I say is calling?"

"Delivery. Need a signature."

Brief consultation on the phone, then—

"She says to go on up. Room 1211."

The elevator was mirrored. The carpeting was blue. The hallway had that soft, vaguely menacing hum that all hotel hallways have. Room 1211 was at the very end, the last door on the right. It was important not to think, just do. Vera knocked, then, omitting to breathe, knocked again.

Inside Room 1211 of the Holiday Inn, Charlene was attempting, without much success, to master the game of Nintendo. The joystick came with the room, and, like a zoo animal that had exhausted all other sources of stimulation in its cage, she'd worked her way around to it at last. She'd felt bored and draggy all afternoon, shifting herself from one bed to another for a change of scene, barely attaining the upright position en route. One bed was littered with magazines and half-melted M&M's, the other with Doritos and the *TV Guide*. Even with the air conditioning on high, the room smelled of sleep, fake cheese flavor, and something metallic—empty beer cans, perhaps. Too bad the windows didn't open. But then, she thought, some lonely guest might jump.

Not Vera, she reminded herself, as she did whenever her thoughts strayed in that direction—not now. Because she had a plan, a program of action. Charlene, in fact, had made a bargain with the Universe. A few days earlier, slumped on the creamy leather sofa of her Royal Suite, trying to decide whether to drink Baileys or beer with her croissant, she'd caught herself wondering whether the hair-dryer-in-the-bathtub thing would really work, outside of the movies. And, catching herself, she'd realized that she might just be at that very moment "hitting bottom," Dr. Laura's dreaded verdict on the deadbeats who called in. Charlene could almost feel the thud, the hollowness inside, see how a person who'd hit bottom might just not bother getting out of bed one day. And then the next. How such a person might just find herself swallowing too many Xanax with too much Jack. And if this wasn't "hitting bottom," Charlene thought, she didn't want to find out what was. She owed at least that much to herself. To Vera.

So that was when, addressing the Universe out loud, she'd proposed her deal—had even stood up, senator-style, to do it. She would, she pledged, go back to work; she would move into cheaper digs until her apartment was free; she'd ask Cindy, just by the way, over the cotton balls, how a person might go about resuming her interrupted education. She'd lose ten pounds this time for sure. She'd never touch a drink before 6:00 P.M., no, make that 5:00. She would even—to balance things out—transfer half the cash in her Bank of America account to the Prof in New York—yes she would, that very day—if the Universe would just, please, let her not go crazy. There in that hotel room, alone.

And the Universe, streaming in brilliant stripes through the eponymous shades, had seemed to acquiesce. Had seemed to shine down on her plan. Otherwise, why else would Charlene have begun feeling better immediately, better still once she'd moved into the Holiday Inn? Where she was not only saving 800 bucks a night, she reminded herself, but feeling less stressed, living more the way she imagined a normal person would live, in a normal room, with a normal bed, a normal shower, and a normal TV.

When the room phone rang, mid-Nintendo, Charlene started. Her startle reflex seemed to be set on high these days— she'd become as jumpy as a Vietnam vet. But it was only that attitudinous bitch from downstairs, asking if she could send someone up with a delivery for Dr. de Sica. Hell yes, the Doc said, entertaining visions of the UPS guy. In fact, she'd been expecting an important piece of mail all week: a brand-new, gold-lettered, multiply embossed diploma granting Vera de Sica a Ph.D. in English Literature—a recognition long overdue, in the Doc's opinion. The diploma had cost $25, plus tax and shipping, from "Mill University" in cyberspace; as required by law, it would bear the legend "Novelty Item" in a visible spot. However —as both Charlene and "Mill University" were fully aware—the law didn't specify in what kind of ink or what size type "Novelty Item" had to appear, so "Novelty Item" was destined for a disappearing act. Charlene didn't really see what good the diploma would do her right now, but she just wanted it all the same.

Neglecting to peer through the fisheye lens, she unbolted the door.

A woman stood there, disheveled and hesitant-looking, resting one elbow on the raised handle of her rollaway bag. Judging by her appearance (shiny nose, messy hair, weird crease marks on her face), and by her attire (wrinkled khakis, crumpled blouse), she'd recently arrived on a very long flight.

"Wrong room," Charlene said, preparing to close the door.

"I don't think so," the woman replied. She appeared slightly stunned, jet-lagged perhaps. She pushed some errant strands of hair off her face, then kept her hand uncertainly on the back of her neck. "Are you, uh, by any chance, Vera de Sica?"

"Who're you?" Charlene asked, on immediate alert.

The woman gave an odd smile, more like a grimace. "Me?" she said. "Oh . . . I'm Vera. Vera de Sica."

"No you're not," Charlene said. Her response was instantaneous, panicky, and heartfelt. She recognized at once that the Universe had reneged on its bargain, that the Universe, in fact, had screwed her royally, but she also knew that this woman—this unkempt creature who could stand to lose a few pounds off her ass—couldn't possibly be Vera.

"I'm not?" the woman replied, with the same odd smile.

"No."

"Then who is?"

"I am." And, as she said it, Charlene felt, with every fiber of her being, that it was true. She *was* Vera de Sica, Vera by right if not by birthright. She'd worked so hard, with such dedication, such application, to become her—harder, she was sure, than this "Vera" had ever worked to become anyone. So how dare she show up now, this impostor, and tell her, Vera, who she was?

"In that case," the woman said, tilting her head in what looked to Charlene like a sarcastic manner, "who would I be?"

"I have no idea who you would be," Charlene said, blustering, affecting indignation, the way she'd learned from Howie, "but I do know that if you don't leave right now I'm going to call security."

The woman gave an abrupt, incredulous laugh. Her color heightened, a perfect match for Oriole's Mediterranean Fire. "So let me get this right: *you* are threatening to call the cops on *me*?"

Charlene had to concede, silently, that her visitor had a point. All the bluster drained out of her, all of the hope. Why, she wondered, had she ever thought she could get away with this? That she'd even had a chance? It had been a terrible idea, born of desperation, a pathetic attempt to grab something she wasn't entitled to—some kind of self. You could get everything you wanted, she understood, but you couldn't get that.

"OK," she said, leaning against the doorjamb, suddenly limp. That feeling came over her again, that helpless sensation, needing to weep. "What do you want?"

"I'm not sure," the other admitted. She looked baffled,

sheepish, fiddled gracelessly with the handle of her bag, trying to make it retract. She gave up on that task, looked back at Charlene, who, among other things, was quashing the impulse to intervene, show her visitor how the mechanism worked. Some people were just useless in the physical world. "I don't really know. I just wanted to find you, see who you were."

"Well, now you've seen me," Charlene said, folding her arms across her bathrobe. They looked at each other in silent, mutual appraisal. "And I've seen you. So can we call it a day?"

"No," the other said. "Could I please come in?"

Inside the room were two enormous, unmade beds—what kind of ménage had the Holiday Inn been anticipating?—each, in its own way, resembling the lair of an East Village street person. Little else offered itself in the way of seating. After a moment of hesitation, Vera sat down on the corner of the nearest bed, in front of the TV. Wordlessly, the other followed, plopping herself on the matching corner of the matching bed. On the screen a video game was frozen in mid-play; with the incongruous gesture of a thoughtful hostess, the woman picked up the remote and killed it. Then, still without speaking, the two women turned, knees angled towards each other, so they were almost touching. It was an absurd posture, Vera thought, a posture of intimacy, of confidences, the orientation of lovers or girlfriends, cellmates perhaps.

In fact, Vera thought, the entire situation was absurd. She felt stunned, dizzy, as if her brain were misfiring, struggling to process the information before her. This, her brain told her (180-degree pan), was a hotel room. And this, it tried to assert (three-quarter angle, medium close-up), was Vera. Make that "Vera." But it couldn't be. Vera tried, and failed, to resolve the cognitive dissonance, to wrap her mind around a ludicrous idea: that this dumpy woman in the none too clean bathrobe, this sullen woman who smelled of beer, this rumpled woman with the bloated face and bizarre hairdo, was the person who had managed, somehow, to devastate her life. (Not to mention that, frankly, if a person had to parade around Southern California in Vera's name, she'd have preferred someone better-looking.)

Instead of the rage, the grandiose self-righteousness she'd anticipated, Vera felt hugely embarrassed, as if she'd made a giant *faux pas.* She adjusted her watch on her sweaty wrist, gazed at the blank screen. Her entire body was prickling with self-consciousness. Perhaps, after all, everything did come down to this: to the body. One body, or two; hers, the other's, generating all this heat. Getting in the way. Insisting on the old physics: that two objects couldn't occupy the same space at the same time.

Some dialogue was evidently called for.

"Who are you?" she asked. It was a question, she knew, without an answer.

"I already told you," the other replied, truculently. "I'm Vera de Sica."

"No you're not."

"Yes I am."

"You're not. I know you're not." The woman shrugged.

"Look," Vera said, exasperated, "we can't just keep on saying the same thing over again."

The other woman shifted her position on the bed, turned to face Vera full on. She opened her arms like a carnival barker, then pointed to her chest, or rather, to the logo on her grubby bathrobe. "OK, then, you tell me: if I'm not Vera de Sica, who am I?"

"I have no idea," Vera admitted. "That's my problem right

there." The woman opened her palms again, as if she'd made her point. "But I'm sure," Vera added spitefully, "that the LAPD could find out in no time."

The woman's face—or its lower half, anyway—crumpled. She stared at her bare feet, puffy and misshapen, testimony to years' worth of too tight shoes.

Vera was beginning to feel cruel, a joyless kind of power. And with that sensation came an image: a man's face, with dead eyes and slack lips, the face she'd recently adopted as her familiar. "Who's Howard?" she asked, a non sequitur for sure. "Howard J. Hoffner?"

"Howard," the woman said, still staring at her feet, "does not exist."

It wasn't an answer, but, judging by the other's silence, it was the only one she was going to get. They appeared to have reached an impasse. After a long pause, during which she gnawed at a hangnail like a worried dog, Vera tried another tack.

"So, if it's not impolite to ask or anything, how long do you intend to keep this up? This 'Vera de Sica' routine?"

Despite something curiously, and unnaturally, affectless about the woman's face, she managed at that moment to look stricken. "As long as you let me," she said quietly. "Otherwise, I guess, as long as it takes for the LAPD to get here. There's the phone." And she gestured again, with a bravado that was almost dignified.

"Why would I let you?" Vera asked, a rhetorical question, she knew.

"I tried to make things right, didn't I? When I found out."

"Found out what?"

"Who you were."

This was a line of thought that Vera was reluctant, even afraid, to pursue.

"How?" she asked, after a pause.

"How what?"

Vera gestured helplessly. Everything, she wanted to say.

"Look, I gave you half," the woman said. Her tone was sullen, obdurate.

"Half of what?"

"What I had."

"But whose, whose . . ." Vera tried, and failed, to come up with the right word. "Where did all that . . . come from?"

The other looked sheepish, mumbled something.

"Say again?"

"Cash advances. Against credit cards. In your name."

Vera shook her head rapidly, as if to clear it. Cash against credit, assets that didn't really exist. In the name of someone who didn't really exist either. Present, in New York, as pixels on a screen, signifiers that might yet be exchanged for real things: freedom, travel, something like life.

"But who *does* it belong to? Really?" Vera insisted, after a while.

The other shrugged. "You tell me."

They looked each other straight in the eye, for the first time, and a current of something passed between them, complicity perhaps. Then, at the same moment, each looked away.

"I tried to make things right," the woman repeated, doggedly, digging a hole with her toe in the pile of the rug.

"Is that what you thought you were doing?" Vera asked, her voice rising. "Making things right? After all the damage you'd caused?"

"What damage? Tell me, what damage?"

At that moment, despite the lengthy disquisition she had prepared, Vera found herself at a loss for an answer. "Um," she said. "Lots."

But what, she asked herself, had in fact been lost—apart

from all those hours of her life, which would by now have been lost anyway, grading student papers, reading the *Times,* sitting on the subway, surfing the Net? Her creditworthiness?—the (illusory) power to buy things she didn't need, that weren't worth having anyway? Her "security"? Her "peace of mind"? Both, she now understood, fictitious in the first place. Her *identity*? She wanted to laugh.

It seemed, perhaps, that she might have no case after all—no cause, no leg to stand on, not even a phantom limb. Perhaps, she thought, it was time to leave.

"Listen, I'm going to be away for a while," Vera said, after another gap. "Out of the country. Traveling. Like I always wanted to."

"That's nice," the woman said, warily. "Bon voyage." She mispronounced the French, but it was, Vera realized, no longer her job to correct anyone.

"So let's leave it like this: You keep what you have. I keep what I have. Of yours. Mine. Whosever's. Just don't pull any more stunts on me."

"I won't," the woman said flatly. "I can't, anyway. That identity is all used up."

"Gee, thanks," Vera said, mildly offended. "Myself, I was hoping it might still have a few miles left on it."

The woman shrugged again. She was getting on Vera's nerves, with her fat, masklike face, her slitty, calculating eyes. She was unreadable; she absorbed all the energy around her, emitted none. Vera had imagined, somehow, that she might have known her, but it was clear now that she didn't, that she'd never set eyes on this person before. This wasn't at all the confrontation she had planned, the resolution, the—what did they call it in Greek drama?—anagnorisis. Recognition. She felt, if anything, obscurely ashamed.

"OK," she said, "I don't really know what else to say. And it's getting late." She half rose, then changed her mind. "But before I go, please just tell me one thing."

"What?"

"Why?"

"Why what?"

"Why did you, you know, steal my identity?"

The woman met her eyes again. She gave another shrug, almost a tic. "You kind of left it lying around, didn't you?"

"No, I mean: Why me?"

The other looked startled, embarrassed, as if Vera had just made a remark in extremely poor taste. Lowering her gaze, she busied herself untying and then retying the belt on her robe. "Do you really imagine," she asked at last, "that any of this had anything to do with you?"

As the woman stood to leave, Charlene felt—along with a numb, woozy relief—that she could restrain herself no longer. Until this moment, she'd been discreet, reticent even, but surely she had some kind of responsibility, professional responsibility, towards her guest? It just wouldn't be right to let her leave like that.

"Listen," Charlene said, rising as well, "I hope you won't take this the wrong way, but that lipstick you're wearing . . ."

Vera touched her lips, in puzzlement.

"It's Insouciance, isn't it? By Oriole?"

"Um . . . yes."

"Well, honey, I just have to tell you that that color really doesn't do anything for you. With your olive skin tone, you need something warmer, more bronzy. That's washing you out, you know, making you look a little . . . yellow."

"Yellow?" Vera asked, peering aghast into the mirror over the dressing table. Beneath the mirror, though she didn't notice it, lay a driver's license: her name, the other's face.

"Yes, definitely," Charlene said, firmly, "it's that color. And what on earth are you using for blush?"

"Um, don't remember," Vera admitted, weakly.

"Well frankly that's not doing it for you either. Too rosy— I'm thinking Mediterranean Fire or maybe Etruscan Gold, seeing it's summer."

"Mediterranean what?"

"Along your cheekbones, right there." And Charlene mimicked a dabbing action on Vera's face. "You've got good bones, you know, but you're just not making the most of what you have."

"I know," Vera said, "but I just never seem to have the time. Never get around to it, somehow . . ."

"Well, you should," Charlene said, sternly. "You owe it to yourself. Don't you?"

Vera nodded, abashed. She re-examined her face in the mirror, more anxiously now. "And my skin gets so oily, too, especially when I travel—"

"Look," Charlene said, pushing a pile of crumpled clothes off a chair, which she then dragged closer to the mirror. "Before you go, why don't you sit yourself right here"—she patted the seat invitingly, unzipped an enormous makeup bag—"and we'll see what we can do with you?"

Acknowledgments

I would like to thank the Bogliasco Foundation, the Château de Lavigny, and the Julia and David White Artists Foundation for their support. Thanks, too, to Michele Berdy, Elena Georgiou, Maurice Isserman, Robert Ji-Song Ku, Mary Murfitt, Le Anne Schreiber, Marcia Williams, and the rangy young driver, who doesn't wish to be named. I'm also immensely grateful to Jane Rosenman and Betsy Lerner for their work on this book.